Teardrop in My Eye

Country Roads Series: Book Four

Grea Warner

Teardrop in My Eye
Copyright © 2019 Grea Warner
All rights reserved.

ISBN: (ebook): 978-1-945910-98-2
(print): 978-1-949931-00-6

Inkspell Publishing
5764 Woodbine Ave.
Pinckney, MI 48169

Edited By
Cover art By Najla Qamber

OTHER BOOKS BY GREA WARNER

All My Memories in Can't Buy Me Love
Boxset

Country Roads

Almost Heaven

Take Me Home

The Place I Belong (coming soon!)

GREA WARNER

DEDICATION

For all the writers I have met on this creative career journey. From screenwriting classes to internships to conferences to writing groups…you have inspired and encouraged me so that there are only teardrops of joy.

And, for my family and all of their support.

CHAPTER ONE

Two strong hands grabbed me from behind, startling me so much that I jumped and let out a partial scream. I hated sudden, loud noises and things that seemingly came out of nowhere. The emotional scars of my childhood still lingered, no matter how far I traveled or how much I wished them away.

Thankfully, though, I relaxed just as quickly. It was because I knew those familiar hands wrapped around me now. And I loved those hands holding me close. I had missed feeling them so much while he was away.

"Hi, baby," he cooed in my ear, before having his soft lips survey my upper neck.

Loving the feeling, I let him explore for a moment before turning around and meeting his lips for a legitimate "welcome home" kiss. Wearing gray sweats and a partially unbuttoned gray and white plaid shirt, I knew Finn had just arrived home from the airport. Sure, he had texted me, but it was also in his eyes. Those natural gray eyes were watery and he was blinking—a sure tell sign that he had just removed his performer green contact lenses.

"Hi." I smiled, pleased to see the real Finn Murphy. I took off my silver winter coat and laid it on top of Finn's carryon luggage, which was resting on the tall kitchen counter chair.

"God, I'm glad to be home. Everything good?"

"Mmmm-hmmm," I murmured, and leaned into his fit chest. I had missed him. A week had seemed so long, especially since I had been used to having him around full time for the past few months.

"How's my girl?"

I loved when Finn called me that. It made me feel like I belonged. It made me feel loved…and young.

But it wasn't me he was talking about this time. And I was okay with it. She was the only one I would share my title with.

"She's good," I replied and turned back to the baby carrier which I had just placed on the kitchen counter when entering our New York suburban home.

Our daughter, decked out in a pink fleece hat and black designer jumper, instantly started kicking her little legs and smiling as she watched my face change to her daddy's in her line of vision. Finn removed Arinn's hat and gently kissed her head topped with brown, with hints of red, hair. Witnessing the love via his smile and her gurgles, I couldn't help but give a silent prayer of appreciation.

"Where's Little Man?" Finn questioned.

"We were on a play date with Kai. I mentioned that I had some things to do. So Tina offered to watch them," I spoke of my friend, Kai's mom, who lived in the apartment building I used to live in before Finn and I were married. "By the way, I replayed your half-time show for him this morning. He kept signaling back. That was pretty cool, baby."

Finn had performed at the Superbowl the day before. And he had told our son that he would stick up three fingers during the show so that he knew his daddy was thinking of him. Three fingers because our little boy, Chance, had just turned three years old.

"I just wish y'all could have been there," Finn

lamented, looking back at me once again.

"I know." There was no way, though, that I was going to travel to the chaos of the biggest sporting event of the year with a three-year-old and a three-month-old. "And I know I told you last night, but I'm so proud of you. That was a fantastic performance. That had to be such a high."

"So we're alone, then?" Finn ignored my accolades—modest almost to a fault.

I nodded and glanced down at our daughter. "Pretty much so."

"You have some things you have to do?" Finn questioned before rephrasing my previous comment. "How about some*one* you have to do?"

I softly laughed at his obvious proposition. "Yeah," I self-corrected. "That's what I meant. I mean, it *is* our naptime." I was going along with his promiscuous tone but, in reality, it was naptime. And more often than not, I would find myself falling asleep when one or both of the kids napped. "I just need to get Arinn down."

"I'll do it."

"Thanks. I don't think my lullabies nearly measure up to someone who has a slew of number one hits."

"But your dance moves…"

"Oh, give me a break." I jokingly hit Finn; he knew my distaste for dancing. When his wide, alluring grin emerged, I started giving directions. "Her diap—"

"I know. I haven't been gone that long."

Finn was such a good father. I had never doubted that he would be. He was a natural with his eight-year-old niece, Kelsea, and had also been with his nephew, Wyatt, before the young boy tragically died. When our son was born, Finn's connection was instantaneous. He was hands-on from day one and seemed to treasure every minute. Well, maybe not all of the middle-of-the-night awakenings. He acted as a guardian and teacher to Chance but also his best bud. And the cliché about girls being wrapped around their daddy's fingers? No truer statement than when it came to our latest addition. If I couldn't have had that growing up, then there was no greater wish than seeing my children blessed with that relationship.

Finn gave me a quick peck on the lips and began taking Arinn out of the carrier. "I'll get her changed," he said. "And, you? You can change, too. How about that blue one?"

He shifted his eyebrows at me and started walking toward the nursery. I heard his normally country-rock voice singing a soft version of "Mockingbird," and I couldn't help but think there wasn't much sexier than that sight. Certainly not me in that blue nightie, especially because I knew I still couldn't fit in it.

***

"I can't believe how much she has changed in just a few days," Finn said, entering our first floor master suite and peeling off his clothes so that just his boxer briefs remained.

"Yeah, too fast. I can't keep up," I semi-complained. Already under the sheets, I kneeled up to meet him as he climbed on the bed doing the same.

The look in his eyes changed slightly then. I knew that look. I craved and mirrored that look. It was a look, but it was more than that—it was the pure, undeniable magnetism between us. Our love—our connection—was something that had not dimmed in the slightest since becoming a couple over six years before.

I felt my whole body beautifully languish as Finn brushed my long dark strawberry-blonde hair away from my shoulder and then did the same with the spaghetti strap of the black cami I was wearing. He kissed me then in the same spot, but it was as if he was touching me in others. I drew my lips to his, sucking in my need. As the intensity of our tongues and lips grew, Finn eased me down into a parallel position. Feeling his hands venturing toward my panties, I instead encouraged him to assist me in removing my cami over my head. His hands in mine, I guided them to my breasts, which were still plump despite switching to formula instead of breastfeeding. When his hands started to venture south again, I kissed him semi-hard halting our action so that I could quickly untangle both my underwear and his. Simply watching me, his eyes began to bounce as I purposefully, knowing what it did to him, circled his hips with my thumbs.

"Those hands on my hips…" he hummed. And then when I suddenly cupped his manliness, "I…wow. Lara, I'm rea—"

"Then what are you waiting for, Mr. Murphy?"

Swiftly, he pulled me back into position and planked above me. I grabbed his hands and, intertwining them with mine, placed them above my head. And, then, he was in me. I cried out his name in a mixture of need and something else I couldn't quite place. But it was quickly forgotten as I got lost in the rhythmic rock of our love.

Afterwards, when I went to reach for my clothes, Finn asked, "What are you doing?"

"Just putting something on."

"Why?" He sat up a little straighter at my side.

"I don't know. I—"

"Beauty, let me have a moment to just admire you…all of you."

"Puh – lease," I spit out.

"What?"

"It's just…" I hesitated and then admitted, "It's the baby weight. I don't know what's wrong. I've lost a little, but it's not like it was with Chance. My hips and thighs—" I cut myself off, only then figuring out why I had subconsciously geared his hands north.

"Lara…," he sighed my name.

"It's true," I said. "I haven't lost anything since you've been away. I thought—"

"First of all, you just had the baby a couple months

ago, and…" He paused and twitched his eyebrows at me. I had learned over the years that was his telltale sign when deciding to say something or not. Partially singing, he obviously opted to go for it. "Besides, I'm all about that bass."

I couldn't help but laugh at the catchy Meghan Trainor lyrics as I playfully hit him. "I'm serious." But, I also knew he was right to try to lighten my mood.

"I know you are. But, so am I. I actually really like where you're at right now. You're perfect. The curves fit just right. Not months pregnant and not too skinny."

"You're j—" I started only to be interrupted.

"No, I'm not. You're so beautiful. I don't know why you can't ever see that."

Finn wouldn't let me get a word of protest in that time. His index finger immediately went to my lips to form the quiet symbol. But his gesture was interrupted by the baby monitor announcing Arinn's whimpers.

"There's the little curve-maker now," I jested. "I'll go get her. This is her short naptime. Besides, by the time I get her fed, it will just be about time to go get Chance. Do you want to come with me?"

"Sure. Maybe we can pick up something to eat and have a family movie night?" he suggested.

If the press and fans could see that side of him— it was such a contrast to the rocking cowboy on stage. But Finn was almost obsessively protective of his private life, which I admired and appreciated to the fullest extent. It allowed us to lead as normal of a life as we did, unhindered for the most part by outside forces. As a multiple Entertainer of the Year and Male Vocalist of the Year winner, I'm sure keeping that privacy intact wasn't easy for my husband. But, he knew it was worth it.

"Sounds good." Thinking of his thoughtful heart, I smiled. And then, knowing he had played one of the biggest events in his career less than twenty-four hours before, I asked, "But aren't you tired?"

"Yeah, but I slept a little on the plane."

"Don't know how you do that."

I cringed just thinking of him being in the air. Flight had never been my favorite mode of transportation. It had lost even further ranking after Finn had been in an aviation mishap a few years before.

"Regardless..." He knew there was nothing else he could say or do to ease my phobia. "The four of us—this family time— is important. You just might have to tuck two boys in tonight, though."

"I can do that." Internally thanking him for loving us that much, I outwardly kissed him and then started to get out of bed.

"Hey...in a minute," Finn spoke kindly but with determination. He locked eyes with me and guided me back into a prone position. He kissed me softly on the lips and then brought his hands down to my stomach and then my hips and thighs. "I love you." He kissed me again. "Every part."

There were new tears in my eyes, but I welcomed them. They were security. They were love.

***

"I have a surprise for you," I practically sang to my son while walking down the interior steps of Tina's apartment building and making sure Chance's jacket was fully Velcroed shut.

"Cookies?" Chance guessed, looking up at me with big, expectant eyes.

"No."

"Pizza?"

"No." I shook my head with a slight laugh. "And since when does a surprise mean food?"

I opened the front door of the building to bear witness to the chilly air and snowflakes beginning to swirl from the sky. Our car was in the visitor's section across the parking lot. Wearing khakis and a black leather jacket that partially exposed a dark gray graphic T, Finn was propped up against the car door.

"A pup—" Chance stopped himself from asking what I knew he really wanted but couldn't have because of my allergies. "Daddy!" he squealed with pure childhood excitement. Like a mini-marathoner, Chance started tearing across the lot in the direction of something even better than a puppy.

"Chance! Grab Mommy's hand! Ga—God!" A look of sheer terror streaked across Finn's face as I grabbed our son's hand. "Lara…" The pronunciation of my name was a mix of warning and relief. His hands up to his hair was a reflection of the stress that still remained.

"Mommy?" Those gray eyes, so similar to Finn's, peered up at me, confused with what had transpired. Just a millisecond before, he had been so excited to see his father. He didn't know what had happened to cause Finn to yell.

I did, though. We paused mid-way through the parking lot, and I bent down to our son. "You're fine. Daddy just wants to make sure you're safe."

"I safe."

"I know, Little Man." I kept his hand securely in mine, and we walked the remaining steps to the car.

Finn, who had been pacing in front of the car, stopped and directed his statement to our son. "Chance? Chance, come here." As we walked hand-in-hand toward him, Finn continued in an authoritative voice. "You do *not* let go of your mother's hand."

"But, Daddy—"

"No! No!" Finn interrupted in a voice Chance was not familiar with. "There could be a car."

"There no car." He didn't mean to argue back. He was simply a three-year-old who just knew literal terms. And he stated them.

"Wy—!" Finn started to say the wrong name.

We both froze. Without saying it, Finn and I had both known what had panicked him. Chance had not. Finn had been the only familial witness to his nephew Wyatt's fatal accident. Years earlier, long before Chance was even born, a car had careened out of control and hit the seven-year-old.

"Finn..." I tried calming the situation for both of them. "He understands."

Bringing his hands up to his eyes, my husband turned and walked a few steps away from the car, causing Chance to burst into tears. The surprise was supposed to be Finn returning, but instead our preschooler probably thought his dad was leaving again. His little heart was hurt, and I had to do my best to explain.

Bending down to his level, I said, "You know how much you love Daddy?" I smiled seeing his tears instantly dry and his arms open up as big as a little boy's possibly could. "Well, he loves you that much, too, and his arms are even bigger, aren't they?"

"Yeah."

I couldn't help but hug his innocence and kiss the top of his head. "You're not in trouble, Chance, okay? Both Daddy and I love you very much, and we just want to make sure you are safe. Will you sit in the car for a minute for me? Make those funny faces at your sister. I need to talk with Daddy."

Without a word, Chance obliged, allowing me to buckle him into his car seat and kiss one more time on top of the head. I went to Finn then. His back was toward me. Sidling up alongside him, I took his hand and leaned my head onto his shoulder.

"He okay?" he asked, continuing to stare straight ahead.

"Yeah."

"I shouldn't have yelled."

"No. You should have. He shouldn't have let go of my hand. He knows that."

"I couldn't handle—" Finn finally looked at me…his eyes misty.

"I know." I paused. "He's settled. He just needs to know that what he did was wrong, but you're not mad at him."

"I'm not mad."

"I know. I know the difference between you being mad and you being scared." I continued when Finn didn't comment. "But Chance is scared, too. You walked away from him when he was so exci—"

"I would never leave him."

And there it was. I hadn't even thought about it when I sized up the situation in front of me. It was something both of them had in common. Neither of them wanted to be left. Hopefully, though, Chance would never experience that fear to the magnitude that Finn did.

Chance was just getting to that age where he really understood someone not being around. It had been easier when he was younger and Finn had to leave for a few days or so to perform, or promote, or record, etc. But now he was starting to understand. It was the reason he had been so excited to see his dad after a lengthy week.

And Finn…Well, if anyone else knew that hurt, it was him. As a toddler, Finn had been left by his maternal grandmother in a park. It had been more than twenty-four hours later when he was finally reunited with his family. But he had repressed that memory… only for it to come violently crashing back in the form of PTSD and depression in his mid-twenties—something that only his immediate family and I knew about. But it was because of that incident and the consequences stemming from it that he could not face anyone ever leaving him.

Finn silently went to the open door of the back seat, unbuckled Chance, and, putting him in his arms, hugged him tightly. Chance, his legs wrapped around his daddy's back, gently played with the back of Finn's similar brown hair. It made me wonder who was comforting whom more.

"You want me to drive?" I asked, knowing that Finn was emotional.

"No! Daddy drive!" Chance belted out as Finn brought him back down to the ground.

"See, even the boy knows a bad driver when he sees one," Finn teased, very well knowing I was a fine driver. He just needed to play that macho role when it came to vehicles.

"Whatever," I mocked back. "C'mon, Little Man, let's get you in that car seat. Daddy will drive."

I put Chance back in the car and then entered the front passenger seat myself. As I put on my seatbelt, Finn started the engine and looked into the rearview mirror, signaling the same three fingers to Chance that he had during his Superbowl performance. I turned around to witness Chance doing it right back. I clasped my left hand with Finn's right and silently thanked whatever deity allowed the parking lot scene to be lovingly defused.

GREA WARNER

CHAPTER TWO

We only had a few days to enjoy the exclusive family bubble of just the four of us, since the rest of the collective Murphy/Faulkner/Jamison clan were joining us for an extended family weekend. Chance's birthday party was going to be that Saturday, followed by Arinn's christening on Sunday. As much as I loved our families and treasured the rare moments that we all got to spend together, getting ready for big gatherings was sometimes exhausting.

The night before everyone's arrival, Finn and I had just gotten the kids to bed when our landline and the community gate buzzer simultaneously sounded. Closing Chance's bedroom door, Finn insisted that I get the front door while he saw who was on the phone. I thought it should be the opposite. But, I went along with it since he was already heading toward our guest room, where the only upstairs landline was stationed.

I quickly found out why he made me see who was at the front gate. I allowed the delivery person access and, within minutes, in front of me was the most beautiful arrangement of three dozen red roses. I admired their beauty not only with my eyes but also my nose. They were the non-fragrant variety, due to my allergy to strong scents.

I placed the flowers on the kitchen center island and read the card, already knowing, of course, that they were from my thoughtful husband.

Our babies are both celebrating big threes. I can't believe how time has flown. I watch you with them—your love...your tenderness—and it just confirms to me the fact that I always knew you would be the best mom. I love you more than ever.

I rejoined him in the guest room with the card in hand. Not caring who he was talking to, I wrapped my arms around his strong, lean torso and started letting my tongue lap in his mouth. "I love you more than ever, too," I whispered when I broke our lock.

Grinning from ear to ear, Finn spoke into the phone. "Have a safe trip. Your daughter is manhandling me right now. I'm gonna have to go."

My eyes grew wide in the revelation that he was on the phone with my mother. "Finn!" I lightly hit him as he disconnected the call.

Setting the phone back on the nightstand, he gently tossed me onto the guest bed. Lovingly smothering his body on top of mine, he started planting kisses on my neck while letting his hands roam. "I think we should make sure this bed is comfy enough for your mom."

***

After two exciting and exhausting days, Chance was definitely ready for an early bedtime that Sunday evening. Although, of course, he wouldn't admit it. His droopy eyes and touch of attitude told me it was time to go to sleep, but he didn't want to miss any of the action. And, at the newly-crowned age of three, he had already picked up the act of charming the ladies.

"Your dress pretty, Mommy."

"Thank you, Chance," I said, as he played with the ruffles of my cream-colored dress, which I had yet to change out of since the christening. As a mom to a newborn, I hadn't had many occasions to dress up, and I was savoring it. "But you need to say good night to everyone."

"Mo—"

"Fine, then don't. Let's just go upstairs." I gave the ultimatum.

He pouted and went on his mission, getting big hugs and kisses from his grandparents— Finn's parents, who flew in from Louisville, and my mother from Pittsburgh. Everyone else had already left. The Jamisons—Finn's sister, Nola, and her husband, Will, who lived in a neighboring town, had to take their daughter Kelsea to another event. And my older-by-a-year brother, Lane, was meeting up with a friend in nearby Manhattan. He was staying in our NYC penthouse before returning to North Carolina and his wife.

Still looking so damn handsome in his black suit, minus the pink tie, Finn received the final hug from our son. "Night-night. Sleep tight."

"No bed bugs," Chance finished.

"Nope." Finn winked at me, knowing the phrase that had once been a sentimental one just between the two of us was now shared with our son. "Just sweet dreams. I love you, Chance."

"I wuv you, too, Daddy."

"You good?" Finn asked me.

"Yeah. Stay. He'll be out quick."

Chance relented and turned to me. I hoisted him into my arms and carefully climbed the stairs. Even though it had been years since I lost my balance on those steps, causing me to be in a coma and miscarry, I knew Finn still held the vision in his mind. It was another tragic accident that he had been the only witness to. So I was very conscientious, especially when carrying our children on those stairs.

After putting on his pajamas and brushing his teeth, our son automatically knew it was time for prayers. It was something he definitely got from Finn. Although my mother went to church regularly, religion was not at all reinforced in our house growing up. If I had prayed during those years, it wasn't to an organized holy being—it was to my inner self to get me through. I still did not go to church on a regular basis, but I respected the beliefs of my in-laws and honored their choices by raising my children with that foundation.

Once Chance had finished with his liturgy of names and things to be thankful for, I cuddled him into me securely and told him I loved him. That was my ritual. Just like Finn, I sadly knew how easily things could be taken away. And I never wanted a day to go by without my children knowing that I loved them.

Despite him being asleep at "goodnight nobody, goodnight mush," I continued reading until I got through the famous last lines of Chance's favorite, *Goodnight Moon*. I then quietly extracted myself from his bed and placed the book on the shelf near the glow of the nightlight. Hearing the voices of my mother and Finn's mother coming from Arinn's nearby room, I walked in to see both ladies putting my other child to sleep. When I started to offer to take my daughter, they both instantly protested, shooing me out and insisting they needed grandma time.

Glad they got along as well as they did and, honestly, happy to be relieved of one of the numerous times an infant needs to be rocked, I accepted and made my way downstairs. Finn and his father, both with half-filled glasses of bourbon, were standing in mid-conversation near the towering fireplace. I had to laugh hearing what the topic was.

"Pop? You're sure? You know what Pilates is?"

"Yeah."

"Really?"

"Your mother's always nagging me to get some exercise, and this way, I'll get to spend some quality time with my daughter-in-heart." Zak Murphy looked at me as I joined them.

I couldn't help but smile. My Pilates class was the next morning, and I had asked prior to Chance's needing to go to bed if anyone wanted to join me. I didn't expect Finn's father to take me up on it. I was surprised but honored, as it wasn't anything my father would have ever done—not the actual class or using the words Mr. Murphy had. Even though he didn't need to say them. I knew I was more like another daughter to him than any kind of in-law.

"It's like yoga…a girlie thing," Finn explained as Mrs. Murphy entered the room.

"Bless her heart, that precious little one is asleep. And your mom is just checking on her flight."

"Thanks," I answered and then corrected Finn with a touch of subtle seduction. "Pilates is strengthening and flexibility and core work. You want me to be strong and flexible, don't you, Cowboy?"

He performed in front of sixty-thousand-plus and on live television, but he was still his folks' little boy. "Lara, not in front of the innocent." He nodded his head toward his parents.

"The kids are sleeping." I mocked naivety as he shook his head. "Besides, if I talked about the effects of watermelon rinds the first time I met your parents, I think they're okay with my comment now."

"Love this gal!" Mr. Murphy bellowed out with hearty laughter, surely recalling how at a party years ago—because I tended to be sarcastic and talkative when I was nervous—I mentioned that I heard watermelon rinds had a Viagra effect. "And I can't wait for this Pilates thing."

When I stuck my tongue out at Finn, signaling that I won on all levels of that debate, he swiftly pulled me into his body and whispered in my ear. "I can think of a lot of better things to do with that tongue." And then he dipped his into my ear. Before I could get all squirmy, he turned me around so that his hands were around my waist from behind. "You two have fun tomorrow. I'll make sure your mom gets to the airport, and then I'd like to go into the city if Nana here," —he gestured to his mother— "can watch the kids."

As Mrs. Murphy whole-heartedly agreed, I questioned, "Why are you going into the city?"

"Reese just called," he spoke of his longtime publicist. "She wants to meet with me. It sounded kinda important. That all right? I'll be back before dinner."

"Yeah," I agreed and then turned to Finn's mother. "As long as you're okay with that."

"Putting on tights, being in that crazy city, or playing with two adorable children...I got the best job of them all."

"Hmmff," Finn and I practically grumbled in unison.

But it was so true. I knew I was blessed, especially after I had such a tumultuous start in life. I just had to remember that when I stepped on the scale or missed Finn. Every warm hug from our extended family, every magnetic knowing look of love from my husband, and every pure word or sound from my children...yes, I was blessed.

***

Those kids were happily playing, albeit completely differently, when Finn arrived home late in the afternoon that next day. His parents, who were staying at Nola's, were most likely resting from their active day of exercise and childrearing before heading back to Louisville early the following morning. And I was in the midst of putting away the numerous gifts our children had received over the past couple of days, as well as writing out thank you cards and running the dishwasher.

Finn's greeting was a silent, warm, lengthy hug. Before I could question where my traditional "hi, baby" was, Chance ran up to his daddy and pulled him down to the great room floor where he was building a block creation.

Finn looked up at me with a knowing, parenthood half-smile.

"My mom just called. She's already home."

"That's good," he replied and complimented Chance's tower while adding to it. "How did Pop do? I still can't believe you got him to go to Pilates."

"He did good." I smiled, recalling how Mr. Murphy had tried every exercise and mixed it up with the few guys that were there. "He definitely has the strength. Just had some trouble getting up from the floor as quickly as we did. And I had to park in the bottom lot. So, we had to walk that hill, which he took slowly. But that's age."

"Yeah. I forget how old they are getting," Finn commented with an edge of lament.

"I forget how old *we* are getting," I countered, joining my two favorite guys on the floor.

"Well, we hit that age. Remember back in college when we thought at thirty-five we wouldn't be able to keep up with the pace of Manhattan?" Finn stretched over to Arinn, who was under her baby mobile, and gently cupped her head to give her a kiss.

"Yeah." I laughed. "How *did* you do in the city today, old man? Did you bring your walker?"

"Somehow, I managed without," he joshed back. Finn was years and miles away from needing any walking aide. He was an avid runner, both on pavement and on the treadmill, and kept in prime shape for the energy he used when performing.

"So what's up?" I asked regarding the impromptu meeting in Manhattan.

"Well, there's good news and bad news." He added another block to the tower.

"Oh, yeah?" I asked perplexed but not overly concerned.

"Yeah." He looked up. "The good news is, Reese and Roger are engaged."

"Wow!" My eyes widened. "That's great news. What

made him finally do it?"

Finn shook more than laughed. "Scheduling, what else? A publicist and an agent? It's all about timing."

Reese's now-fiancée managed a couple high profile athletes. He and Reese had been dating for a few years. I understood all too well about scheduling—even more so since having two kids.

"They want Chance to be the ring bearer," Finn continued.

"I wha—?" Chance piped in not missing a beat.

"Oh, boy." I shook my head, both proud and a little leery of an unpredictable three-year-old being responsible in front of a crowd.

"You are going to be a very special part of a big day for Reese," Finn explained to our son.

"Okay," he answered nonchalantly and went back to building.

"When?" I asked.

"Labor Day weekend. Right after the tour."

I couldn't help a quick sigh at the mention of my husband's multi-city summer tour, which would take him away for months. But, I quickly added some positivity. "Tell her congrats from me and the little ring bearer here."

"Will do. Chance, Reese got you something for your birthday. I just put it on the sofa. Go get it, bring it to your room, and play for a little bit. Mommy and I need to talk."

I looked at my husband, now a bit apprehensive. He hadn't told me the bad news yet. And it involved sending one child out of the room— somewhere his curious little ears, which were mighty good at listening, could not comprehend. Luckily, Chance was every bit his father's son and loved to open gifts. He grabbed the bag and did his waddle/run up the stairs faster than I could even stand. Finn, now also on his feet, took my hands.

"What?" I asked slowly and cautiously. I was expecting him to announce additional days he needed to be away or some other obligation that demanded his attention or time.

But that was not the case...at all.

"Lara, I went to the penthouse." There was that twitch. "Your brother wasn't expecting me. He...well, he wasn't with a friend. He was, but his friend... she...they—"

My hands dropped from his. "What? He was with a girl?" I didn't need to say it... not his wife.

"I guess it's been going on. He didn't want me to tell you. But I told him I had to... that we had no omissions." My husband honored our "no omissions pact" even when he didn't want to— one of the many reasons I loved and trusted him.

"What about McEllie?" I asked.

I was shocked and processing like mad. My brother and his wife had been married for over ten years. There had never been a peep of dissension. We had seen them together at Christmas.

"He said they're separated."

"What?" I exclaimed. "When?"

"I don't know, Lar. It's their business. I really didn't want to be in the middle of it."

Trying to remain calm and rational, I used a technique I had seen Finn use plenty of times. I turned around, inhaled and exhaled deeply, and then once again faced my husband. "He's cheating on her." It had started as a question but ended as a statement as reality set in.

Lane was my brother, and I loved him dearly. He had been my protector from as long as I could remember. But, as a woman— a married woman— I was horrified.

"Yeah. I don't know how long they've been separated, though."

"Separated doesn't mea—"

"We don't know the whole story."

"Why? How can someone do that? I mean, they seemed happy. They...you saw them together. If Lane...if it can happen with them—"

"Don't even go there, Lara," my husband interrupted me with conviction.

"Finn—"

"Baby…" He put his hands up to my face. "We are not them. I am not your brother. I love you with a passion that blinds me to anyone else…anyone…anywhere…any time." After a moment of my body melding into my husband's strong, sturdy, secure torso, Finn softly added, "Y'know, I wouldn't mind hearing that back."

I pulled away slightly so I could see into his sincere eyes. "Without a speck of hesitation or doubt. Ditto, ditto, ditto, Cowboy." And, to solidify my response, I sealed it with a kiss.

"Now, I know you, Lara. I know you are ready to find your phone and call your brother and lay into him."

"I—" True.

"I already did." He paused for a split second, took a step away, and said, "How he chooses to live his life is his business. But, first of all, I wish he wouldn't have deceived you." Finn was most definitely my other protector. "And, truthfully, I was pissed that he brought someone to the penthouse. McEllie would have been one thing. But, you know, I— we—have personal stuff there. Who knows who this woman is or how long it will last?" Finn guarded his privacy fiercely, and Lane, most likely without thinking about it, violated that.

"Was she in the penthouse alone? I mean, Lane was with us a lot. Where was she?"

"He swore to me that she was out in the city— visiting other friends, shopping, sightseeing, whatever." Finn paused. "She said the same thing. Besides, you know, anything that is really important, I either have locked up or here. I still don't like it, though."

"I'm sorry."

"It's not your fault. You didn't know."

"What was she like? Blonde? Brunette? Did she do the whole starstruck thing?"

"Brunette and, yeah, a little. It was just awkward all the way around."

"I can't believe this," I said, starting to fume all over again.

"Listen, let it sit for a little bit. You can't call now, anyway. They're on their way to the airport."

"Okay. I guess you're right."

"What? What was that?" he teased. "I'm right? I think we need to add that to a tally chart. I might have just crossed over to five. Five times right since we've been married…"

I laughed and playfully hit him. "Stop it! You're right, especially when knowing me."

"I know I love you."

"Forever." I stated our tagline since even before we were engaged.

"Forever, Beauty."

***

I couldn't let it sit, though. What I had discovered about my brother stirred and stirred around in my mind all day until it was like an infectious tick buried deep into my skin that could only be eliminated through extraction. So, after dinner, while Finn and Chance were starting to play a video dance game together, I brought Arinn upstairs to change her diaper. I also brought my phone. I called Lane in the solitude of Arinn's all-white nursery accented only with a few touches of soft purple and green. I half-expected him not to answer. After all, it had been a long day. He needed to unpack, and he needed to be with "her." On the third ring, I was scripting my sarcastic voice mail message in my head. Right after the fourth ring, though, he answered.

"Hi, Lar," he said with an obvious cautious tone in his voice.

"I can't believe you did that, Lane."

"What?" Like he didn't know.

"What? Let's start with bringing an uninvited guest into

our home when we're not there. Finn doesn't let just…." I was start-stopping like crazy. Both my pacing and my blood pressure had accelerated while, in contrast, Arinn played in the crib, thankfully, oblivious. "How about bringing her in the first place? How about cheating on your wife?"

"Are we going to be able to talk about this rationally?"

"This *is* rational. You should have seen me when Finn first told me."

"He is so protective of you." My brother acknowledged something that he had admired Finn for in the past.

"He loves me. He doesn't want me betrayed."

Lane heard the obvious insinuation in my voice and countered with, "So, we're *not* going to be able to talk about it then?"

Breathe, Lara. Breathe. I did want to talk about it. I wanted to understand. That was why I called.

"Is there somehow you can explain it? Cause, God, Lane, I want to know how you could do it. What's going on? What happened?"

"That's just it. It just kinda happens, Lara." He sounded suddenly older but yet, strangely, content. "I can't really tell you when, but McEllie and I were leading two separate lives…for a while. And then I met Piper."

"I don't want to know," I interrupted.

"She didn't do anything to you. In fact, she really wanted to meet you. I didn't think this weekend was the best idea, though."

"No kidding," I replied with syrupy sarcasm. "Thanks at least for that…for not ruining your nephew's birthday or niece's baptism." I leaned over and stroked my daughter's hair.

"Seriously, Lara, chill out."

"Lane, you're cheating on McEllie." I turned from the crib and went to look out the window; the dark February sky seemed even chillier somehow.

"We—"

"As rotten as dad was, he never—"

"Oh, fuck you! That's enough." His temper really rose on that comment. "I can't believe you just said that. You are seriously comparing me to that asshole? Good God!"

"I'm just saying—" I started.

But now it was my brother's turn to let loose. "You know, I don't know who you think you are. It's finally gotten to you, huh? Living like royalty. You think you're better than everyone else. Like you're above the rest of us and we're always the ones that are wrong."

"Lane, you know I'm not like that. You—"

"Well, I'm not like that bastard that called us his children. I never hurt McEllie. We just faded. You know what? Just go live your pie-in-the-sky life with Mr. Rockstar and leave me alone. Just forget…well, forget everything."

I knew he hung up. There wasn't a doubt. The finality of his words and the silence on the phone told me all. But, yet, I didn't believe.

"Lane?" I tried to no avail.

And then I crumpled to the floor. As Arinn played happily, I began to bawl as if *I* were the infant. I don't remember Lane and I arguing like that… ever. The scarring pain of living with an abusive, alcoholic father had bonded us early in life. We had understood and looked out for one another until Lane finally had the chance to escape upon high school graduation. My remaining year at home without my sibling had been a life-changing one. And Lane and I didn't speak as often due to pure distance, but we never fought. Certainly not like we just had. Certainly not as if we would never fight or even speak again.

"Mommy, Daddy say his gril have to dance wif—" I heard Chance's voice gaining proximity volume as he unexpectedly entered the nursery. He froze, and his gray eyes grew wide at the site of me—his mother a mangled mess on the floor with tears flowing uncontrollably. Before I could stop him, Chance started out of the room yelling, "Daddy! Daddy! Mommy crying. She hurt."

I could hear Finn flying up the stairs as if he was taking them two or three at a time. I tried to shake off the tears knowing now that I had scared both of them. Pushing Chance gently but urgently aside, Finn entered the room purposefully falling in a seated position beside me.

"I'm okay. I'm... I'm not hurt," I said as Finn's hands roamed my body searching for potential injury. When his hands rested on my tear-stricken face and he let out an exhale of relief, I said, "I called Lane. We both said some things."

"Oh, baby, I told you to let it sit."

"Finn, I don't need 'I told you so' right now," I choked out.

"Okay. Okay," he repeated calmly and pulled me into his chest while stroking my hair. "Hush." His soft voice was the one he used on our children when they were upset.

Chance, determining that the scene before him was more settled, sucked onto us, giving a collective hug. "Mommy okay?"

"Yeah." Finn ruffled Chance's hair and joshed, "She'll do anything to get out of dancing."

I chuckled in between my tears. I hated the empty, sickening feeling that my telephone conversation with Lane had left. But knowing that I had such an abundance of love holding me both figuratively and literally definitely helped.

CHAPTER THREE

My text read, *FYI— I'm getting changed in2 something more comfortable.*

Finn's immediate response was, *Send pic.*

He knew I wouldn't send anything even remotely provocative, not only because of my career but because of his. If anyone got ahold of something that was meant to be personal, it would be extremely detrimental to the job I was currently on maternity leave from—a technology coordinator for a private school. But, as the wife of a superstar, it would also be very unwelcomed, national publicity in the hands of the press.

After looking around our master suite, I took the perfect picture and sent it to my husband. The photo was of our red lava lamp. It had been mine in college— the place where Finn and I had first met before losing touch and reconnecting seven years later. Back then, the fun lamp had sparked Finn's satirical "Roxanne" nickname for me. But, since becoming a couple, I had regifted it to him so he would know there would never be another man for me besides him…no one to put the red light out for.

LOL! he replied. *More than that lamp is turned on right now. Just dropped off Chance. C U soon. xoxo.*

It was Valentine's Day. Neither of us wanted to get dressed up and go out, but we both wanted to celebrate the holiday the way it was meant to be celebrated. That was obvious through our mutual soft touches and sexual undertones over breakfast that morning.

While I waited for Finn to return from taking Chance to his biweekly preschool, I played with our daughter. I moved her soft, rubber toys around, trying to improve her hand-eye coordination. And then I used baby oil to massage her belly. I wanted her calm. I wanted her to sleep. Because, I wanted her dad.

Mission was accomplished just before Finn returned home. I was putting Arinn's bottle in the kitchen when he walked through the door that joined the kitchen with the laundry room and adjacent garage. His eyes scanned my new red silky attire with admiration. The way he looked at me, despite my only losing a couple more pounds, made me feel sexy… made me know that his eyes were only for me. And I never, ever wanted that to change. I didn't want us to "fade," as my brother had said.

"Jesus, Rox." He placed a box of chocolates on the counter. "You're…damn!"

"Happy Valentine's Day." I smiled.

Finn removed the coordinating silk cover from my shoulders and let it drop to the kitchen floor. His expert hands started massaging my shoulders and back. "God, I want you," he cooed into my long hair, pulling me then tightly up against him.

I turned around and started kissing him in a way that I knew I wasn't going to stop until both of us were spared any type of clothing. And he had way too much of his on. Releasing my tongue momentarily, I reached for the bottom of his blue graphic T and lifted it over his head.

"You know what happened last Valentine's."

"Mmmm-hmmm," he murmured kissing me between words. "That girl, from being conceived on Valentine's to the day she chose to enter this world, is one hundred percent our daughter."

He pulled me into him again so that I could feel every manly inch of him. Our kissing grew intense once more as my feet became light and I found myself lifted onto him— my legs around his waist and my arms around his neck. He only took a few steps when we both heard Arinn's cries. They weren't horrible, but they were the type that if she was immediately pacified with a cuddly snuggle, she could go back to sleep. Otherwise, we were in for a long haul.

Finn grumbled as I slowly eased my feet back to the floor. "Start the shower," I said, kissing him lightly on the lips. "I'll meet you there in just a few."

"Some of my favorite Valentine memories are in the shower with you."

"I know. Let's make another. Just not with the same result as last year." Because, although we had been trying the previous year for a second child, it definitely wasn't time to even start discussing whether we wanted a third.

I had found out I was pregnant about a month after Valentine's Day the year before. Well, it was Finn who had actually figured it out first. And, of course, it had to be surrounded with drama…

…It was mid-March the year before, and we had just finished making love. "What was that about?" Finn's voice was a mix of exasperation and frustration.

"What?" Bewildered by his reaction, I covered myself up with the sheet.

"I didn't realize it was such a task making love with me."

"What?" I had managed to look at him. "It's not." And then I burst into a downright deluge of tears.

"Damn it."

"I'm sorry." I immediately apologized—for not being quite into our lovemaking, for crying, for making him upset…for it all. "I guess…I guess I'm just tired. I didn't want—" I didn't know what to say because I wasn't really quite sure myself.

"God, Lara, why didn't you tell me? When have I ever, ever gotten even remotely close to making you?" Now he was hurt.

Never. Never was the answer. He was super sensitive to my feelings and my past— a past that included having sex basically without consent.

"I wanted to and then I just...I felt so alone, and I didn't want you to...to go."

"What? What are you talking about? What's going on?" His voice had started to soften. "Look at me." When I did, I saw the concern in his eyes.

"I'm sorry. I know I'm all over the place." I rubbed my itchy and watery eyes and nose. "I don't understand." I definitely wasn't typical Lara.

"Baby, geez, what's going on? I haven't seen you this emotional or this scattered since..." He stopped himself mid-sentence and gently touched my face. "Lara?" He waited until he had all of my attention. "Lar? You're rubbing your face like your allergies are bothering you, and there's nothing remotely fragrant. Are you pregnant?"

"No," I instantly denied. "No. I'm just tired. Chance, and work, and you being away... I..." Was I pregnant? "I...God, I don't know. Maybe." Tired, moody, crying, super sensitive... they were all the same symptoms I had exhibited during the first month or so of each pregnancy. Was I pregnant?

Finn had let out the lightest of laughs as he tried another question in a more relaxed tone. "Do you have one of those tests?"

I wiped the remnants of tears from my wet cheeks. "No." Finn's closed mouth "hmmm" was met by my mind simply demanding to know one way or another if I was pregnant. "Will you go get one?" I propped up more securely on my elbow.

I would have been more amused by the shocked look on my husband's face had I not been so focused on the mission at hand. "Me? Now? You want me to go into a pharmacy or grocery store or whatever and pick up a pregnancy test, and you don't think that will be trending on every——?"

"I…Yes. I want to find out. Don't you? And I'm a mess right now. I can't. Finn, please. You can wear a cap and some glasses. Nobody will know." I rattled off my closing arguments in a hurry.

"If you really want me to, I will. But, Beauty, I don't think there's any doubt. We don't need a test. You…all of this" —he smudged the pads of his thumbs under my eyes and put his forehead up to mine— "has pregnant written all over it."

I was coming more and more to that realization. Trying to add a bit of humor to the situation, I had added, "All we need now is Audrey showing up."

Finn shook his head at the mention of his former fiancée, who we hadn't seen or heard from in years. Of course, the previous two times we had, I had just found out I was pregnant and was ready to tell Finn. Audrey had never actually caused either of us any grief or disruption in our relationship. Yet, just knowing how she had hurt him in the past made me detest the mere thought of her.

"I'll get dressed," Finn had mumbled, knowing better than to continue the Audrey train of thought.

He sat on the edge of the bed and started to string his legs through his jeans commando-style. I was more awake then, and it wasn't just the sight of how his sexy body hugged the denim. It was the anticipation of what that pregnancy test would reveal and the realization of how fortunate I was. Finn could have easily become upset with the scene that had played out. But, he hadn't. He loved me. He loved me enough to figure out what was going on.

I wrapped my arms around his still naked back and let my lips rest there for a moment. "I love you, you know."

His head dipped. I sometimes forgot—despite him commanding a stadium full of people with one lyric, or taking charge of nearly every aspect of his high-level career, or always having a secure answer for our son—how vulnerable he was after being left as a child. With meds and therapy for his PTSD and depression, no one would know the difference… except on nights when he doubted his wife's love for him.

Finn turned and planted a semi-strong confirmation kiss on my lips. "You, too," he said and then softly played with my hair. "Are you ready for our lives to change again?"

I was. It felt right, even though we had just decided to start trying again. And Arinn was definitely meant to be. When she decided to make her entrance into the world was proof enough. I had gone into labor a day before her due date. Of course it had to be that day. It was meant to be.

"I'm sorry," I had legitimately offered to my husband while lying in the hospital bed that November night.

"You better be sorry because you are squeezing the hell out of my hand and not for any other reason," was his response.

"Finn!" I admonished while legitimately trying to ease up on his hand. But the contractions were coming too close, and the memory of each one had lingered.

"Not for any other reason," he reiterated. Squeezing his hand was definitely not the reason I was sorry, and he knew it.

"You can have the TV on." I looked at the quiet and dark television hanging in my private hospital room.

"Nope. Drop it."

"At least put your phone back on." Before he could, no doubt, deny that request, too, another contraction shook my body. "Ahh, Ahh, Ahh, Ahh, God!"

"You're doing so great. I love you, Roxanne." When I released my grasp ever so slightly, he took the opportunity to stroke my hand with his thumb. But, when I didn't respond to his declaration of love, he said, "Lar?"

"I'm debating," I teased and then left him off the hook. "I love you, too. How's Chance?"

"He's fine."

"How do you know? You don't have your phone on," I said, pointedly.

"Lara, I'm not turning on the phone. All of my attention—all of it— is with you. Nola and Will have Chance. They know where we are. And everything else? It simply doesn't matter. It's not going to change anything if I know toni—" He had stopped mid-sentence because, once again, he was probably close to losing circulation in his hand.

And I was screaming. "Ahh, Ahh, God, they're too close. I've got to be ready."

I *was* ready, and so was she. Arinn's birth from first contraction to final push was relatively quick and occurred with the most ironic of timing—she arrived just before midnight on CMA night. It was the anniversary of when Finn and I had first made love. That night had always held a special place in our hearts, and her arrival made it even more so.

Of course, though, on the day of her birth, we were tucked away in a suburban New York hospital—miles and miles away from all the hoopla of Nashville. Finn had declined presenting or performing months in advance knowing that, even if the baby came a few days early, he was not going to leave our sides for the awards show. He had been up for both Entertainer of the Year and Male Vocalist of the Year once again. But, because of her timing, he had not even gotten a chance to watch.

The press release the following day had read, "Finn Murphy takes home ultimate prize on CMA night." No, for the first time since that first night we were together, Finn had not collected a glass trophy and bragging rights. But, he had not seemed to mind. Our healthy baby girl, whose moniker was the combination of Finn's and mine, had been the best award of all…

***

I was fondly remembering our daughter's birth that past November as I sat with her on the low cement wall that lined Nola and Will's driveway. Kelsea, whose ninth birthday we were celebrating, was delighting in her role as older cousin by helping Chance go up and down the slide. They were not in my immediate eyesight, but I knew they were being taken care of. The rest of the Jamison and Murphy clan were gathered close by around the fire pit, relishing the unusually warm March weather. Everyone, that is, except my husband. He had been out of town for a few days and was concluding his trip that night with a meeting in Manhattan.

I was just finishing rocking Arinn and was planning on rejoining the group when Finn entered my line of vision. He must have come from inside the house and out the back door because he hadn't walked past me via the driveway. I could see but not hear as he greeted his family and then looked as they pointed in my direction. I softly smiled, knowing that he would make his way up to me then.

"You're here," I said when he was just a few feet away.

"I am."

"How? What about your meeting?"

"It's bullshit," he said while simultaneously lifting his body up to sit on the ledge next to me. "I walked out."

I couldn't hide the puzzled look on my face. But Finn chose to ignore it. Instead, he softly touched Arinn's whisper of brownish-red hair, so much the radiant combination of both of our shades—Finn's brown and mine dark strawberry blonde. He then offered me the treat in his other hand.

"I stole one from the fire pit."

My momentary concern faded as I took a bite of the s'more still in his hand. He had brought it knowing how much I would appreciate it. S'mores were, after all, our favorite snack— a remembrance of our first weekend spent together.

"You didn't steal it out of your sister's hand, did you, Munch?" I teased, using Nola's nickname for Finn. As a kid, he was supposedly notorious for taking her afterschool snacks.

"You know it." Finn laughed as I took another bite.

He then handed me the cold, green beverage he had managed to hide at his side. I laughed, recognizing the McDonald's Shamrock Shake. It was another of our personal connections. I jokingly always bought him McDonald's gift cards, knowing his love for the seasonal minty shake.

"I forgot they were out."

"You didn't hear the alarm reminder on my phone for the past week or so?" he joked.

I took a long sip from the straw and handed it back to my husband, who seemed to be looking at me with such intense concentration. "What?" I asked.

"Just you."

"Me? Me what?"

"You. Everything. S'mores and McDonalds and sitting here on this ledge. I'm so glad you trusted me all those years ago to tell me...to tell me everything."

He was talking about the night, many years before, when I had told him about giving up a child as a teenager fresh out of high school. Essentially, it had been that honest, open conversation that had launched our friendship into something more. We hardly talked about it anymore, though. There was no need to. I was not, nor had I ever been, a part of that child's life. And my life with Finn and our family was beyond blessed.

"And, God, for waking up from that coma," he continued. "You've given me this wonderful life with these two amazing kids. You are my constant in an inconsistent world."

Sure, he was remembering. And sure, he had been away. And he was always sensitive when it came to me and his family, but...

"Finn, is everything okay?"

"What? A guy can't just tell his wife how much he adores her? You need me to put it in a letter or a song?" He grinned to let me know he was jesting. But he had, in fact, on numerous occasions written both private and public declarations of our love.

"No. No. Saying it is beautiful. It's perfect." Carefully, because Arinn was still sleeping peacefully in my arms, I leaned over and kissed him to confirm my response.

"Daddy! Daddy here!" Chance's excited voice broke our lip lock as he ran up with Kelsea by his side.

"I was wondering how long it would take for him to notice." Finn left out a soft chuckle before letting his feet drop to the ground and scooping up Chance in his arms. "Hi, Little Man. Hey, Kels. Happy Birthday."

"Thanks, Uncle Finn. I didn't think you were coming."

"I wanted to make sure to make i—" he started.

"Daddy, watch me. I slide. Watch." Chance started to wiggle his little body down from Finn's while reaching for his hand to pull him toward the swing set.

"Okay, Chance. Let me see if Mommy nee—"

"All good," I confirmed.

Our two-minute reunion was over. Finn was being dragged to the swing set, and I had to put the baby in her portable crib. Our time alone as a couple was becoming more and more sparse— two kids, his career...But, what time we had, I was determined to make count—to make special— because it was us, and we had to be worth it.

CHAPTER FOUR

Finn doing push-ups was always a sight to behold. But Finn wearing just gray sweat shorts, exposing his washboard abs and insanely sculptured biceps, and going at an unusually menacing pace, was a whole other realm. That is what Chance and I witnessed walking into my husband's exercise area on the last day in March.

While switching off the television, Finn said to Chance, "C'mon, Little Man, I need some more weight, climb aboard." Finn lowered himself momentarily to the floor, allowing Chance to brace himself on his father's back. "Ready? You have to hold on tight."

After a few more push-ups, with Chance laughing out in glee, our son looked at me and cried out, "Mommy turn. Mommy on top."

I tried not to laugh as Finn's eyebrows bounced up and down at me flirtatiously. "Can you handle me?" I asked.

"You're going to ride me on top?" Finn spit out, trying not to laugh himself. "Bring it on, Cowgirl."

I covered my face, feeling slightly embarrassed in front of our three-year-old, although I knew he was completely oblivious to his parents' double-meaning conversation. Nevertheless, Chance and I switched places. I rested my face on Finn's bare back and enveloped my arms around his torso. As Chance cheered, Finn moved his body at a much slower pace—I definitely provided the extra weight he said he wanted— before jokingly collapsing and flipping us so that I was on my back and he was planked above me. He did push-ups again, kissing me as he came down.

Our blissful moment was abruptly interrupted, however, when Finn stopped mid-stream and exclaimed, "Chance, don't touch that. Get down!"

I looked over to see our son bouncing on the large, purple, plastic exercise ball. He had done the same thing a million times before. He was in no danger of harm. Sure, he was reaching for the weight on the floor. Probably because in the past, he had seen Finn use the two in combination. But there was no way Chance could possibly, even remotely, lift the weight.

Eyes wide, Chance listened to his directive and got off the ball. Finn got off of me. My husband wrung his hands through his hair and sat in a way that was reminisce of his meditation pose. He would sometimes use the technique to write new music or calm himself when stressed.

Recognizing in the silence what needed to be done, I sat up to meet them and said, "Chance, go wash your hands. We'll be up in a minute."

"I a big boy. I wash all by myself."

"You are." I smiled, knowing this was a relatively new skill for him. "Daddy and I are very proud of you."

On the mention of his favorite name, Finn attempted a closed smile at his son. Chance beamed, whole exercise ball incident already forgotten, and hurried out of the room. In turn, Finn stood up and turned away from me. Trying to collect my thoughts, I first closed my eyes and then joined him. I knew my husband and all of his idiosyncrasies pretty well, as he did mine. I knew when to question. I knew when to push. I knew when to ignore. I knew when to make it better.

I waited until he turned to me, which I knew he would, and then made a request. "Hold me."

He obliged, wrapping his arms securely around my body and resting his tilted head alongside mine. He couldn't deny my soft voice or his need to touch me and hopefully release whatever was troubling him. I knew that.

"We don't have to go out for my birthday," I spoke while savoring his embrace.

"What?" he questioned, pulling us arm's length apart. "You made me promise not to buy you anything if we just had a night out."

"It's a woman's prerogative to change her mind," I teased.

"Uh-huh." His mumble was accompanied by a semi-smile.

"Finn, we don't have to do the whole dinner and a movie tonight. It can wait. It's not even my birthday." My birthday was a few days away, but Finn would be out of town, as he unfortunately was most years due to the ACM awards.

"It *can't* wait."

"You're..." I hesitated but then knew our "no omissions" pact kind of included being blunt. So, I forged on, alluding to the extra push-ups and worries. "You've been worked up about something. I don't know if it's the ACMs or what, but—"

"I'm all right," he denied. "But I think the night out will actually help."

"You sure?"

"Believe me, Lara, you're not going to want to miss what I have planned." When I furled my eyebrows with suspicion at him, he said, "But since you offered to change your mind, you'll have to be good about getting a gift, too."

"Finn!" I expelled.

I had told him years before that I didn't need gifts—a card would suffice. It had been partially because I wasn't used to receiving gifts. Growing up, my father's hard-earned money was for liquor. My husband was the exact opposite—he overindulged me.

"C'mon, you knew I would." He seemed to stifle a laugh.

I did. And, I knew it would be something with diamonds. He always gave me some sort of jewelry with my April birthstone.

"You'll like it," he said.

"I'm sure I will. That's not the point."

Ignoring that, he forged on. "You'll like our destination even better."

Finn had not told me yet where we were going for dinner— just that it was in Manhattan and that he had already made separate plans for the kids. I wasn't a fan of the unknown. But the fact that he seemed once again animated or, at least, back to normal, made me happy and more willing to go with the flow of the surprise evening.

I brushed my index finger's knuckle along his slight stubble. "Can you at least let me know what to wear and if I should have my hair up or down."

"Doesn't matter. It's gonna end up down either way," he said seductively, not missing a beat.

And there was his beautiful grin again. Thank goodness. Hopefully, the evening would bring plenty more of exactly that.

***

There's advantages and disadvantages to staying nestled in our suburban New York town. Just as there's advantages and disadvantages to going into Manhattan. If we remained truly local, most of the people in suburbia were used to Finn being in town. But if we ventured even slightly into neighboring areas, Finn was destined to not only be recognized but celebritized with autograph and picture-taking locals. Then, of course, there was New York

City. True residents of Manhattan seemed to play it cool… almost purposefully trying not to acknowledge that someone with fame was in their midst. But tourists… well, they were the complete opposite side of the coin. And, that night—my birthday date night—I was both the star-struck tourist and the annoyed celebrity wife.

We went to a movie theater in a residential area of Manhattan. Because of its location and the fact that we did not go to the later evening screening, we got into the darkened theater unscathed by Finn Murphy fans. Shortly after the thriller started, I felt Finn's arm slowly, tentatively wrap around my shoulders. It was so awkward, I even looked over at him. Our bodies knew one another's with precision—the proverbial hand and glove. So, why the tentativeness? But Finn's eyes remained glued to the screen. So mine did, too. Then, after a good moment or so, his other hand ventured onto my inner thigh and his lips nuzzled my neck.

Shocked, I purposefully whispered each word slowly. "What are you doing?"

"You told me you wanted a real date. Isn't this what you're supposed to do at the movies?" he murmured ever so seductively in my ear and then blew into it.

I actually busted out a breath of air, thankfully stifling any real sound. Turning to him and seeing his wide grin, I kissed him quickly and said, "Later, Cowboy." And I leaned my head onto his shoulder—the natural fit found again.

***

"You know that thing…you know how couples have a 'freebie list?' If one of them had the opportunity to have sex with a celebrity on their list, the other would be okay with it?" It was much later that night, and Finn and I were strolling hand-in-hand back to our Manhattan penthouse. "We don't have a list." He continued before I could query or comment. "And when I say we don't have a list, I mean, we will never have a list."

I shook my head, knowing exactly what he was referencing. "I would not sleep with Ben Winthrop."

"You acted like you were a teenage girl meeting the guy whose poster is hanging on her bedroom wall." Finn laughed, obviously remembering the fool I made of myself.

"No, I did not!" I wasn't *that* bad.

"Don't make me mimic you," he teased as he nudged me.

"You wouldn't dare." I shot him a look while lightly laughing. "You know I like that TV show he's on. And, now, with the films, he's a pretty big star."

"What's the difference with me?"

"You're my Finn." I emphasized the word "my" in the phrase I liked to use when referring to my man, lover, friend, husband—not the famous star the world sees.

"Right answer." He pulled me into his side a little closer as I recalled the details from my birthday surprise.

Finn had arranged it so he and I could have dinner with Ben Winthrop at an exclusive club that evening. The actor had flown in from California to do some promos for a film he was in. The guys talked about the entertainment business, and Ben and I shared stories about our roots in Western Pennsylvania. But, rest assured, or, more importantly, Finn assured, I was completely his and no one else's.

"So, no omissions and no freebies. You know I'm more than okay with that," I said, thinking of my brother.

There was no question that Lane and McEllie were getting divorced. It was just a matter of the extensive waiting period required by state law. I only knew this information, of course, through my mother. Lane and I had not talked since the infamous phone call two months before. But he was obviously now confiding in our mother, who, while sad that the marriage didn't work out, was always on her son's side. I wanted to be, too, but there was too much hurtful debris still scattered on my heart from his words and actions. And *he* certainly hadn't made a move to tear down any proverbial walls.

Surely sensing where my thoughts had wondered, Finn pulled me a little closer, only to be interrupted by the shriek of a girl who seemed to be in her early twenties. "Yes, it is! It is Finn Murphy!" She was making the declaration to a similarly clad and aged woman next to her. "You are, right?" she asked my husband.

"Yeah," Finn acknowledged, as I dropped his hand.

"Oh. My. God. I've got every single one of your albums. I've seen you perform like five times. We even drove—"

"I'll be inside," I said to Finn as the young redhead was still rattling on about driving miles and miles and getting only the best seats.

"I—" he began.

"See you in a few." I started in the direction of the penthouse which was just a block away.

"Can we do a selfie?" I heard the young woman ask with a voice that seemed like she could barely contain herself.

"Sure," Finn answered. And just like that, our at-ease, romantic moment on the sidewalk was over.

I knew how important Finn's fan base was to him. So, even though I was a little disappointed, I accepted fate and walked into the towering apartment building alone. Since it was so late, the regular, friendly front desk man, Graham, wasn't stationed there. An unfamiliar nighttime guard, seemingly disinterested in his job, was in position instead.

Walking toward the elevator bank, I removed Finn's dark pinstriped vest, which, because of the beginning-of-spring chill in the air, I had worn over my lacy blue top on our walk back from the club. Before the elevator doors could open, I felt his hand draw a heart on the bare space of my back. Then his lips gently kissed the center of his finger art. My shoulders dipped as his chin sank onto one of them.

"It's okay," I replied to his non-question.

"Really? It didn't feel okay."

I turned, forcing him to lift his chin and look at me. "FYI, mister, *that* was a teenage girl with a poster on her wall. I did not act like that."

"No, y—"

The opening elevator doors caused Finn to momentarily halt his thought. With his hand on my lower back, he guided us inside. After using his special key to access the penthouse floor, the doors shut, leaving us truly alone.

Finn's piercing eyes and the slight shake of his doubtful head made me reinforce my response with a little amendment. "It's okay. It's just… sometimes I wish you had a normal job."

"Yeah? Like what? A plumber?"

"No. That's part of the problem. You already have a job where women are looking at your ass. Being a plumber wouldn't help." I tried to make my voice light and semi-jovial.

"So? What then?"

"You know, suit and tie, nine to five. Look how good you look in this shirt." I pretended to fix his crisp, white shirt, sleeves partially rolled up. "And this vest before I stole it."

"Not as good as you looked tonight." He smiled with his eyes as much as his mouth. "But, nine to five? Not really my gig. I know."

Silently, he pulled me into him running his big hand through my hair, which I had decided to leave down for the night. He was applying just the right amount of pressure, creating a massage like sensation. It made me feel so secure…so right.

"Lar?" My name was the open-ended question.

"It's okay," I repeated once more. And to show that I

truly meant it, I pulled slightly away so that I was looking directly in his eyes.

I think he was still debating on how to reply and if he believed me when the elevator doors reopened. Relenting, he led me through the front door of our mini-palace in the sky. I turned on the light as he tapped something into his phone.

"What are you doing?" I questioned while laying my purse and his vest on the sofa. "Checking on the kids? It's late." Besides, I had already checked on them.

We had dropped the kids off at Finn's uncle's place. Eoin lived above the restaurant he owned just a few blocks or so from the penthouse. And he and his live-in girlfriend, Junie, were watching the kids for the night. Two divorcees, Eoin and Junie were committed to be committed—just not married.

"No. Business," he answered.

"Finn…" I sighed—in addition to the ass gazing and grabbing, the constant hours of correspondence wore thin.

"Sorry. It's all taken care of." He quickly tapped a few more things in his phone and then put it in his pocket to show me he was finished. "The kids are fine, too."

"I know." Thinking back to him being so upset that morning while exercising, I prompted with, "Chance is really growing up fast."

"He is," Finn agreed with a note of sadness and then changed the subject. "I would ask if you had a good time tonight, but I think I know." He smiled in a most self-assured way.

"It was really special," I replied and then added with a smirk, "And thanks for the mental image of a freebie with Ben Winthrop."

"What? Uh-uh. No freebies—mental or otherwise!" he bellowed but started laughing. "Now I might regret the actual gift I got you."

"What?"

He went over to the liquor cabinet and pulled out a flat,

rectangular package. I had to inwardly chuckle. Besides the fact that I was rarely at the penthouse, the liquor cabinet was the perfect hiding spot. He knew I also very rarely drank.

Regardless, I accepted the gift and delicately opened it up. Inside, was an exquisite picture frame. Of course, there were diamonds embedded in it.

"I thought you could put the picture we took with Ben in it to remember tonight. But now with the whole mental freebie business…"

"Hmmm…" I teasingly played along, pretending to gaze at it in a whole new way.

"Give me that back." He laughed, reaching for my present.

"No." I started off with it.

But with his running expertise and my pewter-colored, jeweled, high heel shoes, I was no match in the track competition. And with his muscular frame, I was also no match for him lifting me effortlessly in his arms and carrying me up the stairs. But, then again, I didn't want to be. I wanted to be right there…nowhere else and with no one else.

***

Why the hell was Finn's alarm going off? He never got up early. And we had been up late the night before. There was no reason for him to get up. What was going on?

When I grumbled something incoherent, he kissed the back of my head. "Sorry, baby. Go back to sleep. I don't know what happened."

Grateful for whatever extra minutes or hours I would be granted, I did just that. I turned back into my side-sleeping position and let Finn spoon around behind me. It wasn't long until my eyes and body relaxed back to slumber.

It also wasn't long until I was reawakened. I had never

been a good sleeper, most likely due to growing up with a father who would disturb the peace on a semi-regular basis at night. But, since becoming a parent, I was even more attuned to every sound that a residence can make, whether it was a child in need or otherwise. The squeak of the dresser drawer was what made me turn my body and adjust my eyes that morning after date night.

In front of me stood my husband. He was sharply dressed in a brilliant Persian blue button-down top, black slacks, and coordinating tie. It was far from his normal attire on what was supposed to be a relaxed family day.

"What are you doing? Where are you going?" I sat up a little straighter as Finn reached for a briefcase that I didn't even know he owned.

"I'm going to work," he said plainly.

"What? I didn't know you had something today. What's with the suit? What kind of work? Finn, huh? What? You're leaving tomorrow." Leaving for nearly a couple weeks and over my birthday. I was shamelessly beginning to whine.

Ignoring my tone and questions, he asked instead, "How do I look?"

"You look fantastic," I admitted. "But, I don't understand."

"See ya, sweetheart. Have a good day."

"Huh?"

Sweetheart? That was most definitely not a Finn term. Roxanne, Beauty, Baby... yes. Sweetheart? Have a good day? What did that mean? I wasn't going to see him?

"Off to the office—working nine to five, what a way to make a living." The lyric king partially sang and bent down to kiss me. It was quick just like his exit was.

Too stunned, I sat and listened as I heard the finality of the downstairs front door shut. I laid there in bed searching my memory bank for something that I may have missed. Had he told me about some meeting, event, etc. that he had to attend that day and I simply forgot? Or, had he thought he told me and didn't? I couldn't visualize either scenario. As crazy busy as our lives were, we knew of each other's plans and commitments— not only through verbal correspondence, but via the calendar organizer hanging in the house's kitchen, as well as our electronic calendars. I sat up and checked the planner on my phone. No. Nothing. Tomorrow—he leaves. Today—nothing. That's why date night in the city had worked.

My emotions went from shocked to confused to sad to depressed within about a half hour. I gave in to the situation and tried to go back to sleep. But, in reality, it was already a lot longer than I usually had a chance to sleep in. If the baby wasn't crying, Chance would have definitely been up wanting to go, go, go. The night before had been a good night's sleep...once we had gotten to sleep.

Eventually, I muddled down the stairs of the penthouse to make some coffee—extra strong. I felt like I was going to need it. While it was brewing, I took a shower and got dressed. I'm not sure if it was the heat of the shower or just enough time removed from his departure, but my next emotion set in. I was pissed. How could he leave, especially after what we had talked about in that elevator?

I drank a couple good sips of my honey-sweetened coffee and decided to get on with my day. I called Eoin first. After a couple rings, he picked up.

"Hey, Lara. How was your evening?"

Evening? That was great. Today? Well, that was another story.

"Very nice. Thank you," I said instead. "And thanks so much to you and Junie for taking care of the kids last night."

"Reminded me of the good ole days," the divorced dad of three grown children answered.

"I'll try to remember that." I chuckled and then continued, "Everything all right? Did my two munchkins make me proud?"

"Not a problem at all."

"Can I talk with Chance?"

"Ah, well, he's...you know, busy...a game I think. I can see—"

I laughed. "No. You don't want a tantrum on your hands. It doesn't matter. I'm gonna come pick them up pretty soon, anyway. We're gonna head back home."

"Oh." He sounded shocked. "Does Finn know?" He stumbled on his words. "I mean, he's coming with you?"

"No. No. I don't know what he's doing. He already left. He had something." I tried to keep the irritation out of my voice because it had nothing to do with Finn's uncle.

"Should you call him first?"

"I'll let him know," I answered. "I'll be there in less than an hour. Is that okay?"

"Yeah. Yeah. Take your time. Take all the time you need. Call Finn."

"I will," I reiterated, curious about his insistence.

I didn't call, but instead texted my husband after hanging up with Eoin. *Must have forgotten some big meeting?* I typed, thinking that was much nicer than what I was actually thinking. *No sense staying in the city. Picking kids up & heading home. Will we C U B4 U leave?* I hesitated with the last sentence. I'm pretty sure my astute husband would be able to read the spite between the lines on that one. I didn't like how that felt, but I was hurt...more because I didn't understand than anything else. Regardless, I pressed send.

Finn's response didn't come in the form of a text. It came with a legitimate phone call. He started before I even got a word in. "Let me tell you about my morning so far."

"Yes, please." My reply was smothered with sarcasm. "How about if you start with where you went. Where are you?"

"So..." Again, he ignored my very reasonable question. "My secretary spilled coffee all over my desk. The latest acquisition paperwork that was just freshly signed?

Ruined!"

What was he talking about? Who was his secretary? Where did he have a desk?

Before I could actually verbalize my questions, he continued in a flurry. "Stocks plummeted. The CEO is under fire. We're going to have to have an emergency meeting in front of the board in another hour. I have to have all the data from this previous quarter on his desk like... now. And..." He sounded exasperated. "I wanted to have a nooner with my wife, and she just texted and said she's leaving the city."

CEOs? Board members? Acquisitions? None of it sounded right.

"Finn, what are you talking about?"

"You said you wanted normal—nine to five," he answered. "What's today, Beauty?"

Today? God, I don't know. My brain was spinning.

"April fir..." st. "Finn Murphy!"

"Uh-huh?" His voice was sugar-coated with glee.

"No nine-to-five. Get your cowboy ass back here."

Downright laughter filled the line that time. "Nooner?"

"Sooner." I laughed back, full of relief despite being majorly duped with an April Fool's joke.

"Give me ten minutes?"

"Yeah. I have to call your uncle and tell him I'm not going to pick up the kids right away."

"I'll do it." Before I could respond, Finn yelled out but not into the phone. "Eoin, Junie, we'll be back for the kids."

"Got it," I heard Eoin's voice.

"Is that where you're at?" I asked incredulously.

"Of course," he replied matter-of-factly and then followed up with, "Quit shaking your head. I'll see you soon."

I stopped shaking my head. He knew me so damn well, even without a visual. I knew him, too and should have never doubted him that morning. He had gotten me good, and I was happy to play along.

***

The look on his face when he entered the penthouse and saw me standing there was super sexy and just what I had desired. His eyes pinned me with his yearning right before the rest of him pinned me against the entry wall. His hands skimmed alongside my body, which was clothed solely by a full apron and panties. He kissed me quickly and then stepped slightly away.

"You mad?" he asked, wisely assessing my text from earlier.

"I was," I admitted. "Do I look mad now?"

"You look fiery hot," he practically whispered in what I determined was appreciation.

"Just trying to be the little woman for my hard-working man." I grinned, playing my role while giving him the glass of bourbon that had been waiting in my hand.

Without letting his penetrating eyes leave mine, he downed the alcohol, kicked off his shoes, and took my hand to lead me into the adjacent kitchen. Setting the glass down on the granite center island counter, his hands were once again free. He chose to place them around my waist and gently but swiftly turn me around. I felt him untie the ribbon in my hair, releasing it so that my locks were completely cascading down my bare back. When he next kissed my shoulder and untied the apron strings, my breathing automatically intensified. I couldn't help it. I craved his touch. It had been that way since we first got together. And the thought of that ever changing was unimaginable. The depth and commitment of our love was something I never questioned but cherished to the fullest.

Finn peeled my nude colored lace panties down to the floor, allowing me to push them aside with my toe. His hands found their way up to my bare backside, which he softly rubbed in a slow motion. I think I may have moaned, but it could have been him, too. He was kissing every inch of me and, by all due purposes, I was completely melting.

Finn's voice was filled with awe. "I love how you come undone like that."

By planking my hands on his shoulders, I was silently prompting him to lift me onto the countertop. I welcomed my warm bottom meeting the coldness of the sleek surface. Finn lifted the apron up and over my head and began working on his belt and fly at a faster pace. I started assisting by loosening his tie and unbuttoning his shirt. But I only succeeded in getting about three fourths done when his lips met mine. And then he was in me…masterfully…beautifully…lovingly…again and again.

When I called out his name in adoration, his face nestled into my chest and my chin dipped onto his shoulder. And when our breathing subsided, Finn kissed me sweetly a couple of times and allowed our bodies to disconnect. I slid down and immediately went toward his pants, which were gathered around his ankles. I slowly, purposefully so, pulled them up his legs. When I got above his knees, I met his eyes, which were somehow all over the place and yet fixated on me. At the last minute, he grabbed the waistband, completed it himself and picked me up into his arms. He carried me into the adjoining dining room and ever so carefully laid me on the dining room table. He then repeated with my panties what I had done with his pants. His hands intermixed with the thin, lacy material traveling up my legs was almost as erotic as when he had removed them only moments before. Once completed, I sat up to see him starting to go back into the kitchen for the apron. But I tugged at his hand.

"No. Your shirt," I said as a simple command.

His closed mouth spread wide as he finished taking off his partially unbuttoned shirt. Putting it on me instead, he opted to fasten only one button—the one right at my breasts. His hand then led me off the table and into the living room where we sprawled onto the sofa and each other.

"How long exactly is a lunch break at one of these nine-to-five gigs?" he murmured into my ear.

"I think you've been fired," I played along.

His light laughter vibrated behind my back. "Good. So does that mean I don't have to wait for a coffee break to sneak off and see my girl again?"

"Nope," I answered and then turned slightly around to face him. "Finn? Thanks. Thanks for this. But I don't want you to change. You are everything I want." And I tacked on one more "Everything" for good measure.

"Ditto," he replied. "But..." He reached for that solo fastened button. "I think even as smokin' as you look in my shirt, it might need to be removed."

CHAPTER FIVE

During the nearly two weeks that Finn was away— at the awards, filming his new video, and doing some promotions—Chance, Arinn, and I managed. It was tough because, although we certainly had the means to, we didn't hire any outside help for housework. Both Finn and I wanted to maintain as much privacy as possible. And that doubled as far as our children were concerned. I didn't want a nanny raising my kids, or, for that matter, becoming a pseudo family member. We had enough aunts, uncles, grandparents, cousins, etc. to provide love and help if need be. But, in truth, I was pretty proud of myself. I was exhausted, but I was blessed with two—for the most part—well-behaved kids and a husband who seemed to know just when to text or call to motivate me through.

Finn won the Vocal Event of the Year award at the ACMs for his collaboration with Danny Roth. It was a first-time award for him and one that really seemed to get him pumped up. However, despite being nominated, he did not win in any of the other categories that had, until recently, become as common for him as bread and butter.

When he returned home, he spent a good amount of time in his studio on the lower level of our house. He was busy recording some of the new material he had been working on. The style was different for him—a little edgier, perhaps. But, I liked it. It was more the type of music that I think he wanted to play—not the type that had been mainstream for years and helped him gain his popularity and fame. Luckily for him, it was a prime time in the music industry for genres to mix and for him to try a little more individualized approach.

Like a reflection of his music, Finn, himself, seemed to be a little edgier. There was nothing definitive. It was just that I knew him so well. For one thing, I noticed how it would take him a few moments after emerging from his downstairs studio to once again find his natural rhythm as father and husband.

That was the case one afternoon in late May. I was sitting outside trying to get Arinn to say "ma-ma" and "da-da," although I knew she was much too young to complete such a feat. It didn't help that Chance was close by in his kid-sized plastic pool wanting me to "watch this" or ducking up and down playing peek-a-boo with his sister. That distracted her in the most humorous way, as, every single time, she would squeal in delight.

"Arinn…" came Finn's melodic voice from behind us.

She knew her name and she most definitely knew her daddy's voice. She looked to him as he sat down on the blanket-covered grass next to me. Finn rolled a soft, plastic ball toward our baby girl, who tried to get it. Managing her mightiest little push, she followed it to the edge of the blanket and then went to grab the grass.

"No," I said firmly, and she looked at both of us, knowing what that word meant… or at least the tone.

Finn picked her up. "Come here, pretty-in-pink. No getting in trouble. You're too cute." He adjusted the bow on top of her head and propped her onto her wobbly legs. He then turned to me. "How was the park?" he asked, stealing a kiss.

"Fine." I spoke of a local park where the kids and I met

up with some other families for the morning. "How was—" I started.

"Daddy, play me." Chance was all about his sister until he saw her getting Finn's attention.

"Chance, Mommy is talking. You don't interrupt." On Chance's pout, Finn answered my question. "It was okay."

"Okay?" I queried.

"It's...I'll never..." He censored himself and let out a frustrated sigh.

"What?"

Bouncing Arinn back into a seated position on the blanket, he turned to our other child. "All right, Chance-Man, what are we playing?"

"Finn?"

"Hoops!" Chance yelled out.

Finn laughed and gave a hand to Chance as he stepped out of the mini-pool. "Hoops it is. You gotta get some shoes first."

"On it!" Our little basketballer yelled in reply, making me laugh and forget any other concerns.

"I'm gonna get Arinn a bottle and put her to sleep. Chance is next. Just a couple minutes," I kindly warned the duo.

"On it," Finn mimicked our son with a wink and put Arinn in my arms.

***

I could see the two of them from Arinn's bedroom window. Hoops involved Finn dribbling the basketball as Chance chased him around like a wild man. It was equally as funny for Chance as it was for any spectator. Occasionally, Finn would lift him so he could shoot a basket.

I saw when he fell. It was just as I had Arinn down. Chance was scurrying about at Finn's legs and just simply tripped over himself. I went down the stairs to get outdoors, more worried about how Finn was going to react than the seriousness of any injury our son would sustain.

When I got outside, our "Little Man" was wiping his tears in Finn's arms. "Mommy," he wailed seeing me.

"Yeah, sweetie, you all right?" I asked, looking at both of them.

"Ouchie! Daddy kisses no work." Chance whined, reaching his arms and fresh crocodile tears out to me.

"Can't even kiss the right way," Finn mumbled.

I took our son from him. "Depends on who you ask," I teased. Doing a quick assessment of a simple skinned knee, I then said to Chance, "We'll go wash it off." I squeezed Finn's hand. "He's all right."

"Yeah. I know." His answer came out quietly. "Go ahead. I'll just gather his things."

***

"Really? That's it?" Finn was talking on his phone as I reentered the great room after getting Chance down for his nap. "Yeah. I mean, no, it's frustrating." He not only verbalized it, but the strain on his face displayed it. "If that's what you're saying." He once again listened to the person on the other end. "Hell yeah, I want to do something." Pause. "I don't know." Another listen as he took a few steps away from me. "I know." Pause. "I know." A longer pause. "I do know that. Okay. Thanks. I appreciate it." He clicked a button and placed his phone on the coffee table. "How's the little guy?"

"He's good. Almost asleep," I said and then added, "Tough as his daddy."

"He shouldn't have to be."

"Finn, what's wrong?"

I had debated about asking him that question so many times before. Over the weekend, I could have blamed it on the anniversary of Wyatt's death. But Finn had been so much better at dealing with that as the years had passed and as we had our own children. And I knew that he knew Chance was fine. But there had been too many half-comments and not-well-disguised down moments to ignore. I was concerned because I loved him so very much.

"Nothing," he denied. "There's nothing to worry about."

But I *was* worried. And just like I feared he was keeping something inside, I had been bottling up my worry about him. As much as I hated it and as much as I resisted it, I couldn't help it...I began to cry. Not a lot. Just a few simple, silent tears trickling down my cheeks.

Because it seemingly came out of nowhere, Finn was most perplexed. "What are you crying about?"

Damn wiping them away or playing his game of "nothing," I thought. I laid it out. "Because you're not telling me something. I know it. Please talk to me."

"Aw, Lara..." He hated when I cried. He hated to see me hurting. And if it was so bad that I allowed myself to cry, he knew it was going to be hard to fix. "I'm anxious about the tour, that's all," he tried. "The long distance and the time away."

Yes, it was almost as traditional as watching *It's a Wonderful Life* at Christmas time. Finn would get cagey and worked up before hitting the road. And this year, he was going without me or the kids. We had decided that Arinn was still too young. And even though Chance had gone on tour with us months after his birth, now there were two kids. The compromise was to build in a mini-break mid-summer so he could return home.

Regardless, I knew the tour wasn't the entire picture. "There's more than that. There's been something bothering you for a while now. I don't know why you can't trust me...why you're not letting me in."

"I trust you," he answered immediately. But, he offered nothing else.

I didn't either. If he trusted me, he would tell me. I just had to hold on. No omissions.

He didn't break our eye lock until the very last second. Then he dipped his eyes and spoke slowly. "I feel it all slipping away. The ticket sales, the nominations,…" He looked up as his voice faded, and I could see the honesty in his words. Some of the things changing in his career were, indeed, affecting him and, for whatever reason, he had been shielding me from how he felt.

"Thank you for telling me. I know I can't fully understand, but I want to help."

"I know."

"You've always told me how fickle and fleeting the industry is. It's a pendu—"

"Yeah, but to say it is one thing. To live it…"

"Baby, it's not like they are giving you a lifetime achievement award. Your career is not over. You still have singles on the charts. You still have fans— tons of fans— coming to every show you play. You just played the Superbowl, for God's sake. So the last album didn't do as well. So there's not another trophy to dust. You told me they didn't matter anyway."

His semi-mellowness raised a notch with agitation. "I don't want to promote a fragrance, Lara. Or teach guitar lessons. Or dance with the fucking stars, for that matter."

"Watch your language." I glanced at the stairs, hoping that Chance was truly sleeping. "And, you're not at that point. Your new stuff is great."

"Music—my career— is my whole world, though."

I very blatantly stared at him. When I didn't receive the slightest ounce of recognition, I shook my disapproving head and simply walked away. Chance, at the age of three, already knew that look. And so did his father.

It took him a couple minutes, but Finn followed me into our master bedroom. "What? What, Lara?" He had followed me, but he still didn't understand why I had left.

"What?" I mimicked.

"Don't," he said. "Don't do that. I have enough—"

"You do!" I yelled out perhaps a little more assertively than I meant. But, regardless, it was accurate, and I forged on. "You do! You have enough. Don't you even realize what you said out there?"

"What? No." Exasperation filled his simple two words.

"I thought *we* were enough. I thought *we* were your world— me and Chance and Arinn. Not your damn music!"

"Christ, Lara!" His hands flew to his head. "I didn't—"

"You said it," I replied plainly.

"Don't talk semantics with me. You know damn well what I meant and how much you and those kids mean to me."

I did. I knew how much we meant to him and vice versa. I had wanted him to open up. And he had. But, unfortunately, it was with uncensored words that stung...bad.

"What?" he spewed when I didn't give him any type of response. "You have no idea how much I love and need you?"

"Yeah," as much as I do you, I started to say but was cut off.

Finn was hitting some other emotional, upset realm. "I ache when we're apart, and you don't know how much you mean to me?"

"Finn!" Crap, I had no idea how the conversation descended so rapidly downward.

"You need me to show you?" Before I could respond, he quickly brought me into his body and held his lips on mine for a strong moment.

I could feel both his anger and desire intermixed with one another. In one way it was erotic. But, in another, it seemed so wrong.

"Finn, stop." I cried out. "You're...no. You're scaring me. You—"

He released me so quickly that I almost fell from the

contrast. His hands on top of his head, he managed to look at me with wide eyes. Mine were threatening to be filled with fresh tears.

"I…God—" The words stumbled out of his mouth only to be interrupted.

"Daddy!" It seemed that the three-year-old voice was coming from the staircase.

Regardless of why Chance wanted his father, Finn was not up to finding out. He knew it, and I knew it. So I took on the task of intercepting our son, secretly kind of glad to be temporarily removing myself from the situation that had somehow almost turned ugly.

"Chance! Chance Wyatt Murphy!" I used his full name for good measure while entering the great room. "You are supposed to be in bed."

But, indeed, there he was at the top of the steps. "Momm—"

"Now! Right now, buddy!" I marched toward him.

Still in semi-slumber mode, he said, "But what—"

"No excuses. Let's go." I grabbed his hand, and we entered his room personalized with his hat collection and his name painted whimsically on the wall. "Please put those blocks away and get into bed." I pointed toward the large multi-colored Legos that were freshly scattered on his bedspread.

Chance did as he was told. He had had a long day already between the park and pool and hoops. I knew he had to be tired, and I was sorry that he hadn't found sweet slumber yet and was most likely privy to his parents' heated conversation.

As I tucked him into bed, he still resisted sleep, though, by asking a question that I was surprised yet glad he hadn't asked at the playground. "Why did dat little boy at the park only have one arm?"

It was one of those tough life questions— the type that makes adults sad and not know the answers to themselves. "Life isn't always fair" was the simple, honest truth, no matter if you are a toddler on the playground or a thirty-five-year-old country music star. But Chance wasn't old enough for that lesson yet. He needed to hold onto his innocence. I opted to go the route of "everyone is different" and gave the example of how he and his friends have different eye, hair, and skin colors but still liked the same games.

"So, the same thing. The boy on the playground was missing an arm, but he liked to play on the swings just like you do, Chance."

"Yeah," my sweet, little guy agreed. "He good. Mommy, how Arinn get in your belly?"

"Chance, I already answered that." I blew out air, thinking how much he was like his inquisitive cousin, Wyatt, who he never had a chance to meet.

"I fowget," he whined.

"Love."

"Daddy love," he added.

"Yeah, Little Man. Daddy and my love. Same with you." I kissed him on the nose and, before I could tear up, I left the room, shutting the door behind me.

***

I couldn't go immediately back to the master bedroom. I wasn't ready to face him yet. I wanted to treasure those words with my son because if there was one truth that I believed in in this world, it was those words. And I knew Finn did, too. We just needed to step back for a moment, remember that, and breathe.

I was sitting pretzel style on one of the outdoor chaise lounges, my back unable to relax or incline fully onto the chair, when Finn stepped from the house out to the patio. A mass of clouds had found their way overhead, darkening the previous spring sky and threatening to immerse the ground with nature's tears. I tugged the blanket that I had been playing with a little more around my waist.

"Are you cold?" he asked.

"A little," I answered, although we both knew that wasn't the whole truth. I paused for a millisecond, considering whether I should edit or delete my thought wanting to come out. But, we were always honest with one another. "You think that, in there, is how I would know you love me?"

"No," he said immediately. "Of course not. Please forgive me."

"I'm getting there," I said, seeing the sincerity in his eyes and knowing his instant remorse.

I waited another moment and then reached out my left hand to him. He accepted it and, with only the slightest hesitation, brought it to his lips kissing my engagement/wedding ring ensemble. Neither of us saying anything, Finn slowly started to pull away. But I denied him, knowing we had to cut through more. He took the space behind me, letting his feet set on the ground on either side, and then he carefully wrapped his arms around my waist. Just the considerate, soft way he touched me almost made me fall apart. It was so different compared to the scene that had played out in our bedroom just a little bit before.

As I remained silent, his secure hold grew stronger. "I love you." He said my name then, prompting me to turn around and look at him. "I'm sorry." I took a deep, cleansing inhale and waited for him to continue. "What just happened...God, I didn't mean that. That wasn't at all how I feel, how I should have...The look on your face...I...I'm sorry."

"I don't understand. What's going on?"

"I promise, Lara, I'm taking—"

He was referring to his meds. But he didn't need to say that. It wasn't that bad. But it wasn't good.

"I believe you. But, baby, I'm worried about you."

"I know," he answered in a way he probably should have in the first place had his pride and feeling like he needed to always shelter me didn't take priority. "I know you are. It's just...I told you, I feel it slipping away. Right or wrong, it's how I feel. And it makes me sad and angry. You asked. That's the truth. But when I stop and think, I know we've been through so much worse." Before I could reflect on Wyatt's death, my coma, Macon's blackmail, etc., he continued. "So, I called Dr. Bartola when you were up with Chance. I'm going tomorrow."

"Yeah?" I quietly asked, while thinking how it would take us mere humans months to get an appointment with any doctor, but, due to star power, Finn had managed one for the next day.

"Maybe it's just an extra session. I need to be more regular with them. Or something with the dosage. I don't like that I reacted that way."

"You're upset. You're allowed to feel, Finn."

"I shouldn't scare you, though. And, I never, ever want Chance or Arinn to see me like that."

"I would never let that happen," I said in a soft but adamant way.

My kids would never live my previous life. They would never experience a life where a parent is out of control and becomes verbally or physically abusive. They would never be scared of their father. They would only have love— love and security.

I didn't need to tell my husband all of that. He knew everything about me. He knew about my past. But, more importantly, he knew the woman I had become and the woman that I would forever be.

"I know," he replied just as softly. "I'm glad."

"And let me tell you something. If all of this—the house, the cars, the money—were all taken away overnight, and it's not going to, all that would matter was that you and the kids are with me and healthy. That's all."

"I know. The same goes for me. It does. I'm sorry I implied otherwise." He leaned in and tentatively, sorrowfully kissed me. "You know, I meant it when I said music is my world."

What! He didn't really just say that, did he? I hadn't truly thought he meant it the first time, but…to repeat it?

Before I could question or even move away, because that's definitely what my gut reaction was, Finn said, "Because you are my universe."

I felt a mixture of relief and love wash through me. "That's a much better line, Cowboy." I allowed myself a smile, and it was my turn to return that kiss.

"I love you, Lara. Thanks for not giving up on me."

***

The next day was the day before Finn was set to leave on tour. I'm not sure who was feeling it more—he or I. But there was definitely a sense of lament and change and stillness throughout the day.

After Finn's early morning meeting with his doctor, the four of us spent the day together without leaving the safe haven of our home. When it came time to put the kids to bed for the night, though, I could see my husband's emotions were getting the better of him. He made it through prayers and kisses but bowed out of the rest—the final touches and words while they drifted off to sleep. And Arinn, usually a docile child, was, of course, abnormally cranky that night, as if she was emulating her father's distress.

I found him, unsurprisingly, in the lower level studio. He was in the booth belting out one of his latest. Eyes shut, he looked so internal, so lost in his music, and so beautiful. I took the moment to just admire the man who was my husband, letting him finish his song, as he was still unaware that I was there. On the last beat, he dipped his head and sat in utter silence for a moment. I pressed the button that I had learned long ago allowed me access into his personal earpiece.

"I think 'Lara's Song' might need a little more work." I

spoke of the song he wrote for me before we were even engaged.

His smile emerged at the same time as his eyes opened. It was a peaceful smile. It was a loving smile.

But when he started to remove his headphones and get off the chair, I pressed the button again and reiterated. "'Lara's Song.'"

He obliged by placing the phones securely back on his head and telling me which buttons to press to produce the instrumentals to my song. He didn't lose eye contact as he began the lyrics or as I stepped from the board and walked into the booth with him. Once I shut the door behind me, I put the child monitor on the floor and walked over to his chair. Not missing a beat, he continued to sing the sentimental lyrics but displaced the earphones. I carefully, due to the wheels on the chair, perched myself snugly onto his lap, resting my head on his chest and listening to the vibrations of his tender voice. At the same time, I felt his hand stroke my long, dark strawberry blonde hair ever so gently.

The song wasn't done, but I couldn't wait. I tilted my head up and let my lips meet his. His lyrical words dissolved into hums. I had come down to the studio to soothe him... to make sure that he was all right. But I realized there seemed to be a reversal. I, too, craved comforting. He wasn't gone yet, but, suddenly, I was already missing him like he was. And I wasn't ready for him to go.

When I embossed my face into his warm, beating chest, he cooed, "You are so beautiful, and I am so lucky to have you." His words made me only more emotional, though, and he could sense it. Taking his knuckle, he tilted my chin up so I could meet his inquisitive eyes.

"It's gonna be weird not to be on tour with you." I attempted to explain the rash of emotions flooding my body.

"Just say the word, baby."

"I…we…can't." I lamented the truth. "It's just… I just didn't expect it to affect me so much. I should be used to you being gone."

"That kills me, you know—you saying that."

"I'm sorry. I don't mean it to. It's fine. Really. This time, it's just—"

He finished my thought for me. "Different."

"Yeah."

"It's because this is *our* thing—summers on the road. It's hard to remember a time pre-Lara. It's not gonna be the same. But you'll be with me every minute. On stage, backstage, in the trailer…" He left his voice fade on purpose, replacing it with a devilish grin before pulling me back into his upper body.

"It's just a little longer until we see you," I said, knowing Finn had it worked out so that his tour started later and ended earlier but was compact with dates except for a mini-break the week of July fourth.

"I love you like mad, Lara Murphy, and I am going to miss you like no one has ever missed someone before."

My heart instantly beat a little faster with those words. "You say things like that because you know they get to me. You like to see me swoon."

"Yeah." He smiled with a mock coyness. "But, also because I mean them."

I nodded my head slightly and then allowed my thoughts to go to the reality of his words—he was going to be gone an exorbitant amount of time. "Will you write me?" I asked in a stillness that mimicked the atmosphere of the room.

"What? You know I'll either be calling or texting a couple times every day."

By his response, I knew he didn't understand my request. But, also knowing how much he had on his mind, I let it go. "I'm gonna miss you, too."

***

The wall that Chance had just built up was brought down thanks to a more and more mobile seven-month-old. "No!" Our son's little voice seemed to mimic one that I would sometimes use when reprimanding his baby sister.

Startled by her brother's insistent voice, Arinn looked to me for some sort of guidance, assistance, or even scolding of my own. But, quite frankly, I didn't have any of that in me at the moment. I was too busy building my own walls. Although mine weren't made of mini-plastic molds. Mine were emotional, inner-being ones. I was trying to secure my heart from Finn's impending departure.

Regardless, I was still "mom." I took a deep breath, bent down to the kids' level, and pulled a block out of Arinn's hand just as she tried to stick it in her mouth. Looking at her instantly weepy eyes and face, I tried to explain to Chance. "She's not doing it to be mean. She's just curious—learning how things go together or," —I added with a note of pessimistic truth— "fall apart."

Entering then, with the ever symbolic suitcase in his hand, Finn joined us. He first picked up the baby and blew bubbles on her belly, causing her to laugh infectiously. Then, after giving her a most sweet kiss on the top of her head, he set her back down and asked Chance to walk him to the front door. I made sure Arinn was secure and joined them.

Crouching down to Chance's level, Finn ruffled our son's hair and said, "You're going to be the man of the house for a little while, bud. You have to take good care of the girls."

"Where are you going 'gain, Daddy?"

I knew Finn had already explained to Chance about the tour. In fact, we both had been preparing him for a while in subtle ways for Finn's departure. But, whether it was because Chance was too young to understand, or he was trying to procrastinate his daddy's leaving like he did bedtime, he asked again.

"On the road." Finn remained patient as my heart pattered a little harder with the reality of his words.

"Which road?" Chance asked, making me smile at his toddler simplicity. He probably thought it was the road where the supermarket or library was.

"Lots of them, Little Man."

"When you coming back?"

"Fireworks day." Finn met my eyes and stood up in front of me.

Emotional, especially upon hearing the second beep of the car service outside, I nodded my head up and down, unable to do much more. His caring hands form-fitted my cheeks before he kissed me. It was long and soft, but it was also goodbye.

"Why you crying, Daddy?" Chance peered up from the midst of our collective knees.

As discreetly as he could, Finn brushed the rare straggler from his eye and looked at me with an actual trace of bashfulness. I couldn't do or say a thing. I had somehow remained stoic—both for our little man and for my big man. And the slightest acknowledgement would destroy my façade.

"Think I must be getting Mommy's allergies." Finn by far stretched the truth for Chance and then mouthed "I love you" to me before turning and walking out the door.

I let Chance stand at the doorway and wave like he usually did when Finn would go away for a few days. I would normally be right beside our son. But I just couldn't this time. Instead, I told him to make sure to shut the door once Daddy waved and to play nicely with his sister for a little bit. In the meantime, I hastily retreated to our master bedroom.

It wasn't long after when the text from Finn came through. *Wipe those tears.*

I did as I was told and then texted back. *Just allergies. LOL!!*

Where R U hiding? Finn texted in an omniscient way.

On your side of the bed, I admitted via text.

Near the door???

I laughed because, even emotional, I wouldn't let my phobia of being closer to the door lead me astray. *Well, I'm on my side but w/ your pillow.*

He sent me a hug emoji. *I miss U already.*

Mine was a sad face. *Me 2.*

I love U, Rox.

Forever, Cowboy.

CHAPTER SIX

Between calling and texting, I was able to keep in touch daily with the traveling musician during the month he was gone. Finn would routinely text me first thing in the morning—either a simple "Good morning, Beauty" or something even sexier from a lonely bunk. And we tried to video chat with the kids during the time right after he had gotten done exploring the new venue and before any fans invaded the preshows. Chance always talked a mile a minute. And, thankfully, Arinn was a lot less cranky since the emergence of her first teeth—the bottom two.

Each time we talked, though, I wondered how he was managing it. His schedule was insanely packed with different cities almost every day, plus the traveling and extra-curriculars like meet and greets, radio promotions, etc. Thankfully, though, although at times tired, he seemed both relaxed and energized. Doing what he loved—the performing side of music—was part of the puzzle that helped keep Finn even and stable.

It was a unexpected gift from Finn's parents, though, that helped *me* get through. I didn't understand why a present arrived about three weeks into Finn being away. It wasn't my birthday, and it wasn't Christmas. So, I said just that when I called to thank them.

"It's made out of baobab," Mr. Murphy explained the material but not yet the reason.

"What? I'm sorry, what's that? Is that the type of wood?" I examined the simple but beautiful wood bracelet more carefully.

"The strongest tree there is. Someone I know just returned from missionary work in Africa and brought a few back. I thought of you because you're one of the strongest branches of our family tree, Darlin'. I know it's hard on you and the kids when our boy is away for so long. I saw it in him, too, when he was here." He spoke of their time together when Finn arranged to play his hometown for Father's Day. "But you're both so good for one another. Dig in deep, stay rooted, and hold on."

***

I did just that until Finn was able to finally arrive home for his break on the Fourth of July. Our exclusive neighborhood was having their annual picnic and fireworks display. It was going to be my day to feel like a regular person— not arm candy for paparazzi at a music function and not a single parent. Some of that anticipatory giddiness of seeing Finn again wore off, though, when I got the message that he wasn't going to be home until much later in the evening due to a flight being rescheduled.

I knew exactly when Finn had finally arrived despite having my back to him and it being dark at nearly nine-thirty at night. Our neighbors, although pretty cool about Finn's celebrity status, gave telltale signs, always looking his direction when he would first enter any venue. A lot of that had nothing to do with Finn being a country music star, though. He just had a special type of magnetism that made everyone want to be his friend. I had been witness to it when we were college co-eds, and I was certainly witness to it as his wife. I also knew, without yet turning around, that he was ignoring all of the casual looks and was making a beeline to me and our kids.

The full view of my husband came as he lowered himself onto the red blanket that the kids and I were occupying. I had purposefully set out our things a little off to the side. I wanted what little privacy we could get while watching the colorful eruptions hit the warm, but no longer oppressively sticky, summer sky. Finn took the top of my hand and gently rubbed it with his slightly-more-callused-than-usual, guitar-playing fingers.

"Hi," he said quietly.

In the second that it took for me to respond, Chance, who had been playing a game on his tablet, looked up. "Daddy!" he shouted, dropping the electronics and jumping into Finn's lap.

After wrapping Chance up in a mutual bear hug, Finn said, "I missed you, Little Man."

"No road?"

"Well, yeah, but I'm here for a little bit."

"We're going to see the fireworks!"

"I know." Finn smiled that damn endearing, wide smile. "I didn't miss them, did I?"

Decked out in his toddler jeans shorts and navy blue, flag shirt, Chance recited something his mother had murmured numerous times during the afternoon. "No. You missed the picnic."

"Did you have a hotdog for me?" Finn asked.

"No. I can only eat one." Our son answered like it was the most ridiculous question ever.

"But he managed to eat two cupcakes." I teasingly nudged the three-year-old.

"Is that right?" Finn smiled my direction, but I could tell it was in a way that he was trying to judge my disposition. "Happy Fourth, baby."

"Yeah, I thought Independence Day was going to have a different connotation." My comment, admittedly, was riddled with sarcasm.

My husband caught my double meaning and astutely apologized. "Sorry."

Despite the number of times in our relationship that I had to deal with him being late or cancelling or interrupting our plans, I knew his love and felt his sincere lament. But, before I could officially let him off the hook—because, after all, I wanted that bear hug, too—Chance questioned, "Why you call Mommy a baby, Daddy? She old!"

I shook my head as Finn smiled and corrected our son, "Chance, you never call a woman old. Remember that. Even Nana who is really old!"

"Finn!" I managed a laugh just as the first firework went off.

Chance immediately screeched and yelled, "What that?" before jumping from his father's lap to mine.

I rubbed my son's back in soothing circles. "That's the fireworks. That's what we're here for."

I glanced over at Arinn. Dolled up in a patriotic inspired dress, she was still peacefully asleep in her portable seat. I was glad one of my children wasn't scared of the sudden loud disruption. And I never would have imagined Chance would be. It was me who had that scared-of-my-own-shadow childhood, not him.

"They scary," he half cried, half whispered from within my embrace.

Finn reached over and rubbed Chance's arm as more and more spectacular lights lit up the sky. "It's a celebration," he explained. "Kinda like a birthday party for the great country we live in."

Ever so slightly, Chance peeked his head up. "New York?"

"The United States," I corrected as a loud boom seemed to shake the ground beneath us.

Chance screamed in pure terror while those around us were screaming in delight. It was really his first experience with fireworks. It had rained the year before on the Fourth of July, and he was too young to remember before that.

"Honey, it's all right," I tried.

"Hey, bud, you know what?" Finn's daddy voice was so melodic, it made both Chance and I look at him in wonderment... like somehow he could take all the monsters away with his next words. "Sometimes, when I'm playing my music, I have fireworks go off as part of the act. We like it. It's fun. It gets us pumped up." He almost had our son convinced until too many fireworks clustered together went off—their sound mimicking a loud machine gun.

"I don't like them, Mommy. Mommy!" Chance reburied his head into my chest, tugging at the V-neck of my red T-shirt decorated with sparkly white and blue USA letters.

I ached for him, feeling his little heart beating so rapidly against mine. Looking at Finn, I said, "He is shaking...terrified."

Finn seemed mystified. "Do you want to go back to the house?"

Gently, I pulled Chance slightly away so he could see my eyes while talking to him. "Do you want to leave? Do you want to go back home? It's up to you."

"Uh-huh." Without hesitation, Chance nodded his head quickly up and down before once again burying it into my chest.

"Is that all right?" I turned to Finn.

"Yeah, sure. I'm here to see you guys not the pyrotechnics." He started to get up.

I tried to follow suit, but Chance was clinging too hard to allow me the leverage to stand.

"Chance, go to Daddy, okay? I need to get the blanket and Arinn."

"Here, monkey." Finn squatted down and reached for our son. "Wanta climb?"

Chance, who normally loved to crawl up Finn's back, started only to be derailed by another, semi-sonic boom.

Instead, he clung to Finn's side. Finn looked at me with a touch of sadness filling his eyes. He absolutely, above all else, could not stand to see his kids hurting. I shrugged my shoulders once and figured it was best if we just got Chance out of the situation as quickly as possible. Finn, with Chance as an appendage, stood up while I shook out and shoved the blanket, along with the few toys, into the tote bag and threw it onto my shoulder. Cooing to sleeping Arinn, who looked like she was threatening to stir, I placed her car seat securely back in the stroller.

"I can get her," Finn offered at my side.

"Neh, I'm used to it," I answered with a soft smile. "Thanks, though."

Finn placed his hand on top of mine and said, "Hey" tilting his chin slightly upward.

That slang-like word was all he needed to say. It told me all. He wanted to slow down for just that second. He wanted to be Finn and Lara. He wanted to feel my welcome home lips on his. I complied and, for that magical moment, I forgot all the noise, lights, and tears around me.

We walked as a family unit through the park. Finn kept trying to talk with Chance about silly things, wanting to distract him from his fears. We would periodically get stopped by neighbors wanting to know why we were leaving. "Finn, you just got here" and "How's the tour?" seemed to be recited every few steps.

"Hi, Lara." I mocked just for Finn's ears. "Yeah, I'm fine, too. Just got here? No, I've been here."

"Beauty, they don't mean—"

"I know," I admitted and truly meant it— most of the commentators were truly good friends. It was just…"Now that you're here, I'm kinda just looking forward to having you all to myself."

"You and me both, baby."

"I'm not a baby. I'm old!" I teased.

"Yeah, like a great granny at least." He grinned, surely

happy that I was in a light mood. "Right, Chance?"

"Don't agree with your daddy, Chance."

"Mommy pretty."

"You're one smart kid, Little Man," Finn agreed. "C'mon, we're almost home. We only have a couple more streets."

***

Of course, just as we were entering the foyer, Arinn decided it was her turn to get some attention. Waking up, she opened her now four-teeth mouth and started belting out her own hysterical tune. I brought her into my arms as Chance, who had just gotten done covering his ears from the fireworks, dramatically placed them back again.

I looked at Finn who rolled his eyes. "Which one do you want?" I asked, referring to our children. "Thing One or Thing Two?"

"I guess I'll take the one I have," he answered, readjusting Chance on his hip.

"Welcome home," I said with a touch of sarcasm.

"There's no place like it." He bent slightly down to peck me on the lips before we walked both the kids up the stairs.

As it turned out, I got the easier of the two. I had Arinn freshly diapered, changed into pajamas, semi-fed, and rocked before Finn had even gotten close to making his great escape out of Chance's room. I discretely stood at the doorway and watched my two favorite boys… only then truly realizing how much I had missed that scene. Under covers, Chance was in his bed wearing his favorite superhero pajamas and looking up at Finn as if *he* was the superhero. Finn, still in black jeans and a white T with faded American flag, had his legs stretched out alongside him.

"Chance, they're done. I promise. That was the finale." He tried to reassure our son about the audible, multiple explosions that had just taken place a few moments before.

"No," Chance denied, and I took note of his nightlight all aglow.

In that sense, our son was like me. He didn't like the pitch black of a nighttime room. It was a fear I instantly developed after coming out of the coma a few years back. Chance developed his only recently.

"It was, Little Man," Finn tried again. "There's lots like that at the end. Everyone is on their way home and going to bed just like you."

"Daddy! Don't like them."

"I know." Finn sighed.

"Stay with you."

"Chance, you're fine. Besides, you've been hogging Mommy for weeks." He smiled and ruffled our son's hair to let him know he was joking. "Daddy needs Mommy time." He winked at me, letting me know that he knew I was there.

"Peas, Daddy. I miss you."

This time, Finn's look to me wasn't one of mischievous, fun adoration. It was a helpless ache over hearing his little boy's words. I knew how much I wanted to be alone with my husband. But I also knew it wouldn't be at the expense of our firstborn, who was pleading for similar time. Finn knew more than anyone how it felt to be left. His PTSD and depression were direct results of that fear, and I knew he couldn't bear that he would do that to our son. So I shrugged my shoulders and nodded my head slightly and affirmatively, letting the final decision be made by Finn.

"All right." Finn semi-reluctantly agreed, looking from me to Chance. "Special. One time. We'll say our prayers here and then, when we go downstairs, no talking. Just sleep."

"Okay, Daddy."

"Prayers," Finn reiterated. "Let's start by thanking God for Mommy."

I air-kissed their direction and went downstairs to start getting ready for bed myself. I hadn't anticipated going to bed that early. I had imagined sitting with Finn on the sofa, sipping some wine, feeling his arms wrapped around me, swapping stories, and then making our way to the bedroom… if we got that far. But, instead, I entered the master bathroom to untie my hair from the patriotic scarf, brush my teeth, and throw on a pair of black pajama shorts along with one of Finn's gray T-shirts.

Finn had just laid Chance down in the center of the bed and stripped off his own T-shirt when I entered. Turning around to see me, his mouth slightly gaped before saying, "You tease."

"What?" I replied innocently yet secretly happy with his reaction. "I couldn't wear what I was going to wear," I continued as seductively as I could in front of our son.

"So you had to pick my T—that T?" he sputtered.

Not only did it have special meaning for us since the shirt's logo was of the college where we first met, but that particular T-shirt was the one that Finn was wearing when we finally, completely reconnected as a couple after splitting up before our engagement years before. It had been right before he had been set to go on a tour all those years ago. And if I hadn't taken the initiative to go to his penthouse that night, we probably would have never made it. It was that T-shirt night that kept us being us.

Finn took my hand and brought me closer. "I've missed you."

I let my mouth wander in and out of his for a few moments as my hands ventured on his bare chest. He was always even more fit in the summer. He had to be to keep up the pace and energy that performing on a near daily basis required. Right then, though, that physique was going to drive me wild if I didn't let go.

"I love you." I tapped lightly on his pectoral before pulling away. "But I guess no one is getting any fireworks tonight."

"Daddy say no talking," Chance chimed in from the bed steps away.

Finn's eyes lit up as he stifled a laugh. When I did, too, Finn brought his index finger up to my lips in the universal quiet sign. I drew it into my mouth causing Finn to shake his head back and forth.

"You're right, Little Man," Finn said, crossing over to crawl onto his side of the bed as I did mine— our son feeling safe and secure in between us. "Good night, Lara." He looked at me with a serene smile on his face.

"G'night back," I agreed and reached my hand over to find his.

CHAPTER SEVEN

I woke to find Finn propped up on his elbow, staring at me across our still-sleeping son. "Morning." I smiled grateful that his arrival home wasn't a dream; it really was our mid-summer week together.

"You looked so peaceful sleeping."

"I was. It's the first time in a while that I think I've gotten a good night's sleep."

"Yeah?"

"It's because it's the first time in a while that you've been here."

"I'm glad you've always felt that relaxed and safe with me." He brushed a loose hair from my face, surely recalling, as I was, my first official date with him in Nashville and me falling asleep on his shoulder.

"I think the wine on an empty stomach helped that first time," I teased, knowing I wouldn't have even drank if I hadn't trusted him.

"I think you're even more beautiful."

"I think you need to come up with some different lines." Regardless, I felt my face flush from his adoration.

"Not if they apply." He touched my closed mouth with his finger, willing me not to disagree. "C'mon, I'm afraid

we really slept in. Summer," —he spoke of his cousin—
"is probably going to be here any minute."

"Really? It's that late?" My voice rose above a whisper
as I straightened up to a more seated position. I hated
being late. It was one of my quirks and one of the things in
which Finn and I were complete opposites.

"We're good. I'm sure you have everything already
packed."

"Yeah, besides some of the toiletries and my purse.
Everything is set for you, too."

"Thanks, Beauty. Do me a favor and add that T-shirt."
He nodded toward my breasts.

I looked down at his college T still strung over my
torso and agreed. "In my suitcase or yours?"

"Either." He smiled back.

"All right. I need to finish packing." I started getting
out of bed. "You take care of Mr. Unpatriotic here."

"Lar, we need to help him with that. He shouldn't be
scared."

"I know." I sighed. "It broke my heart, too, you
know."

***

We were spending the rest of the week as glorious
recluses in the Hamptons. We both wanted to get away for
a real vacation…not surrounded by the everyday objects of
our house or the inhabitants around it. But, with the time
constraints and having two little ones, it needed to be
somewhere close by. The just over two-hour commute to
the seaside resort town was perfect. Finn had arranged it
so that we were staying at the vacation home of one of the
label's higher-ups. And, as an extra bonus, Finn asked his
twenty-two-year-old cousin, Summer, to join us. It was
part college graduation gift for her and part built-in
babysitting service for us. Finn and I, of course, both
loved our kids beyond all imagination but knew, in the

time that was carved out, that we needed to have some private time, too.

The modern, Cape Cod-style house with circular governor's drive in front was spectacular. There were two wings on the first floor, divided by a great room, dining room, kitchen, and laundry room area. On one side of the house, Summer would have her own bedroom and bathroom near the bedroom and bathroom the kids would share. And Finn and I had the entire other wing to ourselves.

While Chance was running around from room to room like a madman and Summer was keeping an eye on Arinn, I went on the mission of putting the groceries away. It was when Finn peeked in on me the second time and sighed, that I turned to him and said, "Go. Go meditate or run or something."

"Really?" he asked as if it was the most brilliant idea he had ever been given permission to do.

"Finn, I get it," I replied.

"It's just—"

"Go. Get it out. Let it go."

He bridged the gap between us with a few steps. Bracing my face in his hands, he pulled me in for a kiss like he was needing air to breathe. "I won't be long."

"Enjoy."

He kissed me again and headed in the direction of his running shoes. Something that I had learned about my husband during the years we had been together was that it took him a little while to buzz back down from being on tour. He had to adjust to being a semi-civilian again. He was used to being the performer—having a certain persona. And that didn't mean just on the stage. In some ways, on the tour bus and with his crew, even though he was very comfortable with them, he was still performing. My husband was used to having to be "on" even if it was eating late night pizza or playing games or shooting the shit. He was the leader and entertainer and person in demand. He didn't need to be that with me. He was at his most honest self with his family and me. So I understood that the wound firecracker, known as country megastar Finn Murphy, first needed to debrief and defuse.

***

My hair pulled back in a ponytail and earbuds blasting music in my ears, I was laying on the cushiony green lounge chair and soaking in the hot summer sun. Suddenly, my large, round, brown sunglasses were removed from my face. Jumping slightly, I immediately extracted the buds, having not heard the culprit approach me from behind.

"That better be a Finn Murphy song you're listening to." Finn grinned, dangling my shades in his hands.

"Finn, you scared me." Squinting, I sat up a little straighter.

"Sorry, baby." He leaned down to ever so smoothly and slowly give me a kiss. He then pulled a second chaise lounge so that that it was flanked up next to mine. Instead of lying down traditionally, he flopped horizontally so that his swim trunk covered bottom was on his chair and his bare torso and head were resting on my lap looking up at me. "Those are the gorgeous turquoise eyes I wanted to see." When I touched his wet hairline, he put one of my earbuds in his ear. "Good choice, Mrs. Murphy."

"It just happened to come up on shuffle." Finn's "Love Letters (to my wife)" was a song he recorded just for me when I was about a month away from giving birth to Chance, and it had since held more meaning and love in my heart than any other song.

If he were to check out the music mechanism, Finn would recognize the repeat button and my tall tale about the shuffle. But, I think he already knew by the smile on his face and the change of topic. "Where are the rugrats?"

"I asked Summer to take them to the beach. Chance wants to build sandcastles. I'm surprised you didn't see them. They just left."

"Huh. No. I rinsed off in the shower and changed real quick. Maybe we missed each other."

Sitting up, Finn adjusted our bodies so that I was now propped on his lap. His kisses tasted like sweet tea, which I figured he took a swig of from the fridge before coming out to the patio. "How was your run?" I asked in between the soft feathering of his lips.

"Almost everything I needed."

"Hmmm…" I murmured knowing what else he needed… what we both missed.

"Want to test out the pool?" he asked after another smooch.

"Sure."

Gallantly, because I was more than capable myself, he took my hand and helped me off the lounge. He didn't let go as we walked the steps together into the elongated, rectangular swimming pool that the owner had someone get ready for us that morning. The water was a little cold for my taste, but I eased myself into it. Finn didn't seem to have as much of a problem, probably because he was still trying to cool down from his run. Bringing me into his aquatic embrace, he rubbed my shoulders as we stepped even further into the water. We started doing an erotic kind of water dance intermixed with delicious kisses. I felt Finn's hands go to the back of my neck where the tie for my bathing suit top was. I smiled. I was so at peace, so in love, and so wanting him. He smiled back as the tie loosened causing the top to expose my breasts and fall to my waist remaining there because of its tankini style.

"Lara, Chance wants his kite. Do you know if you brou—" Summer, obviously having not left yet for their stroll to the beach, stopped mid-question and mid-patio, seeing Finn and I only partially emerged in the pool.

Mortified, I clung to my husband wrapping my arms around his back and ducking my head onto his shoulder. His upper body thankfully covered my naked top half.

Finn slowly turned us around so that he was the one facing Summer and that she would only be able to see my exposed back.

"The trunk of our car," I whispered to Finn as I was still unable to collect myself.

After echoing my answer back to Summer, he added, "My keys are on the kitchen counter."

"Oh, okay. Oh, good," Summer answered, sounding equally as mortified as I was. "I'll just go…Chance, I'll be right there. Stay there." Her voice cautioned, and I sunk my head even deeper, if possible, into Finn. "Okay. Good. We'll stay a while," she said once again to us.

Embarrassed or not, I played my motherly part and managed to regain my voice. "Not too long. You got sunscreen, right?"

By the way Finn's body shook in a laughing kind of way, I knew he was starting to actually enjoy the humor in the scene unfolding. "Take them out for ice cream or something, too."

"Yeah. Got it," his cousin replied rapidly. "We'll—Chance stay there. I'm…we're going."

My eyes were closed as I heard the patio door click shut and felt Finn's lips on top of my head. I pushed him out of pure need to get some aggressive embarrassment out. "Go. Go check and make sure they're really gone."

"They're gone," he laughed more than said.

"Don't laugh. You're not the one who is partially naked."

"Um, yeah, I am."

I squinted my eyes at him—his chest exposed was worlds different than mine. "Finn, go. Please. Make sure," I pleaded while stretching my hands behind my neck in an effort to retie my tankini top.

"Okay," he agreed with the slightest scent of lament.

Instead of walking up the steps, however, he reached his hands out to the exterior rim of the pool and, in one swoop, masterfully pushed his body out of the water. With my bathing suit now refastened, I admired the back view of him as he went toward the house. His well-defined back, muscular calves, and the curves that ever so slightly outlined his ass, really were a magnificent sight. Craving that body more and more by the second, but knowing I was not going to risk another peep show in an unescapable pool, I got out of the water myself.

I was using a towel to dry myself off when Finn reentered the scene. "Huh? Uh, no. They're gone," he said noting my status.

"You're sure?"

"Yeah, and by the expression on Summer's face, they'll be gone for a while. Why are you out of the pool?"

"Finn, no."

He looked almost pained. "Baby, I want—"

I intercepted his thought. "You want to sleep with me?" I semi-teased, now a little more secure knowing that Summer and the kids were definitely gone.

"Uh, yeah," he said in a way that he may as well have added "obviously."

"Prayers first and then no talking," I teased, recalling his deal with Chance the night before.

Surely relieved, Finn produced the slightest of smirky smiles. I inched closer, dipped my hands into the sides of his shorts, and slowly circled his strong hips with my fingertips. I watched as his spectacular, natural gray eyes bounced upon feeling the touch that I knew always intensified his desire.

"Oh, dear God," he stated as my hands moved more central to his manliness. "Jesus."

"That *is* how a prayer begins, Mr. Murphy." I smiled in a naughty girl way.

"I might have to ask for forgiveness for the lustful thoughts I seem to be hav—"

"Shhh." I replaced my hands in his, leading him toward the chaise lounge. "Grab the blanket just in case."

Finn obliged, quickly taking hold of the enormous teal

blanket that was draped over a side chair. He started kissing me then while carefully lowering us onto the chaise lounge. As he covered our bodies, he said, "You know what this reminds me of?"

Without hesitation, I remembered—our first weekend together… in Nashville with the hot tub, the s'mores, the blanket, and, most of all, the love. "Margarita night. Still no bikini."

"Lara…" He paused planking above me. "You are so beautiful. I've been nearly out of my mind dreaming about this."

His tongue lapped mine while he once again untied my tankini top. I momentarily sat up so that he could lift it off completely this time. Now reclined, I felt Finn's lips all over my breasts and then making their way to my swim shorts. His hands replaced his lips then as he teased by encircling the waist line and then a little further south. My head and back arched backward as I stifled a groan. And then we found that sweet, slow, rhythmic mix of rocking, kissing, and touching that was uniquely us.

***

"You look happy," I noted, watching my husband.

While I was on the adjacent grassy area with the kids, Finn was on the patio dismantling the fishing gear from his afternoon of catching and releasing with Chance. It was our last full day before returning to reality. Finn was more relaxed than I had seen him in a while. I think I was, too. Wasn't everyone like that on vacation, though? After all, when growing up, on the rare daytrips that we would call vacations, even my father seemed a little less aggressive and demeaning.

Wearing worn jeans and a faded blue T, Finn looked up, appearing to be a little perplexed by my comment. "Huh? Yeah. Of course I am."

"I'm glad."

When I didn't say anything more, he stopped what he was doing and looked a little more closely at me. It was then that he understood my second, deeper meaning— the mood he had been in before leaving on tour. "I'm good. This?" He swung his arms around. "Being with you guys? There's nothing better than this. And the other crap? I'm trying to put it away. I mean, things change. But, being on that stage…having the crowd support me in the awesome way that they do? It's empowering. The awards and sales…they're backburner. What about you? You're happy, right?"

"Yeah." The word came out just as relaxed as my unconditioned, wavier-than-usual beach hair. "I wish I could lose a few more pounds, but, yeah. Plus, us girls got to go shoe shopping in town today…and got bargains." While shoes were my only true girly obsession, I was still small-town at heart and never bought without finding a sale.

Sarcasm hadn't been the way to go, though…Finn knew my masks. "Lar?" he asked now a little concerned.

"Baby, yeah," I answered his "happy" question again. Throwing on my black and white flip-flops so I wouldn't burn my feet on the patio's hot concrete, I went over to where he was squatting near the outdoor storage container. I bent down and reassured him with a kiss. As I started to get back up, I casually said, "I turned in my resignation."

"You did?" Standing up to join me, he touched my shoulder, which was adorned by a black eyelet cover-up. "Why didn't you tell me?"

It wasn't necessarily a surprise for Finn. We had talked about me quitting my job many, many times. And I had pretty much come to the conclusion that I would do it after my extended maternity leave. After all, we didn't need the money. And my job had been changing in ways I didn't necessarily like. It was just hard to let it go. It was hard to understand that I was such a different person than I was when I moved to New York as a single woman years before. And, no matter how much I knew beyond any reasonable doubt that Finn and I were eternally committed to one another, it was hard to think that that aspect, the biggest part of my independence, would be gone. But, in the end, the reasons to resign far outweighed the reasons to stay.

"I just did it before you came home. I wanted to tell you in person."

"You're okay with it?" he asked, directing both of us onto the chaise lounge where we had just made love a few days before.

"I actually felt such a wave of relief…the decision had been made."

"Good." He touched the side of my face with the soft back side of his hand.

"It really hasn't sunk in yet, though. We'll see what happens when everyone returns in the fall. I know *you're* good with me quitting."

"Lara, it's not…" He stopped and started again. "I know this is huge for you. I know what that job meant. I understand because I know how I feel about my career. I would never ask—"

"I know. I know that. You never have. It was my decision. You've done so much to make all of this work. You made the sacrifice by living in New York so I could keep working. It's my turn, and it feels right. It does."

"You know I would do all of it again. And despite some times when I didn't like the long hours…" His eyes skimmed mine. "Didn't like" was being kind, and he knew it. My long hours while I was pregnant, especially after the coma, had been a bone of contention between he and I. But he had only been concerned about me and always respected the work that I did. "I am so happy that, for whatever reason in this cosmic world, that you got a job there… at that particular school. Otherwise… "

I caught his smile and mimicked it. It was because I worked at the school that I had met Wyatt and, therefore, reconnected with Finn in the first place. "You would be dating America's next top model." I finished the sentence for him.

He shook his head, but I think we both knew it wasn't too far from the truth. "And neither one of us would be happy."

"Nope."

"Lara, listen, I'm not going to lie to you. We've talked about it. I like the fact that you will be able to be with our kids more and—"

"And you."

"Yeah. Honestly, yeah. It opens up more possibilities. It won't be like I'm leaving so much."

One of the possibilities was that I, and the kids sometimes, could travel with him to more special events because I wouldn't have to take time off of work. He tried not to say it, but I knew he would have liked me on his arm more often—not only to eliminate any speculation but just because of the pride and love he felt for me. The other "possibility" was for the four of us to permanently move to his house in Nashville. He had sacrificed living in Music City for my job when we got married. And that meant he had to make little trips to Tennessee periodically. That wouldn't be the case if we already resided there. But that would be something we could decide after the tour…once everything became more settled again.

"I know what that means to you. And I guess it wouldn't be so bad having you around more often," I teased.

"Oh yeah?" he mocked back and kissed my forehead.

"So, I'm kinda retired, huh? This does sort of resemble the retiree's life."

"You and Pop," he spoke of his retired father. "Maybe the two of you can take even more of those tree-posing classes."

I lightly pushed on my trying-to-be-funny husband. "Yeah. And then we can eat from the senior discount menus, and he can introduce me to his community center buddies."

"You would drive those old guys wild." Finn semi-laughed.

"You better not be gone too long, then, Cowboy."

"Not funny, Lara." He wrapped me up in his arms and then threw in an extra squeeze.

While the conversation had turned lighthearted, the topic of cheating also reminded me of my brother. We had yet to talk with one another since our fallout phone call in February. I wanted the subject briskly out of both my husband's mind and mine. So, I promptly changed the subject.

"Y'know what's not funny? How hungry I am. I thought you were grilling tonight."

"I am." He tapped me twice on the spot where my tan shorts met my knee. "Let me grab a beer, and then I'll get the chicken started."

"Good. We still have some bread from Eoin's, too." It was Finn's favorite brown bread from his uncle's restaurant. "And Summer just went to the bakery for a dessert."

"You gave her some money, right?"

"Yeah," I answered, knowing Finn always wanted to be the provider. "Chance! Please try not to poke her in the eye." I called out to our son, who was in the yard poking Arinn in the stomach and making her giggle.

"I not," he yelled back.

"You want to help get Arinn's dinner ready and feed her?" I asked the three-year-old.

"Yeah."

When Finn started laughing, I asked, "What?"

"You're a con artist. You just got everybody else to do all the work."

"I don't work. I'm retired," I smirked my answer.

"You know one of the things I miss about you not being on the road with us?"

"Yeah," I smirked again.

"Yeah." He gave me his sexy, confident smile. "Of course that but also our every city selfies. Whatcha say?" He pulled out his phone from his pocket and held it in front of us. "Say Hamptons Happy."

CHAPTER EIGHT

"Lara…" His tone resonated with warning.

"What?"

"Don't," was his solid, simple reply.

"Don't what?"

"Don't ruin our last night together," he defined more distinctly.

"*Me* don't ruin?" It sounded accusatory. It was meant to be accusatory.

He had been on his phone almost the entire time since we arrived back from our trip to the Hamptons. We had spent the day at the resort town and then made our way back to suburban New York, stopping along the way for a late dinner. That's when the phone calls had really started—the managers, the crew, the driver, etc. etc. etc. But at least Finn had demonstrated good Southern manners and had disengaged during the meal.

Now, standing in the middle of our great room, he knew I wasn't happy with an evening of seeing him attached to his cell. But, he took a deep breath, and I followed suit. Neither of us wanted our discussion to turn into a true argument.

After another moment of us both looking away and

then again at one another, I said in a kinder fashion, "I see you getting ready to go, and I know you have to. I just want all of you while I have you."

"Don't do that to me. You know it's hard for me to leave."

"Sometimes it doesn't seem that way." The words came out quiet but sincere.

"What!" Oops. That touched a nerve.

I tried to further explain my point-of-view— the one he obviously hadn't appreciated from the beginning of the conversation. "You're here, but you're not here. You're on your phone… you may as well have already left."

"Fine. Shit! You know what?" His voice rose, and he actually turned and headed toward the door.

I immediately regretted my words, forgetting, somehow, in the midst of my own self-pity, how much pressure he was under and how much he truly hated leaving. "Finn, don—" I started to plead only to lock eyes with Summer who was standing on the bottom step of the staircase, having obviously descended them without either of us knowing.

Hearing the halt in my voice, Finn turned to follow my gaze. "Sorry, Summer. I didn't realize…" Finn apologized without facing me.

"No. I'm sorry," she countered, looking a little uncomfortable. Funny how, over the week, she had managed to be witness to two awkward moments between Finn and I, albeit completely different ends of the emotional spectrum. "I was just coming down for a drink. I'll grab something quick."

"Please. It's fine," I offered, spotting the book in her hand and realizing she had obviously wanted to sit in the great room and relax. "Stay." I said it to Summer, but I also looked and meant it even more so for Finn.

"I'm glad you came with us and that you're able to help Lara tomorrow."

Summer was staying the night and watching the kids

the next day while I ran some errands—it was just a lot easier getting things done without toting two children under the age of four. "God, no prob. I had a blast," she answered. "The real world is going to suck."

"Yep, sometimes it does." Finn shifted his eyes to meet mine.

I tried to interpret his response. Did he mean getting back to his job and the phone calls, etc.? Or did he mean us and the argument we seemed to be in? I didn't have a chance to find out, though, as, within seconds, his phone chimed again. He looked at it, shrugged his shoulders, and walked off to answer it.

***

I was in bed long before Finn found his way there that night. The last time we had been in that bed together, I had fallen asleep almost instantly, feeling so safe and relaxed with him there. This time it was quite the contrast. I was wide awake and unsure of what to feel or do.

"Finn?" I questioned after giving him a few minutes to adjust to the bed and the nearly complete darkness.

"What?" he first replied in a neutral tone and then a little more kindly, "Yeah?"

My back still turned toward him, I breathed a little more easily. "Just wanted to make sure—" I stopped myself.

Sure of what? Of him? Of us?

I started again. "I wanted to know that you are talking to me—that you would answer me."

He breathed like he had been holding it in. "Always." He paused. "Look, you know I hate all of it— the phone calls, the time…leaving."

"You're not the only one that doesn't like you leaving, you know."

"I know. Let's try not to hurt each other in the process, though, okay? It only makes it worse." When I turned and grabbed his hand in mine, he took it, squeezed, and then softly said, "Can we just be for tonight?" He must have felt or read my puzzlement because he readily clarified. "Forget before, forget tomorrow—just be. The kids and Summer are good. Just lay here with me. Please. Just let us be." When I laid my head against his T-shirt-clothed chest, I felt his exhale which I knew, just like I knew nearly all of his sounds and motions, was a sign that the tenseness he was feeling was starting to dissipate. "This was always us. I remember being on that sofa in your dorm and your head on my shoulder like—"

I interrupted, but I didn't lift that aforementioned head. "I thought we weren't looking forward or back."

"Okay," he agreed. "*Now* then. Feel that? Hear that?" He paused and let me listen to something much greater than the absolute silence of the house— his heart beating solid and steady. "That's now, and it was before, and it will be tomorrow, too."

"Finn…"

I felt his lips rest on my head before saying, "Get some sleep, Bed Bug."

"K," I managed.

It wasn't the best goodnights we ever had—far from it, in fact. But it also wasn't as bad as it could have been. It just hurt knowing that it was the last in-person good night we would have for nearly two months, which was double the amount of time we had just suffered through.

***

"Lara, Jesus! Why aren't you picking up? I heard what's going on. I need to know you're all right. Please tell me you're not in that bank."

The day had started off fine. Finn and I were okay, despite the friction from the night before. In hindsight, I knew myself well enough to know that I had subconsciously built up walls to guard my feelings over him leaving. And he, in return, had been too quick to anger, probably for the same reason.

So, amongst not-well-disguised tears, I had wished him a safe flight and watched, once again, as he got into a waiting car and set off to the airport for "his summer job." Not wanting to wallow or overthink, I first made sure the kids and Summer were all right. Then, ready to start my day of errands, I stepped out to meet the spectacular, sunny outdoors, which seemed to dare me to forget any woes and concentrate on the good things in life.

The day, however, had other plans. I was, indeed, at the bank— in the temporary upstairs office of the branch manager, Whitney. My direct deposit paycheck obviously wasn't going to be happening anymore. So, I was closing out that account and merging the balance into another of our accounts along with a CD that was maturing.

Whitney and I should have been at the point of idle chit-chat but, instead, were crouching side-by-side under a big oak desk. Our eyes were on the rolling cabinet that we had quickly used to barricade the door at the onset of the ordeal. And I had my cell phone up to my ear, listening to my husband's frantic voice mail message.

I had put my phone immediately on vibrate once everything started happening. And even though I desperately wanted to answer Finn's call, I knew I couldn't. Any noise could let the perpetrators on the main floor know that there were two scared souls trapped in the only occupied room on the only floor above them. We had no viable means of escape, since the staircase led directly to where the danger was occurring and the room was windowless—an old storage area being put to use while Whitney's front office was getting remodeled. And since no one had made any motion to check upstairs, we weren't eager to promote our presence.

I responded to Finn's message via text. *In bank. Can't answer. Need 2 B quiet.*

I saw that he had picked up the text immediately, but it

took him a little bit to respond. *R U OK?*

Hiding, Cowboy. I confirmed with my special name for him.

Where? Near it?

They're downstairs. I'm upstairs. Back room. Just me & manager.

His response this time was immediate. *Cops R outside. Hold still. B safe. I love U.*

We no longer had any idea what was going on in the main downstairs area of the bank. Initially, the silent alarm, set off by one of the tellers, had registered in Whitney's office, letting us immediately see the footage on her monitor. There were two masked people—presumably men based on their build—at the counters. They were holding guns. Patrons were on the floor. And then the cameras had gone dead. The silent alarm had alerted the cops. But, we didn't know if they had arrived because of our room's lack of windows and the fact that there was no noise coming from below.

Finn's text not only gave me some comfort knowing that the police had arrived, but it reassured me of something else, too. And, it was just as important. His statement of love was something I never doubted but, nonetheless, needed to hear so much in that moment.

Not knowing how long we would be entombed, and especially understanding the importance of silence, I, regrettably, sent the next text. *I will. Don't want 2 text much. Want 2 keep cell battery strong. Forever, Finn.*

Remember we have many more years in Forever.

I sent back a smiley emoji. But, truth be told, I had tears in my eyes. They were a mix of fear and love.

It had been a little before noon when I had entered the bank—shortly before closing time. I rarely stepped into a bank because nearly everything was direct deposit and paperless. And now I knew I would never want to again. My initial telephone call from Finn had come in around twelve-thirty. He knew pretty quickly what was going on. I couldn't help but wonder how he not only found out about it but also knew the police were present. I ran my hand back and forth on the wood bracelet the Murphys had given me earlier in the summer. I had put it on that morning, thinking I was going to need the reminder to keep strong with Finn leaving. Little did I know, though, how much strength and love I was going to have to pull from that thoughtful symbol around my wrist.

***

Over an hour later, my mother started calling. Cramped up behind the desk, I listened to her frantic voice mails and wondered who had informed her. Had the hold-up made national news? We could hear helicopters periodically circling and assumed they were local stations. But, national? Finn surely wouldn't have called just to worry her. And I knew she was worried. She was a mom. I was worried about my own kids, and I knew they were safe with Summer. But even though I empathized with my mother, I could not have her bombarding my phone every five to ten minutes or get into a texting circus with her. I knew it was asking a lot, especially because someone needed to be there to calm him, but I texted Finn for help.

Call my mom. Tell her 2 stop calling me. Calm her.

I'll try, he replied via text. *She just tried calling me. I ♥ U.*

It was so frustrating to not know what was going on. But we were so afraid to even move. And Whitney was relying on me for information. She had unplugged her desk phone so it wouldn't make any noise, and her husband had, of all days, taken her cell phone that morning to get an updated version.

***

Another twenty minutes or so passed. I couldn't stand it, even with my mother's calls ending. We needed to know something…anything.

So, I texted Finn again. *Do U know what's going on?*

Police R negotiating. They want U to just stay put. I'm ready to break the barricade & go in there myself, tho.

What? My eyes enlarged. I reread his text and then replied. *You're here?*

Where else would I B?

The first tears of the afternoon splattered on my phone. Where else would he be? In a different state? On a plane? Gone? Right?

But he wasn't. He was near. He was here. A wash of comfort cascaded over me. Suddenly, I felt safe.

I love U. I texted and then added, *U stay put, too, Finn.*

I could almost hear the frustrated sigh as he typed back. *I am. They're not letting me near the place.*

Following police directives, Finn kept our messages brief and acted as a liaison, giving information to both Whitney and I and to the officers in charge. But then another agonizing hour of silence entailed. Silence from outside, from downstairs, from my husband, and from my "cellmate." We ate the protein bars Whitney had in her drawer while still trying to relax and keep each other as calm as we could.

***

Silence was a much more welcoming sound than the one that finally tipped the day to the other side of the pendulum. A number of loud, vibrating sounds, like wood snapping fiercely on metal, pierced the air. It was obvious what they were and the direction from which they were coming. The gunshots, ringing out just below us, startled me so bad, I broke all rules and screamed. Luckily, I'm sure no one was too concerned about one scared woman blurting out a quick screech. But I don't think I was the only one, though. There seemed to be screaming coming from below us, too.

My phone instantly buzzed a vibrated text. With bile threatening my throat, I slowly looked at the screen. He couldn't have heard me scream. But, had he heard the gunshots, too? Or, did the police relay that to him?

With a one word text, I could see the ultimate fear. *Lara???*

My shaking fingers texted back. *We're OK.*

Baby, B safe. I love U so much.

U 2 I texted back, not being able to breathe or type much more.

Silence again. And then yelling. Not screaming but booming, male yelling. Was it the cops? Was it the men in the masks? We couldn't make out anything that was being said. I had my fingers on my phone ready to text my questions when a text from Finn came through.

They R securing. Stay put. I'll keep U posted. Before I could reply, he texted again. *U OK?*

I was shaking and more nervous than I had been the entire time. I didn't know why because I was pretty sure "securing" was a good sign. But, ironically, it was the anticipatory thought that everything was about to be over…the thought of being able to truly breathe that made me hyperventilate. Could Finn sense that, or was it just another one of the many times he felt a need to ask me that question?

I texted back with honesty. *Trying 2 B. U?*

I will B just as soon as U R out of there. Finn sent that text and then followed up immediately with another. *Cops said to wait til they open the door. And have your hands raised.*

I showed Whitney the text, and she had me send a question—a very astute one. *How will we know it's them?*

It took a couple minutes, but Finn answered back. *I told them 2 say Bedbugs.*

I quickly stopped myself when I laughed out loud at Finn's personalized password. But I continued to smile internally. My hands were knotted together trying to release the excess tension. But, I could feel it. We were almost free. I was almost safe. It was almost over.

Moments later, the pounding on the office door caused both Whitney and I to yelp. The person or persons on the other side were trying to turn the knob but to no avail. It was locked and the rolling cabinet was in front of it.

"Hey, bedbugs," A burly voice boomed with the slightest of amusement. "It's all right, ladies. Open up. It's the police."

Everything from that point on seemed to take place in an alternate universe. Things were happening so quickly. Yet every step down the stairs and into the crime scene, sedated by closed window blinds, seemed to be going in slow motion.

Whitney's co-workers came to her side, while the doe-eyed customers seemed to be in shock. And then there were the two tarp-covered bodies lying on the ground. When I stared at their lifeless figures, the chief of police introduced himself and verified that the potential bank robbers were the only victims after having drawn their weapons on police first.

He then explained what was going to take place. They understood that we all had been through quite an ordeal. So, first they were going to reunite us with our families in the local public high school which was vacant for the summer. However, we would then need to give individual statements before being able to go home. I didn't know what I could contribute, having not heard or seen much, but I was willing to do whatever the police needed in order to get to Finn and finally back home to my babies.

There was a van waiting to take us to the school to meet up with our loved ones. Before opening the door, the chief cautioned everyone that there was a lot of activity going on outside— police, medical personnel, and, just beyond the yellow police tape, onlookers and numerous news media. He requested that everyone get into the van without engaging with anyone so that we could expedite the process.

Accompanied by cops, we started in stunned mob fashion toward the front door. I was in the back of the group and within just a few steps of freedom when I felt a hand on my arm. I turned to see one of the officers who had originally gone upstairs to retrieve Whitney and I.

"Mrs. Murphy?" Completely bald with a towering build, he said my name in the burly voice that had called out "bedbugs" earlier.

"Yeah?"

"Ma'am? You're going to come with me."

"Uh…" I started as he led me in the opposite direction—toward the back of the bank.

"Your husband's not at the school. We have him at the Rotary Club. I'll take you there. You were our only connection inside this building." He continued talking as I followed him down the hallway. "So we had him with us. Plus…" He opened the back door. "Ma'am? With him being in the public eye, we really don't want to add to everything that is already happening. The press? They're out front and at the school. They won't know to look—"

"Oh," I agreed, understanding the dilemma and solution. Welcome to the world of celebrity, I internally sighed.

"I'll walk you to the location. It's just a couple down."

"Okay. Thanks." I think I got one semi-formal word in. We walked a few more steps or so before I realized the ground was wet. "It rained?" I questioned.

"Yeah. Briefly. Just got done."

"Oh." Of course I hadn't seen that, having been scrunched under a desk the entire day. I felt zombie-like as we continued to make our way down the back road. Even though I was trying to focus on what was at hand, my brain just wanted to replay what had happened, especially the sight of the main bank area at the end of the ordeal. I looked over at my makeshift bodyguard. "Everybody's okay, right? I mean, except…" My voice trailed. What do I call them— the bastards…the stupid, cowardly scum? "No one else was hurt? The people inside or you guys?"

"No. Everyone came out physically unscathed."

I took in another deep breath. Would my lungs ever be able to resume a regular pattern? "I'm glad."

"Sorry, ma'am, I don't listen to his music, but your husband... he seems like a good, real stand-up guy." Officer Bell, as I now knew him by, opened the front door to the Rotary Club.

"The best," I agreed, thinking how on a normal day I would have found something sarcastically sweet to say. But, on a day where Finn had been my lifeline, I had no other words—just the honest truth.

CHAPTER NINE

We walked through the lobby area, where a few police officers nodded in our direction. They seemed very preoccupied with their own conversation, as well as the paperwork spread out before them. I didn't care. I could feel him. He was near. He was—

"He's in here, ma'am." Officer Bell stopped in front of a closed interior door. "Please, just a few minutes. Then we've got to get you to the school for some debriefing."

"Yeah, okay. Thanks. I got it." I almost hugged the man, but he didn't really seem like the huggy type. And, besides, just behind that door, there was someone else I would much rather wrap my arms around.

The police officer opened the solid wood door for me. The unveiled room appeared to be an office. There was a formal leather sofa off to the side and, taking main stage, there was an oak desk with accompanying chairs. I couldn't help but shudder looking at that desk and revisiting being stuck under a similar one for the majority of the day. When Officer Bell shut the door behind me, Finn, who had been standing solo staring out the window, swung around in my direction.

"Oh, God." He wrung his hands through his already

ruffled hair.

"Hi, Cowboy," I tried, but instantly my voice broke on my favorite name for him.

Finn put his hand up to his mouth, took a deep breath, and walked over to me with purpose. Without saying a word, his hand went up to my face pushing an imaginary piece of hair repeatedly away from my cheeks. He then gently palmed my face, starting from my eyes down to my chin. He would sometimes do that to get me to go to sleep peacefully. But, this time, it was as if he was double checking to make sure I was real. He secured me tightly into his body then, and we remained like that—still and silent—for countless, secure minutes.

Eventually, pulling me only arm's length away, he said, "You're okay. You're okay, right?"

I nodded my head affirmatively up and down. "Finn?" I got his name out before needing to be closer in his arms again. "I think," I said.

"Yeah, you're fine. You're with me. You're okay. We're gonna get you home."

"I know." I looked up at him, trying to take another deep breath before sinking my head back into his torso.

"Oh, baby. Oh, God." Hearing his voice threaten to tremble made me ache for the agony he had been going through. His misty eyes caught mine before he swiftly picked me up and carried me to the sofa. First taking the phone from his pocket and placing it on the end table, Finn then cradled me on his lap and held me silently for a moment or two. "Talk to me," he finally said in a hushed voice.

My breathing, and my senses in general, had become a little more regulated. So, I was ready to talk. I was ready to get some of it out.

"I wasn't scared at first, you know? I was mad. I was just mad. Can you believe that? I was holed up in this little office. How selfish. Those people downstairs..." I shuddered just thinking of the horror they saw and went through. "I guess I just wasn't thinking clearly. But when the terror *did* start to sink in, I just kept thinking of our kids."

"You're a good mom," he said with conviction while playing with my hair.

"Do you know what happened? I mean, obviously, we knew about the silent alarm, and we saw the gunmen on the monitor until it went dark. And then, eventually, we heard those shots. I was hearing bits and pieces once we eventually made it downstairs, but, at that point, all I wanted to know was how to get to you."

He brushed my cheek slowly, softly with his knuckles. "There were—" He started, but the sound of his phone ringing cut his sentence off mid-way. Looking at the mini-screen, he said, "It's your mom, Lar."

I lifted my head and reached my hand out for his phone. "Momma?" I cried into the phone, using a childlike term I didn't even remember using as a child.

"Oh, my God, Lara, is that you? Lara?" My mother's voice practically screeched across the line.

Still embraced in the comfort of my husband's arms, I replied, "I'm all right, Mom. We're out. I'm fine."

"You're safe? You're okay?" she questioned as if she hadn't heard me in the first place. But I knew better—she was just a worried mom. "Lara? Where are you?"

"I'm in a building near the bank...not in the bank anymore. I'm with Finn." I guess talking on his phone would have signified that, but my mind was not altogether clear yet. "I'm fine," I tried again.

"Oh, my God. Sweet Jesus. Thank you, Mary mother of God. Oh, thank you. You sure? You're sure you're all right? Did you see the guys?" Her words were so rapidly strung together, I wasn't sure if I actually got all of them.

"No. And, yes, I'm fine," I answered not sure if I had done so in the right order.

"I need to call your brother. He's been calling me non-stop, and I think he's been calling Finn, too."

"Really?" I asked.

There were a lot of things that shocked me that day. My brother calling was definitely another to add to the list. It had been five months since we had last spoke.

"Yes," she confirmed.

"Oh. Tell him I'm all right," I partially stammered.

"I will," she agreed.

"Mom, I only have a couple minutes with Finn, and then I have to talk with the police and the bank people."

"You tell him he got me through. He got me through," she echoed. "I don't think I would have made it without him."

"I feel the same way." I looked at the man, who despite his own angst, had helped so many of us that day. "I'll call you tomorrow," I said back into the phone and then tacked on, "Mom?"

"Yeah, honey?" Her voice still wavered although was much calmer than the beginning of our conversation.

"I love you, Mom."

"Oh, baby girl, I love *you*. Tomorrow," she confirmed like she was already counting the minutes until she could hear my voice again.

I pressed the end button and placed the phone back on the table. I sat up a little straighter and then spoke with sincerity to my husband. "I love you, too, you know."

Finn put his forehead momentarily on mine and said, "Knowing that you were in there and I couldn't get you out? The thought of losing you today—"

"I'm okay," I interrupted with determination and love.

"Nothing else matters," he replied with equal conviction.

My voice softened. "I'm sorry about yesterday." It was something I thought a lot about underneath that desk.

"Hey, don't." His voice creaked as he placed his hand on top of mine. "That? That was on me."

"Finn—" I started, not believing that to be the case.

And then I stopped. It didn't matter. What mattered

was the love—the undeniable, forever love—that we shared. I took the initiative and kissed him, feeling every ounce of that precious love.

"Ditto," he said once our lips parted.

I smiled—probably for the first time that day—and then rattled off some questions. "How did you know about all of this so fast? And how did my mom know I was even in there? You didn't call and tell her, did you?"

"No," he replied instantly to the last question. "God, do you think I wanted to deal with an hysteric Elise Faulkner during this?"

"Well, me either!" I exclaimed.

"It was Joe Roberts' wife." Finn spoke of one of our neighbors. "She saw you go in the bank. She was sitting in the parking lot when it happened. She's an eye witness and loving it. Getting her fifteen minutes," he added with a semi-grunt.

"Geez, no doubt." I agreed, thinking of Mrs. Roberts—the stereotypical, older, busybody housewife in our housing development.

"She called the police and then Joe, and then he called me. But now it's all over the news because—"

"Because she knew I was there and told the press when they came."

"Yeah."

"And because you're 'you.'" I tried a smile, acknowledging the power of celebrity. "It's national, isn't it? That's how my mom knew?"

"Yeah."

"And Lane?" I remembered still astonished. "My mom said he's been calling you."

"He's pretty damn worried, Beauty. He's been calling almost as much as your mom."

"What?"

"You should call him. This thing with the two of you ne— "

"I know," I interrupted Finn kindly. "I will. I'll call him.

But you know who I really want to talk with right now?" I answered my own question. "The kids. Is Summer still with them?"

"Yeah, she texted. They're at the house. She can be there as late as we need her to be."

"The kids… Chance doesn't know, does he? Finn, he would be so scared."

"No, baby." He brought his hand back to mine. "Summer knows not to tell them."

It was something else I had thought about while being holed up in that bank all day. Why had Chance been so scared of those fireworks? He was being raised in a loving, solid household so unlike the one I had grown up in—full of anger and uncertainty. Maybe it was because Finn and I doted on him when he was first born. I had a miscarriage before becoming pregnant with Chance and, between that and Wyatt, we knew how quickly a young life could be taken away. Or, was it that he noticed his daddy being away more, and he didn't feel as stable? I hadn't come to a conclusion, but I knew I was bound and determined to protect my child from being scared.

"Do you think we can call?" I asked Finn.

His answer was to pick up his phone and dial. I put my head back on his chest, such a secure place I never wanted to leave, and felt the vibrations of his melodic voice as he spoke with his cousin. Then I sat up as he handed the phone to me, knowing Chance was ready to get on the line.

"Mommy?" His sweet little voice emerged.

"Chance, sweetie, hi!" And for the first time since knowing that Finn was still in town and nearby, tears flooded my eyes.

"Where are you, Mommy?"

"I'm at…" I didn't want to lie, but I couldn't tell the truth. "I'm with Daddy."

Finn, seeing and hearing my emotions erupting, wrapped his arms around me as Chance's question gave me a half-chuckle. "On road?"

"No. No. He's not there yet. Chance, I—" I started getting even more choked up just thinking of telling him that I loved him.

My efforts were thwarted momentarily, though, as our son said, "I dwawing you a picture."

"Are you?" I wiped a silent tear. "I can't wait to see it. I love you, Little Man."

"I wuv you, too, Mommy," he said, and I couldn't take it anymore.

Finn took the phone from me as I pushed it backward at him and rapidly tried to dry my tears. "Hey, buddy, it's Daddy. We're going to come see you and your sister real soon." He paused, obviously listening to our son on the other end. "Yeah, I'm sure Arinn is." Finn and I both looked up as Officer Bell entered the room.

I wiped my eyes on Finn's charcoal shirt which, thankfully, absorbed the color of my mascara. "We need to go?" I asked, standing up to meet the officer.

As the cop nodded in agreement, I could hear Finn's voice become more hurried on the phone with Chance. "Listen, Chance, we gotta go. Put Summer on the phone." Pause. "No, put...No." I almost laughed seeing Finn, a nationwide country music superstar, being out-powered in a phone conversation by a three-year-old. "Okay. Yeah." Finn stood up now, too, while trying to get a word in. "Okay. Put Summ—Hi, Summer." He seemed to say "finally" to me with his eyes.

"Our three-year-old," I explained to the police officer.

"Ah, enjoy these days. They grow up too fast. My thirteen-year-old won't talk to me—phone or otherwise!"

While Finn talked with Summer, the police officer explained what was going to happen next. Part of it included leaving that room and Finn behind while our collective group of victims were debriefed. And then I would have to be individually questioned. Finn, now off the phone, was not about to let it happen that way. He was adamant about going with me. And, admittedly, I didn't want to be apart from him, either.

Realizing the drama that it would create, especially if the press—who were for sure growing at the high school—saw him, I said, "Go ahead. Go home. I'll be all right by my—" I didn't get any further.

"Lara, if you think there is a chance in hell that I am leaving without you, you don't know me at all." Finn took his stance.

I wiped the last of the straggling tears and turned to the officer. "He's serious."

"I can't promise to keep you out of the press. We'll try to go in through a back door. But when we take her statement, we'll need you to be in a separate room."

"Sure. Whatever. I don't care. But I will not leave her. What you have to understand is…my wife? She trumps everything else—absolutely everything."

***

After a couple hours, all the necessities were completed, and we were finally able to make our exit. Finn shook a lot of hands, especially those of the police officers he dealt with during the time I was trapped. Brimming on showing too much emotion, he managed to articulate the gratitude he had for their service and for keeping me safe. He had a special thanks for Officer Bell, who not only managed to get us inside the school unseen but coordinated our final departure out the back while the press conference with the chief was happening in the front.

When Finn drove us, via his rental car, back to the bank, there was still yellow police tape securing the building and surrounding area. But a police officer waved us into the now almost vacant lot. Finn pulled into the spot directly to the right of my red Jeep Wrangler—the thoughtful gift he had given me because of its connection to our college days. When I got out of his car, he followed suit, assisting me in a gentlemanly fashion to the driver's side of mine.

Ignoring any onlookers that were still mingling in the background, he kissed me ever-so-sweetly and unlocked and opened the Jeep's door. "I'll be right behind you," he said as I slid into the driver's seat.

"I know."

He looked at me for an extra second and then went back to his rental. I started the Jeep's ignition. I had driven it for years and just that morning, yet it seemed so foreign to me. As typical as me sitting up against a wall in a restaurant, I had backed the car into the spot that morning. So, now, I was facing the bank. There were a few officers still abuzz outside, a black and white forensics van parked haphazardly in the lot, yellow crime scene tape drooping and straightening in a dramatic fashion, and blinds still drawn. I lowered the driver's side window, suddenly needing fresh air. Then I looked to the second story of the building. That had been my torture chamber for the day— the spot where I thought I might actually lose my life. God, I really could have. I was a step away, a bullet away, from never seeing my beautiful kids again or that amazing man who was such a godsend in my life. I stared straight ahead, and then I started to shake. It was my driver's leg, and it was uncontrollable. Finn started to pull out until his open car window was now face to face with mine.

"Finn?" I partially quivered his name.

"Yeah?" Even though I had only spoken one word— his name—he saw the trepidation and threw his car into park.

"My leg. I…I don't think I can drive. My leg won't stop shaking." I physically pressed my hands onto my right leg to try to compress the seizure like spasms that were taking place.

My husband got out of his car and opened my driver's door. "It's all right, Beauty. Let's just leave the car here.

We'll get it some other time, okay?"

"I don't know why my leg won't stop shaking." I stared at it. The more I pressed…the more I thought…the more it shook.

"Lara, it's all right. It's okay, baby. You're okay." Somehow he had managed to get his hand in mine and direct me out of the Jeep.

"I know. It's just my leg." My eyes pierced and stared at the appendage as if it were possessed.

I did know I was okay. Obviously, everything was over. I was safe. Finn was there. What the heck was this about?

Finn kissed me carefully on the forehead and, without letting go of the grasp he had on my hand, he climbed into the driver's side of the Jeep, got the window up and turned off the ignition. Once he secured my car, he guided me to the rental's passenger side, watched as I got inside, and closed the door behind me. Then, after getting in on his own side, he reached over and buckled me in like a child before doing the same with his seat.

Nothing was registering clearly in my brain. Everything—the bank, after, even Finn sitting next to me—suddenly seemed as if in a fog state. Why? I had been good after seeing Finn at the Rotary Club and after debriefing at the high school. But, now, my world was becoming hazy, as if I was on the outside of my body looking in.

"What about my car?" I managed to ask as we pulled away from it.

"We'll get it tomorrow or some other time. It's okay."

"Tomorrow?"

Sheez! When was that? What was today?

"Yeah, baby." I heard his voice as if it were on the other end of a long tunnel.

We were on the main street now. Traffic lights, buildings, and yellow stripes on the cement road were in my line of vision. When Finn put his right hand on my left thigh, it startled me. I flinched and looked in his direction.

He didn't remove it but instead caressed my leg with small circles.

"I want to go home," I said plainly.

"We'll be there soon, okay?" He turned that right hand palm up and said, "Hold onto my hand. Squeeze as tight as you want."

I did. And we drove for a couple more minutes in silence—the scenery changing ever so slightly from a small city-like atmosphere to a more suburban one. I tried hard to concentrate only on Finn's hand…on our hands together.

"Hey, you can squeeze tighter than that. I've been through labor with you twice." He smiled, seeing if he could get a similar reaction from me.

But I couldn't manage one. "Do you remember that rainbow we saw driving back from Wyatt's memorial service?" I recalled the miracle in the sky years before.

Finn didn't answer immediately. Wyatt's name always seemed to momentarily take his breath away. The ride back from that memorial had been emotional, just as this one from the bank was. Back then, there had not only been one rainbow but two at the same time, creating a secure, serene setting. It was something that had calmed us and made us believe in the beauty of the world even through tragedy.

"Yeah," he finally acknowledged while quietly glancing over at me.

After an elongated exhale, I explained. "I need a rainbow."

He brought my hand up to his lips and held it there for a good few seconds. "I love you so much, Lara." There was a tear in his eye as he brought our entwined hands back down to my leg, and I squeezed… I squeezed hard.

CHAPTER TEN

Our home was uncommonly quiet when we arrived back. It was around five-thirty. Normally, I would be starting to make dinner and the kids would be bouncing around in some kind of energetic state. But, this had, by far, not been anywhere near a normal day.

Summer greeted me with a "thank God you're alive" hug and filled us in on what we needed to know. I was hearing everything she was saying—Chance wouldn't take a nap and finally just went down for a little bit...Arinn was awake in her crib...the kids did not know anything about where we were...the news was covering the bank situation pretty extensively...she talked to all close Murphy relatives letting them know of our status...she had not picked up the landline...But, it was as if she was in that "tunnel" I had experienced on our car ride home. I could *hear* her, but I couldn't really comprehend anything completely.

Finn extended our gratitude. "Thanks, Summer. We really can't thank you enough."

"I'm glad I was here."

"Ingo? Is he still coming to pick you up?" Finn spoke of Summer's boyfriend, who she met in college and had just started working entry level on Wall Street.

"Yeah," she said. "He's actually already here."

"Oh yeah?" Finn questioned. "There wasn't a car in the drive."

"No. He's outside the neighborhood gates. He got here a couple minutes before you."

I hadn't paid close attention to the cars at the gate, but there had been a few. Finn and I, recognizing the persistent press, had kept our heads down and avoided being seen as much as possible when we had entered. Now, not seeming to have control over my limbs or nervous system, I was vaguely aware that I was swaying back and forth as I managed to respond with a, "Hmmm."

"Why didn't you have him come in?" Finn's use of language was much clearer.

"I know how you are with your privacy. Besides, I wanted to concentrate on the kids." She smiled over at me.

"Oh." Finn sounded shocked but proud of his cousin for her understanding. "Well, you could have." Looking at me with obvious concern, he once again spoke to Summer. "I really hate to ask you this, but do you think you two can do us another favor?"

"Name it," she answered without hesitation.

"Can you drive over to the bank and get Lara's Jeep? Just bring it back here? And then I promise you can be on your way. I'll even throw in dinner and a movie or backstage pa—"

"Finn, my dad owns a restaurant, and I know you will let us go backstage anytime. Sure, we'll do it for you. You're family. Ingo won't have a problem with it and, if he does, he's not boyfriend-worthy."

"I'm sure he is," Finn replied.

"He needs to step up his game then," Summer lamented. "We've graduated. Time for something. Not a ring. Just let me know where we're going...who we are."

"Hey, you know, Summer...college guys? They're just scared big boys. Maybe he's tried." Finn looked over at me. If I didn't immediately know for sure that he was making reference to us during our collegiate days, I was certain with his next comment. "Did you tell him? Let him know to try again. You don't want to risk seven years. Or worse."

I smiled and touched his hand then. It had taken us seven years to find one another again. And on one Saturday in July, inside a bank, it could have just as easily been all taken away.

As I started up the stairs, I heard Summer teasing Finn, "That sounds like lyrics to one of your hillbilly songs."

"No. Country songs don't usually have a happy ending, kiddo, and this one definitely needs one."

I couldn't have agreed more. I knew I had a happy ending. I just had to somehow find it under all the clouds and suffering.

Once upstairs, I checked on my firstborn. He was sprawled haphazardly on top of his black and white comforter hugging his guitar pillow. Our little rock-and-roller looked so peaceful in his sleep, thankfully oblivious to what was going on around him that day. I resisted touching his hair —the same brown as his daddy's—in fear that I would wake him. I knew he needed to get up soon or else he wouldn't go back down for the night, but it was also nice just knowing he was safe and happy.

Next, I went into Arinn's nursery. She was in her crib cooing and gurgling and seemingly having a grand ole time. As I brought her into my arms, I heard the security system announce a departure—surely Summer going with Ingo. Arinn squirmed and bounced in my arms until I brought both of us down to her plush, carpeted floor. I reached over for some of her favorite stuffed animals and enjoyed the simplicity of life via the eyes of an eight-month-old.

When Finn appeared in the doorway, he posed the same question he had been asking all day long. "You all right?"

"Yeah," I answered as he sat down directly behind me, wrapping his arms securely around my waist. "I guess. I'm so glad to be home and see my babies."

"I know." He seemed to echo my sentiment. "You're—hey, hey, Lara, look." Finn pointed to our daughter who had managed to crawl her way over to the crib, hoist herself up to a standing position, and take a couple steps while holding on to the posts. "She hasn't done that yet, has she?"

"No. Hey, cutie, you go. Good job." I commended our baby girl.

Sensing her parents' attention, Arinn turned around, instantly lost her balance, and plopped her diapered butt back onto the carpet. Her eyes, which closely resembled mine in color, got wide with the most startled look, causing both Finn and I to laugh. When it appeared that she wasn't sure if she liked the action of being upright or not, I quickly stood up, put her in my arms, and smiled.

"Don't cry," I soothed. "That was brave. That was good."

Making silly faces at our little girl, Finn stood up to join us. "There's your rainbow, Beauty," he said to me.

I nodded my agreement while adding, "And you got to see it. That's one positive thing, I guess." I leaned my back lightly into his strong torso while still caressing our daughter in my arms.

Chance, doing his best drunken sailor impression, stumbled into the room to join us. I have always treasured that part of our son's persona—the time when he first awakes from slumber and is all soft and quiet and cuddly. I handed Arinn over to Finn and sat down on the floor so that Chance would automatically go into my arms.

Talking to him on the phone earlier had been emotional, but this was overpowering. "Hi, buddy." I managed.

"Too tight, Mommy," he complained but still snuggled into me.

"Sorry, Little Man. I just love you too much, I guess," I said and loosened my grip a little.

Finn's phone chimed for the third time since we had been in Arinn's nursery. With a grimace, he took it from his pocket and glanced at it. When his eyes reclaimed mine, I could see they were filled with uncertainty, and I knew why.

"I know," I reassured him. "I get it."

"It's just the press and my crew and fa—"

"Finn…" I interrupted. I knew he was walking on eggshells, considering our argument the night before. "I understand," I emphasized. "Go deal with it. I've got great company." I smiled, soothing Chance's hair.

"I won't be long." He placed Arinn down next to me and kissed the top of my head. "I love you."

"Love you, too."

He paused, softly smiled at all three of us, and then exited to take the calls somewhere more private. I sat Chance in my lap, and we talked about his day with Summer and Arinn. It all seemed so normal and right. It was such a contrast to my day. It made me happy. But it also made me incredibly sad.

As Chance woke up a little more, he began playing with his sister as I sat against the wall and simply watched. When Finn popped his head in a little later to check on our… well, *my* status, I called a time out. I wanted a shower. I wanted to get out of the clothes I had been in all day. I wanted to discard the summery, casual pink floral dress—possibly forever—and feel clean.

While Finn watched the kids, I made my way down to our master suite and the penetrating beads of the pounding shower water. It was the first time since driving to the bank that morning that I was completely alone. I thought the warmth and the repetitious sounds of the water would relax me. They did… but not necessarily in a good way. The solitude and monotony gave my mind nothing else to think about other than what had happened. The intermittent foggy state that I had been in since leaving the bank was gone. In its place was reality. And the tidal wave of the cold hard, frightening fact of what had happened was crashing down full force into my psyche.

I could hear Finn's voice but couldn't really make out anything distinctly. Maybe his words were about wine or needing something. I don't know. Regardless, I couldn't respond even when his voice appeared louder and a bit more concerned.

Then the shower doors were thrust open. All of my senses, with the exception of touch, seemed to have disappeared. I felt my body being pulled into Finn's. But why couldn't I see him? Because, I realized, my hands were covering my entire face. And why couldn't I hear him? There was noise...so much noise. What was that? The water—yes. But there was something else. It was sobbing. And it was coming from me. I was crying...hard. Finn tugged me in tighter, and I felt the water stop its relentless beating over us. He must have shut it off. And, thankfully, with the stillness of the water, I managed to slow down my tears, too.

"God, I wondered how you were doing it. You don't have to be so brave, baby. It's all right. Let it go." I could hear my husband's voice again and couldn't help but think about how I had just given our daughter the opposite advice.

I felt him draw my hands away from my face. And when he looked me in the eyes, I wondered whose were sadder. He took my hands and guided them around his neck before carefully sweeping me up into his arms.

Then, with just as much care, he carried me into our adjoining master bedroom. My crying had almost completely ceased but in its place was trance-like Lara. With his strength and guidance, my feet were brought down to the soft plushness of the carpeting. He put his hand on top of my shoulder for a second or two and then held it up in the universal stop sign. It didn't matter. I had no notion to move. I didn't think I could make myself if I tried. I was vaguely aware of his actions as he pulled the comforter from the bed behind me. After drying me with it, he wrapped it securely around my body and eased me into a sitting position on the bed. I looked up as he walked away. But, thankfully, it was only a few feet to the armoire and back.

As if he were dressing Arinn, he pulled the comforter from my shoulders and kindly urged my arms up in the air so he could slide a top onto my torso. His hands then went to my feet, lifting each as he strung some sort of light bottoms onto my legs. When he got to my thighs, I robotically knew to lift so that he could finish getting them up to my waist.

Having seemingly expelled all energy, I immediately sat back down and dipped my head onto his shoulder when he sat down next to me. But he was soaked. And he still had his clothes on. He had been in the shower fully clothed...a fact that had not even registered to me until just that moment. I retracted my head, not liking the contrast of my dry body against his sopping fabric.

"Hold on," Finn said.

He got up and, in rapid pace, discarded his charcoal tee and jeans. He made an attempt to throw them into the master bath, but instead they laid haphazardly somewhere between the two rooms. Now, just in his boxer briefs, he reclaimed his spot on the bed and brought me into his arms. His chest was still a little damp, but I welcomed it with the undeniable need for comfort.

"I love you. I love you. I love you. I love you. I love you," he repeated into my ear countless times.

"Finn?" I eventually managed to retract my body ever so slightly. "God, that really happened, didn't it?"

"It's okay," he answered as soft as his touch was to my face.

"The alarm? Is the alarm on?" I asked, suddenly thinking of our own personal security system.

He brought me back into his body. "We're good, Lara. You're safe. Everybody's safe. I've got you." And I knew—or at least had to believe—it was true.

***

Feeling that security, I must have drifted off quickly. Because, the next thing I knew, I was waking up with a start. I was in bed, but I really wasn't sure of the time or even the day. All I knew was that I was alone. Then, flashbacks of what led me to be in that bed, cocooned like a china doll in an antique store, suddenly crashed back.

"Finn!" I yelled out. After a minute, which seemed longer but was probably less, I screamed out even louder. "Finn!"

And he was there. Finding me pushed up against the leather headboard with my hands cradled protectively on my drawn knees, he eased his body around mine. "Hey...hey..." His voice soothed while his thumbs rubbed my arms.

"I...I just didn't know. I didn't know where you went." I may have sounded worried, but my initial anxiousness had dropped about seventy-five percent when he entered that room.

"I just got the kids to sleep and was talking with Mom and Pop." He continued in a slow, calming voice. "They send their love."

I glanced over at the bedside clock. It was well past the kids' usual bedtime. But, then again, there had been nothing usual about our day.

"Kids okay?" I asked.

"Yeah. Fed, changed, stories, prayers... everything's good. Summer and Ingo brought the Jeep back, too. So there's no need to go back." He paused— it had been an emotional day for him, too. "There's no need to go back there."

"Good." I never wanted to even drive past that God-forsaken bank ever again. I relaxed my legs so they were now outstretched. "Good."

"What can I get you?" he asked while intertwining his legs with mine. Sometime during my slumber, I realized, Finn had put on a pair of pajama bottoms and a dry T-shirt. "You have to be hungry."

"No. I'm not." Although, God knows, I should have been between just a protein bar crouched under a coffin-like desk and some juice and cookies the police had offered us.

"You sure, Lar? I can make a sandwich quick."

"I just need you to hold me. Please."

He, of course, already had been. So, he squeezed a little tighter. "If it's too tight, it's because I love you too much."

I managed a half-smile at his echo of my earlier words. "Don't let go."

"I'm not, baby. Believe me, I'm not." He kissed the top of my head. "You are not leaving these arms tonight."

***

The next time I woke, it was morning. Well, barely. Even though we had the shades drawn, I could tell the sun was just trying to rise. Finn was asleep next to me, one arm slung across my waist as if it were a seatbelt. I smiled and almost cried at his protective stance, even subconsciously in slumber. That was until further examination. I looked down to notice, for the first time, what he had dressed me in post-shower rescue. I had on the most mismatched combo of colors and patterns— a floral purple T and red and white checkered shorts. I lightly laughed, shaking my body along with Finn's hand on top of it.

The movement must have caused him to wake because he began squinting and adjusting his eyes to the room and then on me. "What? What are you thinking?" He propped himself up on his elbow and went for my hand.

"I'm thinking you are never allowed to dress me again." I smiled, shaking my head.

Examining his handiwork, it was obvious Finn was

trying not to laugh himself. "You look beautiful— ready to rock any stage."

And, it hit me. "Oh, God. Your concert. I...I didn't forget. Where were you yesterday when you found out?" I propped my body up a little straighter.

He sat up to meet me. "Literally getting ready to board. The flight was delayed. And I'm so glad. Another few minutes and I would have been locked in that plane and airborne. If I found out then, I would have went absolutely insane."

I raised my eyebrows. "You mean you weren't already?" I knew he had to have been pretty darn close.

"Maybe a little," he admitted. "When you texted me and said you were in there? Shit, my heart just bottomed out. It took me a while to even get my fingers to work so I could reply back."

I dipped my lips onto his shoulder and then said, "Thanks for not letting me know how scared you were. I knew you had to have been, but your texts were what held me together. You have no idea."

"I'm pretty sure I do. When we weren't texting, and I knew we shouldn't, I was going up the flipping wall. I felt like I needed to double my meds."

"Baby..." My eyes started to mist, and I could see his dared to follow. Not wanting to replay any more of the horrifying day before, I forged on with the future. "But the concert is tonight, right? You have to go."

"Right now, that's not important." He pulled me into him. "Knowing you are safe... that I have my wife... that my kids have their mom...that's what matters."

But not reality, I internally finished his sentence. "But you do. You have to go." I pulled away to meet his eyes.

"Yeah. I do." His voice was flooded with regret. "All right?" he asked and then kissed me ever so gently. "I have a little time, though. Luckily, it's Philly. I won't be able to do all the preshow routines. But that doesn't matter. I need to make sure you're okay."

"I am," I said because "okay" kind of summed it up. "Okay" was a whole lot better than the previous day but nowhere near where I normally was or achieved to be. "Finn?" I asked and then chose my words creatively. "Can I ask you a favor, though?"

His hands parenthesized my face, while his words told me he knew exactly what I was referencing—the first time we had made love. "If the favor involves getting you out of this lovely ensemble, you don't have to ask."

I half laughed but turned serious. "It is. I just need to feel us as close as we can be. All right?"

"Lara, there is nothing I want more." When he kissed me then, I could feel the truth in his words. He needed our love…our connection… us… as much as I did. "But," — he stopped— "only if I get to say thank you this time."

"What? I'm not sure why."

That had been the regret of that night so many years ago. I had said "thank you" to Finn after we had made love because my insecurities had led me to believe he had done it out of a sense of obligation or pity. Of course, nothing could have been further from the truth.

He looked at me earnestly. "For being here in my arms, for being my girl, my love, my heart, my forever."

"Thank you for making me want to be. I love you, Finn." I couldn't have felt more loved or safe.

And then, before I knew it, he was gone again. And despite putting on my brave face, I felt so, so alone. It was as if another silent alarm was triggered—this time on my heart.

***

I finally got around to looking at the text Finn sent while I had been talking on the phone. *Backstage. Missing U. Luv U.*

By the time I picked it up, I knew he was already on stage. So I went about the other tasks of the evening. And,

God knows there were many because the day had kept me extremely occupied. I actually empathized with my husband. All during that day after "the event," my phone had been going non-stop with concerned friends and family. And, for the most part, I had tried to answer or reply in some manner. This, in between follow-ups from the bank and the police, as well as giving Reese my formal statement for the press, and dealing with two tiny tots begging for attention.

Finally, with the exhausting day settling down and all my calls returned and tasks completed, I went to brush my teeth and crawl into bed. I needed to de-stress. But my phone rang again. I silently cursed the call until I realized it was Finn's designer ring— "Roxanne."

Well aware of the time and knowing his show schedule like the back of my hand, I answered a tad bit concerned. "Hey, what's wrong? Shouldn't you be on stage yet?"

"Just got off." He sounded it. His voice was winded and throaty. "No encore."

"Oooo, that couldn't have gone over well," I said, knowing that Finn always did an encore and, most of the time, was overly generous with his fans—singing a number of extra acoustics and sometimes signing autographs.

Before I could inquire why, my husband jumped my thought. "Lara, why didn't you text me back?" I could hardly hear him with all the commotion that post-show backstage creates.

"Huh? I knew you were busy. I was thinking maybe I could catch you after the show." Like in another hour or so—after the encore, after the accolades, after he showered and got a chance to chill.

"Baby, I was worried," he articulated. Although, he didn't need to— I could definitely hear it in his voice.

I sank onto the bed and hugged his pillow. His concern crushed me. I knew I was going to have to deal with the aftermath of what happened at the bank. But I didn't want Finn to have to. He had done enough for me. And he had other priorities and concerns now.

"Finn…" I managed, feeling the tears instantly develop. I adored how much he cared for me, but with the memory of his arms wrapped around me that morning still lingering, it only made me sad.

"You okay?" he asked now with the absence of the extra noise. He must have ducked into one of the private green room areas, I decided.

"Yeah," I lied but then continued with some truth. "The other reason I didn't text back was I was on the phone with Lane when you texted."

"Good. Good, right?"

"Yeah. It was good. It felt good to talk with him."

It had. It was weird. It was awkward. But, in all, it felt really good. Although we didn't really talk about what had caused the rift—the penthouse, the girlfriend, McEllie. But, it didn't matter. It was his life, and he seemed happy. And I had my life, and I was grateful.

"I'm glad, baby." Finn said not pressing for details. "I know what it's like to be on the opposing end of your silent treatment. It's not pretty."

"I'm sorry," I lamented.

"No. I didn't mean for you to—"

"I love you." I interrupted because, all of a sudden, I needed him to know that. I'm pretty sure he already did as I him. But when an almost life-altering event happens, it makes you regret the past pain and appreciate all the beauty of what you do have. "I'm glad you stayed last night." Because, God knows, he could have been on a new plane, and I could have drowned in that shower.

"There was no way I wasn't," he said with conviction before adding, "Shit, I hate that I'm gone now."

"Don't," I said with more bravado than I actually felt, especially in a quiet house and an empty bedroom. "You're where you need to be right now…where you should be."

"I love you. I love those kids."

"Back at you," I managed, but I knew I wasn't going to

be able to handle much more. "Call tomorrow, okay? I'm tired. It's been a long day."

"I know, Beauty. I will. I'll call when I can talk with the kids, too."

"Okay."

"Get some sleep. Don't let the bed bugs bite."

"I'll try."

"Lar? I—"

I know. I know. Don't say it again. I might just lose it.

"Me, too." I cut him off. "Forever."

"Forever," he repeated.

And the second the phone went dead, at least I hoped I had managed to hit "end" first, I cried out. I sat with his pillow smothered into my stomach, and I bawled. And then I cried some more.

CHAPTER ELEVEN

The sun rose and the sun set day after day, which turned into week after week— as if things were perfectly normal. But so much of that time was not. Sure, from the outside looking in, it would have appeared to be. But just like the rain seemed to dampen and destroy most of the summery July activities, this overwhelming sense of being lost seemed to beat up my heart and brain. I knew a lot of it was simply missing him—his touch, his strength, the way he made me laugh. But there was more. I just didn't seem to have any direction or harbor to hold onto. And, after getting much better over the years at hearing sudden loud noises, my jumpiness was back in full force.

One Wednesday morning, I decided I needed a change. It was something I thought might brighten whatever funk I had been in. After all, I had done it once before during a traumatic time in my life—giving my child up for adoption and, consequently, starting fresh at the college where I ended up meeting Finn.

When Finn and I spoke via video chat later that day, he commented immediately. "Blondie, you're back!" he exclaimed.

"You noticed."

I brought my hand protectively up to my now platinum, home-colored hair. Inwardly smiling, I thought about the first time Finn and I had reconnected years after college. He had asked me where "Blondie" went because I had allowed my hair to go back to its natural dark strawberry blonde. And I had kept it that way ever since.

"What? Of course."

"I just didn't know how it would look to those damn green contacts of yours," I teased, noticing his non-prescription contacts were already in place. I think the blonder hair was making me feel a little better…a little feistier.

"Ha. Ha." He didn't like any more than I did the Irish green eyes his record label insisted he wear when performing. "What made you do that?"

"I don't know. I guess I just needed a change."

"Yeah?" I believe I detected a twinge of concern in his voice. After all, he knew my back-story. He knew what had made me go platinum blonde before.

I didn't want him to over analyze or worry about it, though. So I deflected by asking, "Do you like it?" And then I tacked on with levity, "No omissions."

He chuckled. "Yeah. It reminds me of when we first met. It was how I always pictured you."

The thought of him thinking of me during those missing years made me smile and murmur a "Hmmm."

"But, the natural, freer version was beautiful, too. I love it either way…just so you're still my girl." He gave me that smile that reached his eyes and my heart. He knew how much I loved hearing him call me "his girl."

"Is that Daddy?" Chance, not having the best timing, interrupted by joining me in the kitchen.

"Yeah, sweetie. Come here." I hoisted our son onto my lap so he could see the laptop on the counter.

"How ya doing, bud?" Finn directed his comment to the preschooler while I glanced over at Arinn who seemed content playing with a well-loved gray stuffed mouse in the great room. "I could hear you and your sister laughing. Whatcha doing?"

"Karaoke," he proclaimed.

"He's your mini-me through and through, Finn." I kissed the top of Chance's head.

"How do you like Mommy's hair?" Finn asked our son.

He hadn't at first. His eyes had gone wide when he watched me finish drying it. But now, instead, he said to his role model, "She look like *Tangled*."

"Tangled?" Finn asked perplexed.

"The Rapunzel movie," I clarified and realized I truly did since my hair was not only golden blonde but in a long braid.

Finn started laughing, "Rox, I think I called you that once, too!"

"I think you did." I played with the ends of my hair on his recollection.

"Yeah. It was at Sam and Olivia's wedding. You chopped all that golden hair off —like the witch got to you," he recounted.

That had been another lost time in my life. It had been my last year of college. And everyone else seemed to be moving on but me. I was still in school. But all of my friends, including Olivia, Sam, and Finn, had graduated and were living their own lives with their own loves far from me.

"Geez, Finn, how do you remember those things?"

"I remember you," he answered simply and added a wink in the most romantic way.

"Daddy, when you coming home?" Chance instantly brought me back to kids and tours with the only question that had been on his toddler mind during nighttime prayers.

"A little bit. Not too long," my musician husband answered.

"I want you to come home," our son partially pouted.

"I wish I was there, Little Man. Just keep counting the

days on the calendar with Mommy."

I held him a little closer. "We're ready to turn it to the next month." Thank God for August and a fresh start, I thought silently.

"We drawing triangles and circles on the days."

"What's that called, Chance?" I prompted him.

"A pattern," he answered with pride.

"Yep. Good job. And tell Daddy about the number line. That's new."

"I going make a hop every day with the bunny. You holding the carrot at the end."

"I am?" Finn asked puzzled. If he saw the ridiculous photo of him at the end of the number line in Chance's room, he would have been laughing out loud.

"Yeah. Bunnies like carrots!" Chance may as well have tagged "Silly Daddy" to the end of his statement.

"Oh, of course. How many hops left?" Finn questioned.

"There too many!" our little guy exclaimed with pure sadness. "I can't count that many!"

"Mommy can help you."

"I don't want Mommy. I want you!" His voice and his little legs burst at the same time as he scrambled off my lap and out of the kitchen.

"Chance..." I tried.

But it was true. He didn't want me. In fact, he really didn't want either of us right then. Because he knew he couldn't have both, and that's what he really wanted. Didn't we all?

"Lar, go." Finn's voice directed me back to the screen.

"He's all right," I answered as Chance, now back in the great room, brought his body down onto his ankles and went into my Pilates child pose. Yes, that was the perfect name for it, I thought. "He just... he needs a break. He's had a tiring day, and he misses you."

"Me, too."

"Me, too." I honestly echoed.

"It won't be too much longer."

"Good try. I know how to count, Finn." As I was completing my sentence, I could hear someone on Finn's side calling for him.

"Shi...eez!" Finn started to curse but changed the ending aware of the little ears on my side.

"I know. Go," I lamented, knowing someone was tugging my husband away just as Chance was tugging Arinn's stuffed mouse away from her.

There were going to be tears. Some were going to be from Arinn, who did nothing to deserve her brother taking his anger out on her toys. Some were going to be from Chance because he was upset, tired, and about to be reprimanded. And some were going to be from their mom...just because.

"It can wai—" Finn started.

"No. I actually should make sure Chance and Arinn are all right. Call me again tonight after the show?"

"It'll be late," Finn cautioned. "I'm in a different time zone." Denver.

"I know." I looked at my dual time zone watch that Finn had bought for me— the feminine version of the one I had given him our first Christmas together.

"You all right?" New hair and now an unusual late night call request surely prompted the question.

I blew it off with my typical Lara sarcasm. "Yeah. It's just seeing that photo of you holding, mind you, a very big carrot. You know, it kinda—"

"Oh, dear God!" Finn bellowed out with humor.

I smiled, seeing him relaxed and amused. But then added, "Seriously, baby, it's just...I do... I miss you. I'd kinda just like to see you as I'm falling asleep."

"That sounds nice," he replied just as serenely.

"I know it will be hard with everything that goes on after the show...just when you can."

"You go to sleep, and when I get back to the bus, I'll call, okay? Just keep it nearby."

"I'll set the video to automatically answer and you can sing me a lullaby to wake me up." I expected him to say something, but he just stared at me as if our eyes were actually a foot away from one another. "What?"

"Something about that really turns me on."

My lips found a closed mouth smile again. "I love you, and I miss you. I'll talk to you tonight, then?"

"Absolutely... to all three."

***

"Lara? Lara, wake up!" It was Finn's voice.

What? Where? I adjusted my eyes. Oh, the screen. He was supposed to call me after the show. Damn it. What did he say?

As I woke up a little more, he continued, "God, you looked like you were being tortured."

"That sounds like pretty crappy lullaby lyrics." I rotated my neck to stretch it out.

"Don't deflect." He immediately called me on it. "What were you dreaming about?'

"I don't know. Didn't even realize. How was the show?" Yes, I could be a deflection extraordinaire.

"Good. Everyone's chillin' outside...giving me some private time to talk with you," he answered but immediately got back to his initial query. "You having a lot of those? The bad dreams?"

"No," I lied.

"You were all curled up in a ball and your head was thrashing back and forth. It sounded like you were grinding your teeth. Lar..." I could hear the concern in his voice. "You haven't done that in forever. Bab—"

"Huh." I tried to pull off innocence, knowing the nightmares were happening at a good enough frequency and always centered around either needing somebody to be with me or someone dying. A lot of times I was in that damn bank. I shook the thoughts from my head. "Sorry. I just remember hearing you. Did I say your name?"

"Yeah, at the end as you were waking."

"Hmmm. See, it couldn't have been bad, then," I tried. "Hold on, the light's kinda harsh, I'm just gonna…" I had left the bedside light on hoping to stay awake for his call, but I guess I hadn't. I reached over toward the lava lamp and turned it on before stretching even further to turn off the side lamp. That's when I heard Finn's low groan.

When I looked back at the screen, Finn's eyes were examining my body, which was clothed in just a lacy dark blue bra and boy-cut panties. He breathed in heavy. "Damn you."

"I'm sorry." I softly laughed. I hadn't done it on purpose.

When I tried to slip back under the sheets, he urged. "Please, leave it. That light and—"

"No one else is around?"

"No. I promise. Actually, give me a minute. I want to crawl in the bunk." I lost the visual of him when he did, but I still heard his voice. "Almost like we're in bed together." And when I saw him again, he was stretched out under the blanket in his bed.

"Hmmm."

We looked in each other's eyes for countless moments. I was still self-conscious, though, knowing that people were just outside that trailer door. Because of that, my hand was kind of protectively playing with the front section of the bra that connected the two cups. It was a motion that I don't think helped Finn at all.

"I was serious before," I interjected. "Would you sing for me? I know you just got done and your voice is probably raw, but—"

He didn't hesitate. "What do you want?"

"I don't know," I started. I just wanted him and the peace he could bring me. And then something came to me. "Wait, you know that Three Doors Down song? The one, uh…" I wasn't good with titles, and I certainly wasn't the singer. I just knew the sentiment behind it.

"Three…?" His eyes started darting around as if he were cycling through songs in his mind. And then, "Yeah" with a soft smile.

Finn started singing the chorus of "Here Without You," and I hugged his pillow up to my chest. The verse he started singing I think was the second one, but it probably resonated closely for him. And then he went onto the chorus, singing this time a little more softly. My eyes were starting to drift. I could feel it, and I am sure he could see it.

"Lara?" he asked after he had started to repeat the chorus one more time.

I opened my eyes just enough to say, "I love you, Finn."

"Sweeter dreams, baby. Forever you and me." And he reached for the end button at the same time I did.

***

If the first couple of weeks after the Hamptons and the bank were difficult, adding more time without Finn/Daddy certainly didn't help. While I was trying to come to better terms with the hostage aftermath, Chance's behavior only disintegrated. He was a victim, too. He had been left with just a computer screen version of a dad, a baby sister who could not hold a two-way conversation, and a mom who was just trying to keep it together.

Our precocious three-year-old was mastering a lot that summer. He was becoming very good at puzzles, he could write his own name, and he was helping out with simple chores like making his bed, setting the table, gathering the wastebaskets and putting toys where they belonged. He wanted to vacuum and do laundry, but his little body just wasn't strong enough. One of the reasons why he liked doing the chores was because I made it fun by telling him he had the length of one song to get a particular chore completed. Of course, he would often pick one of his daddy's songs to get the job done. I would catch him shaking his little booty to the music and sometimes spilling out some of the words.

But those were the good moments with Chance. Then, there were the others. He developed a fear of monsters, both under the bed and in the closet. I couldn't understand the origin of his angst, besides maybe hearing some tale at preschool. I had gotten into the routine of squirting potion—a.k.a. water— in the places he feared and double-checking the nightlight so he could go to sleep. He also was becoming very possessive of me—not wanting me to hold Arinn and practically trying to tear her from my hands. And, he would ask me if I was going to leave like Daddy did. That nearly broke my heart and was something I decided not to tell my husband. With his personal neurosis of being left, it would absolutely shred Finn.

But the latest was the tantrums. I enrolled him in a soccer group that Kai was in. It gave Tina and I a chance to catch up and the boys time to learn just the basics of kicking and running. It wasn't competitive and they didn't work as a group, but there was an instructor on the field as we watched on the sidelines. Chance quit halfway through the first day. He came over to get his snack and refused to go back out. I tried to encourage him to keep at it— that Kai was doing it. But he said he hurt, he wasn't good at soccer, and he wasn't going to do it anymore. He even started walking toward the car. I apologized to Tina and, not wanting to cause a scene, left with a sulking child and a screaming baby. Chance pouted the entire way home, even when I agreed that he didn't have to go back.

And his temper continued with pure defiance as he refused to eat dinner. So I let him be, figuring his stubbornness could only last as long as the next cookie. I fed Arinn within eyeshot of Chance, who was in the great room stomping and rolling. When Arinn had the audacity to be having a good time with me, Chance flipped out so badly that he actually started spitting out mucus. And then, he basically fell asleep out of pure exhaustion.

Having just finished telling Finn this tale over the phone, I concluded with, "And sorry, Daddy, but I am not going to wake the beast," I teased but meant it in the most sincere possible way.

"Geez, Lar, are you sure he's all right? He's not sick is he?"

"No. I did check his forehead for a fever. But he's fine. I almost wish he was sick. That would explain what happened to my sweet little boy."

"What are you thinking?"

"I think he just picked now as the time to go through his terrible twos—pouting, sulking…"

"Here we thought we lucked out."

"We did. He's a good kid. He's just testing and…"

On my hesitation, Finn prompted me to continue. "What?"

"Well, it's anxiety." I knew it. I recognized it. I had to admit it. "You were worried about what you would pass onto the kids and, see, it was me all along."

"But he shouldn't…" Finn knew of my anxious tendencies and the past which had contributed to their onset—tendencies that thankfully had mostly dissipated since his love. But he also knew that Chance had a cherished childhood. "I don't get it. What's he have to be anxious about?"

"It's kid stuff," I tried. "You know, monsters under the bed…where I am…sibling rivalry…any change, really."

"Oh, man. That's not right. I don't want him—"

I cut him off because that was exactly why I hesitated telling him in the first place— he would feel bad and helpless. "Finn, he's fine. It's nothing to worry about." When I heard my husband's laughter, I questioned, "What?"

"You're asking me not to worry about him worrying."

"Yeah." Glad for levity in the conversation, I laughed

along with him. "I guess I am."

He turned serious. "Are you all right? I know it's a lot."

I took a deep, silent breath. It *was* a lot. I wasn't truly all right. But I had to be. There really wasn't an alternative. I needed to be—both for the kids and for their dad.

"Yeah." I finally managed the one word answer.

He took a moment, too, and said, "I love you."

I sighed, recognizing those words as a signal for the conclusion of our conversation. Although they were sincere and special and never lost their meaning, hearing them instantly deflated my soul. When I was speaking with him, I felt secure. I felt serene. But I knew the moment we would lose that phone connection...

"Lar?" he queried.

"It's just...sometimes I wonder if that's enough."

"What?" His one word started with puzzlement but concluded with fear as he realized that the last comment he had said was that he loved me. His next two words were even more pronounced. "Lara? What?"

"I'm sorry. I'm just tired," I tried with what was mostly the truth. "Go. Have fun. Make that crowd light up."

"Lara!" He immediately admonished me before trying to take the lead in rectifying how I felt and what I said. "No! What did that mean? What do you need? What can I d—?"

"I need *you*, Finn," I blurted out and then more softly echoed with, "I just need you."

Oh, man. I really hadn't wanted to lay that on him. I was just having a rough day and a moment of weak self-loathing. While I realized as partners we needed and should share our thoughts and feelings, there wasn't anything he could do all those miles away. He didn't need that burden, especially when he was mere moments from prepping to perform.

"I'm trying." His words came out just as softly and angst ridden as mine.

"I know."

"Do you want me to stop touring, recording, what? Because—"

"You know that wouldn't work. You would be living a lie— a half-life."

"You can't give up on us, Lara." In that moment, he sounded a lot like our son when all of his resistance was down and he was giving in to sleep.

"Finn…no. I didn't say that," I replied, now really regretting the initial words that sparked that part of our conversation. "It's the opposite of what I want. I would be absolutely miserable if we—"

"Don't. Don't say it." My husband couldn't bear to even hear words that would signify "leaving."

"I just need to find my balance," I explained for both his sake and mine.

"I don't know what to do. I don't want you unhappy, especially if I'm the reason for it."

"Hey, I am ultimately responsible for my own happiness. We all are. Besides, I knew what I was getting myself into when I fell in love with you."

There was a mini pause before I could hear the ever-so-slight hint of hope in his voice. "And you still did."

"I did." I tried to smile and wondered if he could sense it across the line. I hoped he could. That smile, although forced in the moment, had a legitimate, honest meaning behind it.

"I do." He changed tenses on me.

So, I did, too. "Me, too."

After a moment, "Baby?"

I could hear the hustle and bustle getting louder from his end of the phone. If the words "I love you" hadn't meant he was needing to go, the familiar sounds of crew and other personnel bellowing things behind his voice surely did. I took a deep breath.

"Yeah. I know. Hang up, Finn, before I miss you even more."

He knew I had a hard time hanging up first. So he

obliged after telling me we would talk again the next day. As if I had any doubts.

CHAPTER TWELVE

I didn't hear from Finn that following morning, though. But, it was the day after a concert and a traveling day. So he was probably—especially more than half way through the concert season— sleeping in and going in as slow of a motion as he could. Because during the rest of his time on tour, he was the exact opposite—moving and working at an extremely fast pace.

My day with the kids, as usual, began at the crack of dawn with their high energy and constant needs. Chance, unfortunately, started out nearly the same way he had left off the day before. There wasn't any mucus or stomping, but there was definitely attitude.

U should hear what YOUR son did 2day. I texted Finn from the comforts of a quiet patio later that afternoon. Both kids were in their respective bedrooms and mommy had a moment of peace.

I was shocked that I didn't get an instant reply. Or even one in the next few minutes. Besides when he was on stage, Finn was glued to his phone, especially when he knew it was me contacting him. I placed my phone near the rocker I was sitting in and closed my eyes to savor some more of the warm, but not oppressive, sun.

Finally, the text from my husband came through. I picked it up and read. *MY son? Uh-oh.*

I was in the middle of typing back my joking response of, *Yeah all Y-O-U* when I saw another text coming in. So, I saved mine to draft.

What? Did he make fun of his mom's pink poodle flip-flops?

I looked down at my feet and the ridiculous flip-flops that Chance had picked out when Finn had taken him shopping for my Mother's Day gift. Then I typed, *No. LOL!*

Say how beautiful she looks sitting in the sun twirling that straw in her mouth?

I sent back, *Def. not.*

As soon as I pressed "send," I took the straw—the glass of iced tea had long since been emptied—out of my mouth and peered at it. There was no way he could have known what I was doing...down to the precise objects. We were texting. We weren't on any kind of video chat.

In the second right before I connected all the dots, I heard his live voice. "You are."

I quickly twirled around to see Finn leaning against the side of the patio door simply staring at me. "What? What are you doing here? Is everything okay?" My mind went immediately to worst case scenario as I practically leapt off the chair.

"Yeah." He stepped out to the patio. "I...it...you know, it was bothering me... what we talked about yesterday and Chance—"

"So you flew back?" I wondered if my eyes were as wide as they felt.

"Yeah," he answered matter-of-factly. "I wanted to see you and Chance and Arinn. I don't have much time, though. I have to be out before sunrise tomorrow. My team isn't happy at all. They're worried I won't make it."

"You didn't need to do that," I protested, thinking that originally he only had a small commute from Kansas City to St. Louis with a day in between, and now he was going to be flying on the day of the show.

"You told me you needed me. What else was I supposed to do?" Before I could rebut, Finn put his index finger up to encourage me to stop. "Where's my hug?"

I magnetized instantly to him. Only then did I realize how much I truly needed our traditional greeting of love. I took a moment and simply relished the strength of his embrace.

"Hi, baby," he recited.

"Hi. This feels so good," I admitted.

Finn's hand methodically rubbed my back, adorned by a light tank top, before pulling me slightly away. "God, look at you. You're too skinny."

"No, I'm not," I denied but felt a need to cross my arms in front of my body. "You're just used to me being fat."

"You were never fat. You're beau—"

"Please don't."

"tiful." He did a mock sneeze of the word.

"Ha. Ha." I couldn't help but smile…and it felt good.

"Where are the kids?" He astutely changed the subject.

"Arinn's napping. Chance is in time out."

"Time out?" he asked a little taken back. "When did he start getting time outs?"

I tried not to think he was questioning my practically-single parenting skills and answered, "When he started acting like he needed them."

"After I left," Finn said plainly and with a definite twinge of remorse.

"It did happen to coincide with you going on tour." I didn't lie.

"What did he do?"

"He had a complete fit at the store when I wouldn't buy him a toy. He told me he didn't like me and then when we got home, he threw his art set."

Finn reached out and stroked my hair before holding my hand. "Let me give you a time out. I'll go talk to him.

That's not right."

"No." I released my hand from his. "I'll be the bad guy. It's okay. What little time he has with you should be good. I don't want him thinking you're upset with him."

"You don't need to do it all, Lara."

"Believe me, I—"

"Mommy!" Chance's voice traveled from what sounded like the top of the inside staircase to the patio where we stood. "Timer done. Timer done." He spoke of his talking stoplight timer—one that I had picked up from a teacher friend of mine. It served many purposes but most recently as his time out countdown. "I sorry."

"Okay, Chance," I called back. "I'm on the patio. Come down. I want to see you." I curled my mouth up in a half smile to my husband who mimicked me back.

Within seconds, we heard the telltale pitter-patter sound of our three-and-a-half-year-old's feet. But, poor Finn, who was so excited to see his son, got the exact opposite reaction than either of us had been expecting. Chance stopped cold after closing the screen door and spotting his dad.

"Hey, bud," said a jovial Finn.

But Chance actually growled at Finn as if he were a dog ready to attack an intruder. He looked at his father with intense, furrowed eyebrows—a kind I had never witnessed before on a toddler— and stood his ground. Finn laughed not realizing, as I did, that Chance wasn't playing around. He was truly angry and, for a change, it wasn't at me.

"No laughing!" Chance bellowed out.

"Sweetie…" I tried. "Daddy's not laughing at you. He was just trying to cheer you up."

"Buddy, I missed you," Finn interjected. "I came home just to see you and see how you are doing."

I could tell Chance was still twisting everything around and around in his little mind. He was, of course, startled because he hadn't been expecting his father. The bunny still had so many hops, after all. Plus, he was upset about being in time out and hurt because he felt left by the man standing in front of him. But, yet, he—I knew because I felt the same way— was overjoyed at the sight of him...of the sight of Finn standing right there in front of us.

"Come here, Little Man. I need a big boy hug." Finn bent down to our son's height.

Three-year-olds, even stubborn ones, have their limits on holding on to anger, though... thank goodness. Chance gave in and dove into his father's body. In return, Finn pulled Chance to him and lifted both of them up. I could see the relief emerge in both of their faces. And if I had a mirror, I am sure mine was just the same.

"Mommy, I hungry!" Chance stated directly after the father-son embrace was broken.

"All right. It's just about time for me to ma—" I started.

Putting Chance back on his feet, Finn interjected with a parental inflection. "What do you say first?"

"Peas." Chance might have missed the "l" in the word, but we both knew what he meant.

"No," Finn corrected. "Well... yes, but what about how you behaved today? What do you need to say to Mommy about that?"

Those three-year-old eyebrows slightly twisted again before he glared at me. It was obvious Chance did not like the fact that I told his dad about his behavior. When I definitively looked right back at him, I saw the slender line of a pout appearing.

Finn must have also because he stopped our son's action with a semi-warning voice. "Chance."

"I sorry."

"Yeah?"

I knew Finn doubted the validity of the apology, but I also knew that was the extent of what a preschooler was capable of. "That's fine."

"And we love Mommy, right?" Finn continued his line of questioning/teaching our son.

"This much." Chance spread his arms out as wide as they could go.

I smiled softly at my husband before gathering his mini-me in my arms. "I love you, too, Little Man. Now, what do you think you might want for dinner?"

"Nugs!" he joyously yelled as I let him back down.

"Nugs, huh?" I looked at Finn, letting the recognition pass between our eyes. We had taught Chance the nickname Wyatt had given chicken nuggets.

Finn's eyes seemed to glisten as he said, "Sounds good. But what about Mommy? What's she gonna have?"

"She no eat dinner."

"What?" Finn swirled his concerned eyes to me.

"Chance, I eat dinner." I corrected, feeling the tables turn—my son was now tattling on me. "I finish whatever he doesn't." I felt like I had to explain to Finn. But, in reality, I knew it was more of a rationalization. I, indeed, had not been eating well. I was too busy feeding the kids and, most of the time, didn't have much of an appetite. "And, I usually settle down with some popcorn after they're asleep." I looked back to Chance briefly. "And sometimes an adult beverage."

"That's not a meal. I eat better on the road. You—" Arinn's cries from her nursery momentarily interrupted his disapproval. "You're gonna eat," he finished more conclusively. "Go get her. I'll get you that adult beverage and then let Chance and I make dinner for the girls tonight."

"Finn, you just got home. Just...*you* relax. I'll make something."

"Lara, so help me, I'll leave right now if you don't sit down with a glass of wine and let me feed you."

I knew he wouldn't leave just as much as he knew he wouldn't, but I obeyed, anyway, shaking my head as I did so. "You're so used to being in charge." I referenced his career in a joking way.

"I'm used to getting what I want," he amended before

kissing me.

The concern in his eyes was one hundred percent evident as he looked at me before I turned to the sounds of our daughter's "come get me" tears. And that look remained throughout the evening…whether it was watching me holding Arinn, sipping sangria, or eating a turkey hot brown sandwich across the table from him. His dinner choice I found very enlightening. Sure, it was pretty easy to make. And sure, we had the ingredients. It was also a famous Louisville cuisine, although one we didn't make often. It told me my husband was craving simplicity—the kind that his own childhood in Louisville had brought. I didn't mention that observation, though. I knew we both just needed to escape and cherish the moment we were in.

***

A combination of guilt and love led Finn and I to the decision to let the kids stay up later than usual that night. We both wanted to give them as much time with their father as they could. And, despite not having a nap, Chance did really well.

Finally, though, after a second riveting family game of getting lost in Candyland's Lollipop Woods, I let Finn complete the bedtime routines while I made my way down the stairs to our master bedroom. We hadn't discussed it, but I knew it was just about our bedtime, too. Finn needed to get up extremely early to catch his flight. Plus, I knew he had to be exhausted.

When he entered the room, I was sitting up in our king-sized bed. "That didn't take long, did it?" I noted.

"No. Chance conked right out," he answered, while walking into the adjoining master bath.

"Well, he had a pretty exciting day." I elevated my voice slightly so it could be heard above the running sink water.

A moment later, Finn turned off the bathroom light.

Now, just in his dark boxer briefs, he lifted up the cream-colored, silk sheet and stretched out beside me in bed. "God, when he first saw me, he was really mad." He turned off the side light so that only the illumination of the lava lamp remained.

With the purpose of reassuring his concerns, I placed my hand on my husband's well-defined, bare chest. "At first." I repeated. "He's good now. He just misses you."

"He's my little boy. I love him so much." He tried to disguise it, but I heard his voice crack with emotion.

"He knows that," I answered his unsaid question. "God, Finn, you're his hero. It's in everything he says and does." I couldn't help but admire our son for his choice in a positive role model.

"This life wasn't made for a family." Agitated, Finn stirred a little beneath my touch.

I propped myself up on my elbow so I could look at him more directly. "It's not easy right now, yeah. But this is us. This is our family, and it's what's right." It was the truth. I believed it, and I had to live by it.

"It's been really hard this summer." Finn glanced over at me, looking as if he were unburdening a deep, dark secret. In a way, he was. He was holding things in just as I had been—both of us trying to protect each other from worrying. "Everything is harder— the press, the label, the fans. It's like they're expecting something more, and I don't know what it is. And then…" He shook his head negatively and looked up to the ceiling. "Lara, to know that our little guy feels abandoned—"

I couldn't let Finn project his own fears any further, even if there was a glimmer of truth in his statement. "He's fine. You saw that. He just needed a moment to know that you were real."

"And you?" This time he looked directly at me.

"I'm all right." Did I meet his eyes? I had thought about telling him that I was still having nightmares about the bank, but now I knew I had to keep that buried. With all he already had on his mind, it would have sent him over his limit. "You really didn't need to come home like this," I bravely said instead.

But, selfishly, God, I was sure glad he had. Everything seemed more put together, more calm, more right when he was there. And I was glad to have that, even if it was for less than a day.

"What you don't understand, Lara is, yes, I did it for you and for Chance and for Arinn, but I did it for me, too. I needed this. I needed to see them and have you here in my arms...to hold you."

God, I loved that man. Despite him saying those words and knowing he meant them, I still knew he was saying them for me, too. He knew I also needed to be wanted and missed.

I took the initiative and kissed him softly and repetitively before readjusting myself on his outstretched lap. Pulling my lotus-hued cami over my head, I exposed my breasts. Finn watched as I dipped my head down and butterflied kisses on his chest. But when he didn't react in any way, I sat back up and queried a version of his name. "Baby?"

There had only been one time that I remembered him turning down my advances. It was before we were even engaged, and he had been running himself ragged traveling back and forth from Nashville to New York to see me. It had led to a major blow up and ultimate separation between us. I certainly didn't want a replay of that scenario, especially because I could see how he might be even more stressed and exhausted than that time years before.

I halted and waited for his response. After all, we didn't need to make love. I just needed to *feel* loved. And he had already done that, not only through his words but by simply being there.

Not moving me, Finn adjusted his body so that his torso was now in a more seated position. He cupped his large, worn, guitar playing hands around my breasts and dipped his head down in between them. I felt his wet lips rest on the spot right below my neck before they turned into a kiss. His gray eyes then ventured up to meet mine.

"Yeah?" I asked now a little more confident.

His hands relocated to either side of my face and he sucked in a strong, passionate kiss. "Yeah," he confirmed.

We simultaneously removed our own bottom-ware, and I laid back down onto the comfort of our king-sized mattress. Our hands and mouths didn't roam like they usually did. We simply melded together and rolled like a lost boat out to sea.

And then he was putting his boxer briefs back on and pulling me into his side. His lips rested on the top of my head before he said, "I love you."

"I love you, too." I echoed, but I'm not even sure he heard me— he was asleep that quickly.

***

I think Finn's grumble was louder than the actual alarm going off that caused it. We both were in the same exact position that we had been when we had fallen asleep the night before. I'm pretty sure that was due to the utter exhaustion we were both experiencing. I had even been too tired to dream, let alone have a nightmare. Or, was it that I felt more safe than I had since the last time he had left?

Finn gently lifted my head from his chest and moved it onto a pillow. Folding his body out of the bed, he first shut off his phone's alarm and then went into the master bath. I turned onto my stomach and hugged the pillow hard. It was still dark out. It was early. I tried to deny that the inevitable was happening...again.

I could make out the imagery of him stringing himself into clothes despite the darkness of the bedroom. "You can turn on the light," I offered.

"You awake?"

"Yeah," I answered while finding my discarded cami and panties from the night before and putting them back on my body.

Finn opted for the light on the nightstand instead of the brighter overhead light. Now dressed, he sat on the bed next to me. "Rox?" he said softly.

"Yeah?" And then, God, I started to cry. Where did that come from? Somehow, I managed to stop.

"Hey." Finn put his hand up to my teary face and brushed the stragglers away. When I managed a semi fake smile, he said. "Lar, we're good, right? You love me, don't you?"

"Finn, of course."

"You know how much I love you?"

"It's more than enough." I turned the regretful words I had misused two days before around and punctuated each of them individually so that he understood my meaning and determination.

By his tight, warm embrace, I knew he did. He pulled me away just enough to look me in the eyes. "Baby, you scared me so much on the phone the other day. What you said? I couldn't get that out of my mind. Our love needs to be enough or there's no purpose…there's no point in any of this."

"We're not going to fade," I replied confidently but also with a mixture of relief and remembrance.

"What?" His eyes thinned in a perplexed state.

"Lane and McEllie. He said they just faded."

"Beaut—"

"I love you across any miles or any universes." I smiled. "And I know how you feel about me—your love, your want—that's not fading."

"More than ever." He pecked me on the lips. "Sorry I fell asleep so quickly last night. I'm just so damn tired."

"I'm sure you are…even without coming back here spur of the moment."

159

"I hope it helped." The way he said it, I could tell he still had some doubts.

"It did."

"I know it's been hard. I admire you so much. Thanks for being our rock— the kids and mine. I am so lucky that you're my girl. I couldn't do it without you."

I managed to nod. "Ditto."

"It's just a couple weeks now." He spoke of his ultimate return at the end of the summer tour.

"That sounds so magically wonderful. I can't wait."

"The car service is gonna be here in a few minutes. Walk me to the door?"

I closed my eyes, trying for a calming effect rather than an excessive exhale. Opening them once again, I nodded affirmatively and let him silently take my hand. He led me off the bed and out to our main living area where he turned on one of the lamps but did not let go of my hand. We walked together up the stairs so that Finn could look in on the kids without waking them—he had said his good-byes the night before. And then it was back down for that last gut-wrenching kiss.

CHAPTER THIRTEEN

With just a couple weeks, you would think things would have seemed easier on the home front. After all, the finish line was in sight. But it was sort of like the times that summer that I had attempted to run on Finn's treadmill. That clock ticking down should have encouraged me to run faster or push through, but the last three or four minutes always seemed the longest and the hardest. Breathe. Just breathe. When running or when living, I suppose.

I was so anxious to have Finn back home. On top of the nightmares, which thankfully were happening less frequently, I had begun feeling like I was losing all sense of identity. My role as "mommy" had been my sole existence for months. With Finn on the road, I barely claimed the role of wife or even Mrs. Finn Murphy in the eye of the press, for that matter. And now, with all of my colleagues having gone back to work with the new school year starting, I wasn't even a professional. I needed to feel right. I needed some kind of normalcy. I needed him back.

It was just as the long Labor Day weekend was about to begin that Finn was finally due home. He had sounded worn on the phone that morning before getting ready to go to the airport and head back to New York. And while I knew he would miss being energized by those crowds on a regular basis, I imagined his thoughts and feelings were similar to mine—finding home base.

Chance was on the computer in his bedroom doing some early childhood ABC games, and I was changing Arinn in her room when I heard the alarm system announce that Finn had entered the house. I knew it was him because, as was our routine, he had texted me when his flight had landed. I finished the diaper, brought Arinn into my arms, looked in on Chance, who was oblivious to everything with his little earphones on, and bounced my way down to greet my husband.

As handsome, if not more so, as the first day we met, Finn was standing in the middle of the great room looking at my cellphone when I entered. "This isn't Miller as in Mill-er, is it?"

"Hey, I'm so glad you're home." I brought my arm out to wrap it around him in a semi-hug due to our daughter being between us. "I missed—"

"Lara?" He cut me off with his word and, if I wasn't mistaken, with his half-hearted embrace.

"What?" I asked, pulled away slightly, and put my lips to Arinn's head as she began to fuss and cry—almost as if she had a premonition as to what was going to happen. "Shhh, Daddy's here. Shhh." I looked at Finn. "She was fine a minute ago. Could you hold her for a sec.? I'm just gonna go grab a paci."

I handed Arinn over to Finn who managed to place my phone down on the end table just prior to taking her. As I walked to the kitchen, where I knew there were a couple clean pacifiers, I could see Finn starting to massage Arinn's little back. He already had her calmed down by the time I reentered the room. Regardless, I plopped the pacifier into her mouth, smiled at the two of them reunited, and rubbed my husband's back in a similar motion as he had with our daughter.

"How was—" I started to ask Finn about his flight, but he shook my hand off his back and took a few steps away, bringing a wiggling Arinn down to the floor.

"It is Miller, isn't it?" He turned to me then.

"What?"

What was Miller? What was he talking about? And, most importantly, where was my loving husband and the reunion I had been dreaming for months about?

"He just texted you. The phone lit up as I entered, and it had his name. That means you even programmed it in like he's a regular contact." Finn had picked up my phone and laid it back down during his explanation.

"Finn—"

"What? Tell me it's not. Tell me it's someone's last name." He said it like it was a dare—like he knew the answer and wanted to catch me lying about it.

But there was no reason for me to lie...there was nothing to hide. "It's not. It's Miller." I acknowledged the name of my ex-boyfriend from high school.

"What the fu—" Finn managed to censor himself in front of our ten-month-old who was bound to be a toddler at any moment. Instead of swearing, he turned around and blew out a big gust of air.

His reaction totally caught me off guard. Finn certainly didn't appear tired and worn anymore. If anything, he was ready to bounce off the wall.

"Calm down," I said, glancing from him to Arinn.

But he didn't. Instead, he grabbed my phone again, swiped his finger across it, and read the screen. "They are finally tearing down the vacant drive-in. Thought of you. Call me soon." Finn looked at me with a sting of venom in his eyes. "Calm down? Calm down, Lara?" I took the phone from my husband, glanced at the text to legitimize it, and began to explain that in high school I had worked at that drive-in, but Finn started again, "What's going on? Why are you talking with him? How long have you been...Jesus!"

"I talk with him every so often since the transplant."

Despite Finn's raised temperament, I was determined to stay calm. I had no idea why he was so upset about a text message from Miller. Finn knew about my past with Miller and the horrible, life-altering, summer night right after high school—the drunken night with Miller's brother, Macon, that had led to my pregnancy and giving the child away. Finn had been so understanding about everything and had even helped me track down the brothers when I found out that boy—whose identity I still didn't know—needed a bone marrow transplant. When Macon died and Miller was able to donate marrow, Finn stood by my side. He knew Miller had called to fill me in with a positive update after the transplant. Obviously, I would have his number and he mine.

"Talk?" Finn pursued.

"Yeah, on the phone," I specified, although not sure why I needed to.

"You're talking? And texting obviously. How often?"

"I don't know. Every couple months? Maybe a little more recently because—" I didn't get to complete my sentence because Finn had one of our framed family photos in his hand and looked like he was ready to throw it. "Finn!"

On my voice, he stared at the frame as if he hadn't realized it was there. Placing it back on the end table, he now spoke with a little more reserve. "Do you think about being with him?"

"No!" I immediately and insistently denied. "No! What?"

I hardly ever thought about Miller. Even when we were dating that senior year in high school and the summer immediately following, I knew he was never going to be "the one." He was someone I needed to get me through until I could leave my parents' house and my tirade of a father to find a better life. Ironically, I had found it with the man standing across from me who suddenly seemed to have similar shades of the anger my father had possessed years before.

"Lara…" Again, Finn led his voice as if he were trying to get me to say something to hurt him.

"Finn, we are just talking. That's it. He doesn't even live anywhere near here." I knew as much as Finn did that Miller still lived in my hometown near Pittsburgh, which was hours and hours away.

"Why? Why are you talking with him?"

Why are we talking about *this*? Why aren't we holding one another? Why aren't we saying how much we missed one another? Why are we talking about an irrelevant person from my past?

"I don't know," I said instead and then answered with what really drove my conversations with Miller. "For one thing, he gets updates on the boy. That's a big deal, you know? God, he saved my…" I stumbled, as I always did, with the word for that child because he wasn't mine— he never truly had been, and he never would be. "He saved his life," I edited.

"We all know that. I'm not denying him that. But that was years ago. I'm sure there's not updates regularly— if at all."

That was the truth. Miller only found out annually. And when he did, it was not much more than an "all is well" statement.

"He's just been going through a rough patch, and I guess I'm easy to talk to." I let Miller tell me his woes, and it made me momentarily forget mine. "I don't understand what the big deal is."

"The big deal is…" Finn's voice began to rev back up. "The big deal is, you have been talking," —he put his hands up in mock quotation marks— "with your ex and never told me."

"You're gone a lot. Besides, I didn't think you would want to know," I admitted.

"Exactly!"

"Exactly!" I bounced right back, hating every millisecond of the conversation.

"But that doesn't matter. You've been lying. That's just like cheating."

"What?" What the hell? "No, it's not! And quite frankly, Finn, I'm getting very, very pissed. You're insulting me and our marriage."

Feeling the tears start to take place behind my eyes from the absurd accusation my husband was teetering on, I turned away. Our little girl, somehow completely unaware of the emotional strain her parents were under, was crawling around gurgling quite innocently with the paci still implanted. With that as my stabilizer, I took a breath and looked back at Finn.

"What do you two talk about?" he questioned a little calmer after witnessing my warranted rage.

"I don't know. This summer was rough."

"I know that."

"Yeah, well, that doesn't...it was hard. And Miller's was, too. His job is in jeopardy, he and his wife are having problems—"

"Oh, perfect!" Finn's hands actually flew up in the air. "Don't you get it? What a guy!"

"What?"

Instead of answering, he asked another question. "Do you talk about me?"

"Uh...I don't know. I mean, he knows we're married. Obviously, he's met you."

"Do you talk about me, though? Does he ask about how I am or what we are doing?"

"No. I guess not."

"And do you volunteer that information?"

"I don't know. No."

"No?"

By Finn's reaction, I guessed that was the wrong answer. The fact was, Miller usually did most of the talking. I was the sounding board with a few interjections.

"What? Yes? Is 'yes' the right answer?" I offered, feeling a little like I was a student in a class way above my head, or I was back in that house with my father where nothing any of us could do was right. "I thought your privacy—" I spoke of my husband's notorious push on privacy, especially when it came to his personal life—his family, me, the kids, and his diagno—

"The truth is the right answer. Telling is the right answer. Not keeping it a secret. That is how this *is*, Lara, an affair."

Oh. My. God. He did not just say that!

"It is not!" Wake up! Wake up! I silently urged myself. This scene was worse than any of the bank nightmares I had been plagued with.

"It may not be physical or sexual, but it's emotional, isn't it?"

"I am not doing this," I said it so calmly it scared me. I was suddenly more exhausted and spent than the whole summer rolled into one. I grabbed my phone and started to walk past him.

"What? Where are you going? Are you going to call hi—"

"Ahhh!" I screamed out like Chance throwing a temper tantrum. "No." I breathed in and looked at him with sadness mirroring in both of our eyes. "We're going to destroy each other this way." I spoke with sincerity. "Just give me some time to myself. I think we both could use it. Can I count on you to take care of the kids?" I had been slowly making my way to the adjacent kitchen where my purse and keys dangled on a hook.

"You're going going?"

Don't play the "leaving" card on me, I pleaded in my head. I knew his neurosis, and I was vulnerable enough to it to make me stay. But, rationally, I could see that if I did, it would create an even worse scenario.

"Chance is in his room playing a game. He has his headphones on...I hope. I just need air... to get out for a while. Please give me that."

"Lara…" Just with my name, his voice had come back to the kind one I had always known.

"Please. Please, Finn," I said, knowing somewhere deep down he could not deny me much of anything, even if it was the action of me walking out on him.

"Fine," he said plainly.

"The kids already ate. I was going to eat with you. I thought that would make you happy… to see that I was eating. But I guess you're more concerned about things that I am *not* doing." He looked like he was going to interject something, but I didn't let him. "I was really looking forward to you coming home. I missed you. And now you are breaking my heart."

With that, and not another word said between us, I walked into the garage and opened up the garage door. Just sitting in the Jeep, not even having turned on the ignition, I almost turned around. That damned car was enough to make me remember all the love and concern he had for me. He was tired. And he was trying to come down from a major, crazy, hectic summer.

But, so was I. And I didn't need to be treated that way. I threw the car in reverse, hit the garage door remote to close it, and took off to parts unknown.

***

Without having a specific plan or destination in mind, I somehow ended up at my former co-worker's townhome. Vanessa was someone I could trust. She was one of my dearest friends. Plus, she was already basically part of the inner circle of the massive country music world… or at least my husband's corner of it. Thanks to being my wing-girl years before at one of Finn's concerts, Vanessa had met Finn's best friend and drummer, Carter. After an immediate hook-up, they broke up and, after trials and tribulations, were dating once again. This time, it looked more serious and mature, though. She had even flown to his hometown over the Fourth of July break to meet his family.

Vanessa was on the phone when she opened the door. She looked at me with the most shocked expression on her face. After all, she knew Finn was coming home that day. She knew how excited I was to see him. Surely, she couldn't understand what would possess me to be standing there on her front stoop at the very minute my husband should be on mine.

"Hold on," she spoke into the phone. "Lara's here." She listened to the person on the other end. "No. Here here. Standing in front of me here." Another listen as she looked past me to my car. "No. He's not."

I knew who the "he" she was referring to was, and I started to bawl. I hadn't let a tear fall until that point. But, boy, when it did…

"Oh, shit." Vanessa's eyes grew wide. "Carter, I'm going."

When I realized who she was talking with, I shook my head violently in a "no" manner. I was glad Carter was on the phone and not with her. I didn't want him to have an inkling that something was wrong.

"Yeah. Yeah. Everything's okay," Vanessa spoke back into the phone. "I just forgot she told me she was going to stop over." She listened again. "Yeah, Carter. It's not twenty questions. Let me get her what she needs, and I'll talk with you later." Her voice turned softer as she ushered me into the living room while still on the phone. "Yeah, tonight." Another pause on her end. "Yeah, me, too."

They were most likely telling each other they loved one another or something along those lines. Dare I tell her how hard it was to be involved with a musician? That the distance seemed romantic at first but can ultimately cause so many insecurities?

"Finn?" she questioned after hanging up the phone and sitting down next to me on the sofa.

When she handed me a tissue, I blew very unlady-like and nodded my head affirmatively. "I don't want to get into it, okay?"

"You know you can."

"I know," I said. "Thanks for the cover with Carter."

"I didn't think it was that good, but he's a guy. He won't think a second of it. He's probably got some damn game on already."

"When is he coming?" I asked, knowing Carter and Vanessa were also attending Reese's wedding that weekend.

Trying to keep the wedding to an impossibly low guest count, Reese had invited just the immediate band when it came to Finn's entourage. But Carter was the only other member attending. After a long summer, the others were relishing not having to travel one more day and, instead, spending time with their families— something that both Reese understood and I envied.

"Saturday morning. He'll be here in plenty time for the wedding…just stopped by Nashville first."

I thought of Reese and Roger's wedding. Chance was so excited to be the ring bearer. Between that and knowing his dad was coming home, I could already tell he was starting to come back to being his happy, kind, amazing self. Why couldn't we all be happy at once?

"Lara, what's—"

"I just needed a break. I…God, can I just sit here for a moment? I've been driving around, and the car will probably run out of gas, and then I'd really be upset." I tried to laugh.

"Girl, you can stay here for more than a moment. Where are those two little cuties?"

"They're with Finn."

"So, he is back," she confirmed.

"Yeah."

"Okay. Good. Look, did he do something? He must have." She continued without giving me a chance to respond. "I can tell. You are nev—"

"No," I denied. "He thinks I did something, and he's wrong. And he's tired. And we both needed a break. That's all." That really was the truth, even though it seemed so simplistic in those terms.

"I know *you* need a break," she said. "Let him take care of the kids for a night. Christ, it's his turn." I smiled as she continued. "You deserve a girls' night. Stay here. I have the spare bedroom. If you need something to take your mind off of it, I have lots of wine, and I can bore you to death with all the latest standards and criteria we need to exceed in at work."

I legitimately laughed. That was definitely one thing I would not miss about working— all the imposed regulations. "I vote for the wine." I exhaled before saying, "Let me call Finn, if you're sure."

"Absolutely. Positively," she agreed. "I would tell you to give him hell from me, but I have a feeling he might be getting enough from you. Plus, he really is a keeper, Lar. Space for the night is good."

"Thanks." Bringing my phone out to the patio for a little privacy, I took a cleansing breath and pressed a button to connect with my husband.

As the phone rang, I thought of telling Finn that he was not only a speed dial on my phone, but he was number one. Miller was just a contact among many listed alphabetically. But I knew to resist. I didn't want our conversation to start with an open can of worms.

It was after the third ring that he answered. "Lara," he said plainly.

"Hey," I replied in a shy but relieved voice— he had told me he would always answer me, and he did…even in the midst of one of our biggest arguments.

"Where are you?" His voice was more mellow than when I had left, but I wasn't sure if that was a good thing or not.

"Are the kids okay?" When he didn't answer instantly, I

reiterated, "Finn, just let me know the kids are all right."

"They're fine." It wasn't exactly a mellow tone…it was more similar to weariness—like he was waiting for the other shoe to drop.

"I'm at Vanessa's. I thought you should know. I'm…"

I found myself hesitating. It had sounded so right when Vanessa suggested I stay over. But was it? Should I really leave for the whole night? What would that accomplish besides Finn and I being even further apart?

"What?" he queried after I had stopped mid-sentence.

"I'm going to stay the night." I listened to the words reverberate in my mind in the moment that it took Finn to respond.

"Really?" This time his voice spoke of pure shock mixed with—to only my trained spousal ears—an underlining of pain. "Come home," he said after I didn't answer.

"I don't think so," I found myself saying. "Tomorrow. I'll talk tomorrow."

"To me?"

There was no denying his spiteful tone. And there was also no denying to whom that spite was directed. He hadn't needed to bring Miller back into what had been a perfectly decent conversation up to that point.

"Don't," I said. "Yes… you."

"Fan-fucking-tastic." The hurt version of my husband put up a bravado like I did with my emotional walls.

"Finn, see? That's why I'm here. We're not ready. Do I need to come get the kids?"

"You know our children are fine. They are safe and loved. You know that."

"I do know that," I admitted. I shouldn't have questioned that. I didn't need to question that— ever. "Finn?" I asked a little more kindly and slowly.

He took my lead in how he responded. "Yeah?"

I wanted to ask. I needed to ask. Yet a little part of me was afraid to ask. It was something I had only thought of once I had removed myself from the immediate scene that had transpired in our home. "Are you?"

"Safe and loved? I'm not feeling—"

"Are you okay? You know what I am asking. Have you—" I wasn't going to finish my sentence about his meds because, even though I was out on the patio, I was still in public, and I never wanted to risk Finn's secret.

Regardless, he didn't let me. He answered mid-question. "I ran out. So, I missed a couple. But I had some here. I just took one now. You know, though, basically one day without doesn't—"

"I know," I said, appreciating his honesty. What I didn't like was that it meant he was legitimately, honestly mad at me.

And he basically confirmed that. "This is just me pissed. Not even booze. Just flippin' tired, welcome home, wife texting ex-lover pissed."

"Fi—"

"And for you to leave like that? For you to just leave? Christ, Lara, y'know what? Maybe you're right. We need to talk about this tomorrow. I've gotta get the kids to sleep."

"Tell them I—"

"If you wanted to tell them, you would be here."

If he meant to hurt me even more, he succeeded. He played on my love for our kids. And it almost worked. I should have been there tucking them in… no matter what. But then I thought of all the days he had missed doing just that. How would he have felt if I had said that same thing to him for weeks on end? He would have been crushed, for sure. And in the moment when I was considering how to react, I realized he had hung up.

I let a few more straggling tears fall as I thought of everything I had just learned from our brief conversation. He was tired. He was hurt. He wanted me home. He missed a couple meds. And he was still pissed because of Miller. All of the beginning facts outweighed the final one. But because of that final one—because of his tone—it still legitimized me staying away for the night so that each of us could have cooler heads in the morning.

By the same account, I wanted him to know that I listened and that I understood. So I took a moment, thought of how I was going to phrase it, and texted. *Tell them I luv them … & their dad.*

I waited a few minutes with no response and then checked to see that Finn had, indeed, picked it up. If he wasn't going to answer me, at least he knew how I felt. And that would probably be a little bit better once I had one of those glasses of wine in me.

CHAPTER FOURTEEN

It was mid-morning when I walked back into our home that next day. Finn and I had not corresponded in any form since the night before when I had texted after he hung up. I had no idea what to expect as I made my way from the garage into the kitchen and then into the great room. That's where I found Finn on the floor protectively holding Arinn's hands and encouraging her to step with him.

"Ma-ma," she cried out, wiggled, and plopped onto her bottom which was protected by a dress and diaper.

It was the first time Arinn had said my name with any sort of connection to it actually being me. She had said "da-da" and "ma-ma" before but more in babbling. We may as well have been a ball or ice cream. But knowing she was excited and looking at me when she said that word sent a wash of emotions throughout my entire body.

"Hey, sweet thing." I picked her up as Finn rose from his knees off the floor. I held her close and semi-whispered out of awe, "She's never really done that before—said my name like that."

"Hmmm." He didn't give me much verbally. But his face told me that the pain from the night before was still very prevalent.

"They sleep and eat all right?"

"They're fine, Lara," Finn answered almost robotically.

"Okay. Good." I let Arinn back down onto the carpet, giving her the freedom to scoot on her bottom and find her toys nearby.

Somehow, not having her physically between us changed the dynamics of the conversation instantly. "I'm surprised Carter hasn't called yet." He was obviously referring to the fact that his best friend probably knew all about what was going on between Finn and I.

"Carter doesn't know," I countered. "I told Vanessa not to say anything. Besides, she doesn't even know what we are arguing about."

"Right," he said in a pure sarcastic tone.

"She doesn't," I reaffirmed. "It's not her business. This is between you and I. And, God, I wish I could have went somewhere else. But, besides your sister, she is the only person we can fully trust not to go and tell a news rag that I was in tears and away from you for a night."

I knew adding that last part regarding my emotional state would affect him. And, honestly, I wanted it to. I wanted him to not only understand how hurt I was but also empathize and change how he was reacting to me.

He did pause for a second, absorbing my words. But, he was hurt, too, and he was still determined to continue where we left off the night before. "But you talk with 'him.'"

"Not about us." I immediately rejected the thought. "Miller would never know—"

"And here we go. We're talking in circles again. Somehow, you know…you know that this is wrong. Otherwise, you would have said something to me. God, yeah, I know I'm gone a lot. I have been throughout our whole relationship. But that's not it. That's not an excuse. We have plenty of time to talk. There were tons of opportunities. You just chose not to. We swore no omissions."

It was my time to absorb. If I admitted it, Finn struck the proverbial bull's-eye dead center. I could have told him. I probably should have told him. I pretty much told him about every other mundane conversation I had, whether he was in New York or on the road. Why didn't I ever mention the periodic conversations with Miller?

"I knew you wouldn't have liked it." Subconsciously or not, I knew that was what it came down to, even though I knew there was absolutely nothing wrong with occasionally talking with someone from my past.

"If I knew about it, I wouldn't be happy— no. But I wouldn't feel betrayed."

"I didn't betray you," I partially cried, feeling the sting of that word. I then tried to take a calming breath while looking to make sure Arinn was still in safe eyeshot. "Finn…" I tried again. "Sometimes I just need someone to talk to."

As the words fell out of my mouth, I had no idea where they came from. Miller initiated nearly all of our correspondence. If I called him, it was either because he had called or texted me first. It was only on an extremely rare occasion, like the anniversary of the transplant, when I would reach out.

"What about me? I—"

"Separate from you. Separate from your family…from this world." I tried to explain, realizing that even if Miller was the initiator, I never minded escaping for a few minutes or so from all that was around me and listening to someone who had nothing to do with it. That was especially true over the summer months when Finn was gone and the flashbacks of the bank were still holding me hostage. Listening to Miller lament about his career and marriage helped put my woes on the backburner.

"So, him?" Finn emphasized the last word.

"He knew me before all this. Not that there is anything wrong with this." I immediately tried to explain.

"I knew you before all of this, too." Hurt, he stated the truth.

"You did. And that's what I love about you. The two yous. The two yous that merged into 'my Finn.'" The saying I had used when we were first getting together as a couple rang true as much back then as it did now. The college boy I first met and was friends with had grown into the strong, secure man I was in love with. I wouldn't have wanted one without the other. I wanted "my Finn."

He felt the sentimentality of my words as much as I did. I could see it in his eyes, as well as hear it in his voice's slightly softer tone. "Lara, I just can't understand the connection again with this guy." Finn rarely spoke Miller's name.

"There is no—"

"There is. God, at least be truthful with that."

"No—" I started again.

"Not one ounce?" he asked in a leading way.

I spoke honestly. Finn and I had always demanded that of each other. "I mean, obviously, we have a past. That's what it is, though."

"Then let it be there. There's no reason to talk to him now."

"There's also no reason not to." Stubborn Lara had been the one to give that response. It was the same Lara that had refused to let her father bully her and the same Lara that had not let a man into her life for many, many years after the teenage pregnancy.

And then, the tired, emotional Lara emerged when Finn's reaction was to huff, turn around, and place his hands on top of his head. I couldn't stand the tension between us. I couldn't stand it, and I couldn't *under*stand it. I had been hopping with that damn bunny all summer, too. I had been counting the days until I would see him again. And I just couldn't take one more second. Although silent, there was a deluge of tears streaming down my face.

When Finn turned around to bear witness to my

distress, he shook his head as if trying to shake away cobwebs. "Don't. Don't cry. It's not going to work."

"What? Now I'm getting criticized for having feelings? For having my heart torn apart?" I partially screeched, trying to wipe away the tears.

"Mommy!" Chance's greeting materialized from the top of the steps seconds before he started down them.

I wiped even harder and desperately looked at Finn, urging him with my eyes to detour our son while I got my act together. As suspected, Chance seemed happy and reenergized now that his father was home. And I didn't want him seeing me distraught or questioning me about my whereabouts the night before.

"Uh...uh...uh...let me check hands first," Finn cautioned and slowed our son to a halt as I turned around and finished drying my eyes. "All washed? Okay. We'll be ready to go soon."

I listened, thinking how quickly the performer in my husband could appear. He may not be singing lyrics, but he could put on a perfect act. And for Chance's sake, I was grateful. I turned back around and smiled at our growing young man. I was able to crouch down seconds before he dove into my arms for a hug.

"Mommy," Chance started.

But Finn cut him off. "Little Man, where are your shades? We're gonna need those shades."

"They...they..." His tiny face twisted in a comical way like he was really trying hard to think where his sunglasses were. In the midst of my smile at his innocence, he belted out, "I know where at!" And he ran back up toward the direction of his bedroom.

Knowing that it would only be a matter of minutes before Chance would reemerge, glasses in tow, I tried to conclude my interrupted conversation with Finn in a civil manner. "I know you guys have to go. Just tell me about Arinn so I know what to expect today—when did she wake up, how much—"

"I'm taking her," Finn interjected, speaking about the practically whole-day wedding rehearsal in Manhattan—there was a picnic in the park, followed by the actual church rehearsal, and then dinner at a restaurant.

"What?" That hadn't been the plan when we had spoken on the phone a few days before. "Really? You want to? Because they have a babysitting service at the hotel set up."

I was attending a local hotel's luncheon and fashion show. Proceeds from the day's event went to support battered women. Being involved, as not only as a guest but as part of the organizing committee, was something that made me feel empowered, considering how I grew up. And, financially and notoriety-wise, I was able to bring more spotlight to the cause as Mrs. Finn Murphy. Unfortunately, the date of the event meant that I couldn't attend the wedding rehearsal festivities. So, the plan had been for Finn and Chance to go into the city and for Arinn and I to stay in suburbia.

"I got her."

"Okay," I agreed, not needing another point of contention between the two of us. "I'll just pack up some diapers and pacis, maybe extra clothes for them, and some food t—"

"Already did it." He nodded toward a duffel in the corner of the room.

"Oh." I couldn't help but be a little shocked. "All right. So, she's going to need a nap—about an hour, and she's at that age where—"

"Lara," He cut me off short. "I may have missed a few things, but I am their dad, and I have done this before. Don't—"

"I didn't mean…I was just…I'm just used to doing it. I certainly wasn't saying that you—"

"I got them!" Chance bounded back down the stairs with his white camo sunglasses in hand.

"All right, champ, let's get your sister and blow this

popsicle joint." Finn hoisted Arinn up onto his hip, tickling her little tummy.

"We having popsicles?" Chance asked innocently, causing both of his parents a welcomed, short laugh.

"No," Finn answered and then said, "Say 'bye' to Mommy. I'm gonna put Arinn in the car, and then I'll meet you at the kitchen door."

"Mommy not coming?"

"No. Remember, I told you we'll see her later tonight," Finn answered, picking up the duffel bag and starting toward the garage with a babbling Arinn.

Chance spread his arms wide to give me another hug. "Bye, Mommy."

"Be a good boy." I crouched down to hug him back. "Have fun with Daddy and Arinn."

"I will." He broke our embrace.

"Chance?" I waited for him to look me in the eyes. "I'll miss you," I said as Finn entered the kitchen from the garage. "And, I love you."

"I know—even last night," Chance replied.

I looked up at my husband, knowing he must have passed on my text message to our son the night before. "Forever, Little Man. Forever."

Finn's eyes were locked onto mine a room away. I knew he had heard the last part of my conversation with Chance, and it had to move him somehow. But, yet, he didn't take one step forward to say goodbye to me himself. And he most certainly did not show me any sign of that same love that I knew, under the current pain and hurt, we had for one another. He just simply took our three-year-old's hand and walked away.

***

Finn and I unfortunately deal with stress and arguments differently. If something is extreme, he needs his immediate space to regroup and sometimes talk with his family, and then he'll be all right. In contrast, I want to talk or fight and hash things out right away. If I am given too much space without a solution, I tend to let things fester, which means it only becomes harder for me to let things go.

So the combination of not hearing from him, knowing how we had left things, and spending the entire day listening to stories of women who had been verbally and physically abused, did not help my attitude toward making things better. Instead, I felt my walls of defense creeping up. I was bracing to protect myself from being hurt in another battle round. So to further secure my position, I decided to relocate my physical body from the premises once again.

After the benefit, I stopped by the house to drop off some items, retouch my makeup, and write Finn a simple note. I was just pulling the Jeep back onto the street when Finn drove into the driveway with the kids. Seeing the direction I was obviously heading, he got out of his car and approached my driver's window.

"Where are you going?" he asked, glancing at my hand on the gearshift.

"I just left you a note. I thought I would go get a drink."

"You're getting a drink?" He pronounced the first and last words with expression, surely astonished that drinking would be my choice.

He should have been concerned. My choice of venue should have put up little red flags all over his brain. I wasn't a happy hour kind of girl because of my father's alcohol abuse and the fact that drinking in my teens had led to my unwanted pregnancy. But this was a mess. *We* were a mess.

"A few of today's organizers are meeting up to debrief. You know, Finn, my afternoon wasn't celebratory like yours. And, on top of that, my husband is basically calling me a cheating whore." I didn't give the sarcastic train a moment to slow down on the tracks. "But, don't worry. I'll be home in a little bit, and then tomorrow I'll be the perfect wife."

"I'm not worried about tomorrow," he stated in such a way that I knew he didn't want to wait. He wanted to deal with things. He had his space. He was ready to talk it through.

But I wasn't. I was in my self-protection, wall-building, enough-for-the-day mood. "Bye, Finn." I threatened to move the car into gear.

"Lara," he called out my name and actually ran to the front of the car to block it. "Don't," was his semi-warn, semi-plead.

I knew him so well. He wanted me to stay because he was scared of me leaving. But he also wanted me to stay because he knew that if I did leave, that gully would grow deeper between us. He knew me well, too.

In my hesitation, it was our son's voice coming from Finn's car that broke into my thoughts. "Mommy?"

"Lara, don't leave." Finn inched once again toward my driver's window.

What was wrong with me? I had already left him the night before when I had stayed at Vanessa's. We had never before been apart for a night when we had argued. And now I was threatening to sort of do it again. I really didn't want to get into it, though. I was exhausted. I was exhausted from arguing, from the day, from the summer…I would really, truly break if there was one more hurtful thing said between us.

"Lara," he tried again. "Please."

For some reason, the childhood story that Finn had told me about when his mother left his father for a few days slammed into my brain like a fierce hurricane. Little Finn had watched his mother walk past him, into their garage, and drive off. Now, in present day, I had both an adult Finn and our own little boy both willing me not to do the same.

And, God help me, I couldn't. I turned off the Jeep, opened up the door, and stepped out. Standing in front of my husband, I handed him the key fob.

"Thanks," he said and seemed genuinely grateful.

"I'm not doing it for you," I tried. But, I was, and I bet somewhere deep down inside he knew it.

"Okay," he replied and watched as I walked over to get Chance out of the other car.

"Hey, there's my favorite little guy." I unbuckled our son's car seat.

"Where you going, Mommy?"

"Nowhere." That was the truth now. "Just with you."

"What about Arinn?"

"Daddy will get her." I looked at Finn in a "do it" kind of way. Then, lifting Chance into my arms, I exclaimed, "Gosh, you're getting so heavy. How many of those popsicles did you eat?" I teased.

"There no popsicles!" he screeched.

I smiled. "Tell me about your time with Reese and Roger."

***

I was thinking Chance had a good future as a reporter the way he described and detailed every minuscule second of his day at the park and then at the church. Of course, at that moment, I was grateful that he kept talking and talking and talking. It meant that I didn't have to. Not even when Finn entered with Arinn, brought her upstairs, got her changed, and came back down again. He plopped our daughter on the floor near where Chance and I were sitting on the sofa, poured himself a bourbon, and sat on the recliner.

"He did a great job," Finn interjected when Chance was describing practicing carrying the pillow down the aisle and walking alongside the flower girl—Roger's cousin's daughter.

"I bet you did," I said to Chance. And without looking up at Finn, I commented. "I didn't expect you back so early."

"We kinda skipped the dinner part," my husband explained. "It was a long day. Arinn was getting cranky, and Chance here had enough food at the picnic that he wasn't going to eat any dinner."

I looked at Arinn. "You seem okay." I knew I was using our children as a safe middle ground.

"She is," Finn replied. "But, she didn't nap well. So I think she'll be going to sleep early. Speaking of sleeping, Little Man, I put your pajamas on your bed. Why don't you go up and get them on?"

"No! I don't wanta go to bed," Chance whined.

"I didn't say you were going to bed. I just said, put them on."

"Promise?" He did, indeed, sound like a negotiating little man.

"Of course," Finn secured.

"K. I'll be right back!" our son declared and bounced off the sofa to go up the stairs.

As soon as he got up, I followed suit. I didn't know where I was going. But I couldn't even stand a second of the awkward stillness that was sure to follow.

Finn got up, too. "You're determined to ignore me."

"No," I denied. And I finally looked at him. "I can't do this tonight, though, Finn. I can't. I just want to sit here and enjoy our kids, okay? I dealt with sad, hurt, battered women all day long, and I really don't want to be another one."

"Lara, c'mon, that's not fair." He placed his glass on the fireplace mantle. "You can't compare me to...I wouldn't hurt you."

"Maybe not physically, but emotionally." The words he had used when inaccurately describing what he thought was my relationship with Miller came back to bite him. They came out swiftly before I gave it much thought. But they were accurate, nonetheless.

He groaned and took another swig from his glass. "Fine. You don't want to talk, fine. But I can't sit here and pretend that everything is all right."

"Don't then."

"Lara…" His voice had that plead in it. I knew he didn't want our conversation to be like this, and neither did I.

"Go run on the treadmill or ride the bike or record or write or something," I suggested, recognizing the fact that he hadn't had his needed moment or so to unwind after the tour.

Finn had been thrown—or had thrown himself— into one hectic, stressful, continuous event after another. And so had I. Maybe we could work through it after attending the wedding and truly having a restful moment. But it couldn't—wasn't—going to happen right then…in that great room after an already exhausting, emotional day.

"I think we…I—"

"I can't, Finn. It's too much right now. Can you understand that?"

"I…I…" He hesitated and then said, "You know? I can."

***

It was more than a couple of hours later when I saw him next. The kids were both asleep, and I had found refuge in reading the third book in a series. I didn't want to let those characters go— they allowed me, for a few moments here and there, to escape my hectic life and venture into their dramatic one. I tilted the paperback down and looked to where my husband was standing— at the threshold of the kitchen. He was gulping some water and staring at me. By the look of his sweaty gym attire, I could tell he had taken my advice and had worked out for at least part of the time he had disappeared into his man cave/studio area. The house was silent. It was really the only time when our home was like that with two young children living in it. Between that and the darkness that had settled outside, I could feel a certain element of calmness and wondered if we should dare, indeed, broach the elephant in the room once more. I couldn't fully interpret Finn's look, but I knew, without a shadow of a doubt, his thoughts were completely and solely on me.

That was until the scream. We both heard Chance yell out something unintelligible but as if he was in terror. I'm not sure where the water in his hand went, but Finn was up the stairs in an instant. I was a little slower to react. Between the recent tantrums and fears, I was used to a little drama from our little boy.

Finn was already stretched out alongside Chance in his bed when I arrived at our son's bedroom. "Chance, bud, what's wrong?" Finn used his soft, melodic voice to question.

"Monster," he mumbled, only partially awake.

"Chance." I sighed.

They both looked up at me, but it was Chance who spoke. "Mommy," he called out.

"I sprayed, kiddo, remember? Right after prayers, right before bed bugs." On my last two words, Finn adjusted his legs so I could sit on the edge of the bed.

"But they coming," he said ominously while curling tighter into Finn's side.

"They wouldn't dare." I reached over and stroked the length of his nose, willing his little, tired eyes to close. "Not with both Mommy and Daddy here."

Finn kissed the top of Chance's head and did the softest of hums. It was only the matter of minutes before he was slumbering soundly. The two of us waited in silence for a little bit and then carefully crept out of the room.

Finn followed me down the stairs before saying, "Geez, that was some serious fright."

"Yeah. So when you think you know what this summer was like, remember that scream."

"Ah, fuck, Lara." He drew out his words with exasperation, frustration, and disappointment. "Give it a rest. You don't know everything, either." And he walked right past me and into our master suite.

I shook my head and silently cursed myself for not taking a breath before reacting to Finn's obvious concern about our son. I knew he hadn't been witness yet to some of the fears that Chance had developed, and I should have been more cognizant of that. But it was my automatic inclination to self-preserve and be the victor in any battle when I felt alone and beaten down. I had learned that from a very young age. I shouldn't have had that feeling when it came to the man— the person—I trusted most in the world, though. And if I calmed myself down, I knew I truly didn't. I did want him to know how it was this summer. I just should have found a kinder way to get my point across. Standing in that great room, listening to Finn start the shower in our master bath, I was still too hurt and too stubborn to rectify the situation for my own good, though.

CHAPTER FIFTEEN

I knew I had trouble getting back into my book—to the point that I had to reread a few pages a couple of times. My thoughts were disturbed and not focused on the imaginary people in the imaginary land. And I knew at some point that, because I was not in sync with the characters, my eyes had begun doing the blinking, resting pattern. What I did not know was that I had fallen completely asleep on the sofa.

It was the feeling of being scooped up that caused me to awaken. I felt the book drop from my hands, and I focused to see that I was in Finn's arms. While I was still trying to assess the situation, he hoisted me a little more definitively, causing me to instinctively and securely wrap my arms around his neck.

"What are you—" I started in a semi-coherent mumble.

"Settle." He held me firmer and started walking with me intact. Adorned in a soft, freshly laundered dark gray T-shirt and lighter colored sweats, he said, "You don't have to touch me or even talk to me," he added as we entered our bedroom. "But this is where you belong—in our room ...in our bed."

Finn brought me down onto the sheets of the already

drawn bed. He stared at me for a split second, that seemed so much longer, and then made his way over to his side. Feeling him sink onto the mattress and then turn off his bedside light, I mimicked by stretching out my legs and allowing my body to give at least the appearance of a more relaxed position. Facing the opposing direction of my husband, I felt the sheet being drawn up on top of both of our bodies, and I let my head sink onto my pillow. I should have been tired. After all, I had just been soundly asleep. But now I found myself wide-awake and staring at my nightstand—the one with the lava lamp. It was aglow, and I took note that it had just started to move. Knowing that it takes quite a while for it to warm up and then slightly move before it even begins to bubble, I realized Finn must have had it on for a while before coming to get me. Had he laid there after the shower upset over those last words I had said to him? Or, had he been waiting and hoping that I would come to our bed on my own—waiting until he could wait no longer?

Recalling how Finn had tenderly cradled me as he brought me into what was normally our haven, I watched the soothing motion of the red lava ebbing and flowing inside the glass lamp. Both images were such a contrast to the absurdly unnatural distance that was between our two bodies in that bed. The king-sized mattress never felt so foreign and lonely, even during the times when he was on the road. It made me want to cry.

But, I couldn't let that happen. I didn't want Finn to see or hear me. I was still very keen on his reaction earlier in the day when I had started to cry. And I didn't want him to think I was doing it for sympathy.

I just couldn't help it, though. I was so damn sad. I tried hard to muffle my tears and shakes, but it may have only made it worse. Trying to control the sobs caused intermittent gasps of obvious tear-harbored breaths. I felt Finn's body sag behind me before his huge hand rested on the back of my head. The stability and strength of that motion always calmed me in the past, and it was no different then as we laid there together yet still very much in solitude.

"You don't have to," I tried, but internally, I relished his touch.

His response was to press a little harder as if to confirm his presence and his commitment to his action—knowing that he didn't have to, but he was. And, it worked. My tears were instantly slowing.

His hand trailed down the back of my neck, resting in the length of my hair. "Remember, I have that radio interview in the morning before we go."

I nodded in a positive motion. My body and thoughts were a little calmer. "Good night, then."

"Don't let the bed bugs bite," he recited after a beat and simultaneously let go of his touch.

Finn fell asleep first. It didn't surprise me. I knew, even in an argument, he felt comfort and was more relaxed knowing I was there. I did, too. But, yet, I laid awake for some time wondering if we had made one-step forward yet two steps back...wondering what we were even arguing about at that point...and wondering how we could get back to where we needed to be.

***

As if attending a wedding wasn't enough to deal with for a day, there was also trying to get a three-year-old ready for his big wedding job and packing overnight things for everyone—we were staying in the penthouse since the wedding was in the city. All of this while trying not to disturb Finn, who had been holed up in his lower level studio recording a national radio program. He would be down there for hours.

By the time he reemerged, I was upstairs trying to get Arinn into her jumper outfit and Chance into his ring bearer suit, which included a tan and gray vest with dark bow tie. In hindsight, I should have had Chance practice wearing his suit more than once. He wasn't much in favor of the feel of the material so tight and warm near his neck. He was used to his summer attire of loose T-shirts and shorts. Not wanting an argumentative three-year-old on my hands, I decided to keep his tie and white button down shirt open until right before he entered the church. And, by that time, I knew it was going to be Finn's job to convince his son to do what he was told.

When I finally made it back down the stairs, Finn was emerging from the master suite showered and looking damn handsome in his black suit with coordinating straight tie and white shirt. He stared at me for a moment before saying, "You look beautiful."

It had been my husband's mantra for nearly as long as I could remember. And I knew he believed it—even in that moment. But *I* didn't... especially then. I did have my strapless, floor length, soft green dress on. But my hair, barely blown dry, wasn't fixed, and I didn't have a stitch of make up on.

I guess Finn didn't appreciate my hesitation or glare. Because the next words out of his mouth were anything but kind. "For Reese's sake, can you at least suck it up and pretend for a couple hours that you love me?"

I was thrown...shocked. "What—" I started.

"I'm going to be outside. We should leave in ten." And he succinctly walked past me and out the front door.

I took more deep breaths than a yoga guru takes in a career. But, yet, it didn't seem to help. I was still upset by the time the kids and I met him at his car. I knew we would take his. It was a little smaller than our usual family SUV, but it was safe and easier to manipulate on the streets of New York City.

The silence on the first part of our trip into the city got to me. I couldn't stand the utter absence of any noise because I couldn't stand the reason behind it. More than anything over the past couple of days, I was sick thinking that Finn would even contemplate that I didn't love him. He didn't really believe that, did he?

After fiddling with the air conditioning and playing with the contents of my purse, I finally ventured and looked in the direction of his driver's seat. "Finn?" When he offered me nothing, I let him know what I was feeling. "I can't believe you'd say that I don't l— "

He cut me off. "It's not the time."

"You know what?" I immediately bounced back not liking the parental tone he gave me.

"Not now, Lara." There it was again, but I at least understood why. "You okay back there, bud?" He snuck a look at the kids in the back seat.

Finn was being a parent. Arinn had fallen asleep, but Chance was awake. And even though he was engrossed in his tablet, our son was all ears.

"Yeah," Chance answered. "I good."

"Good," Finn confirmed—I'm sure as much to me as to his son.

I exhaled. He was right. We shouldn't get into anything in front of Chance. And I selfishly wondered if we would have found a way to have gotten through this rift earlier had it not been for our children. Before the curious ears of kids, there had been more time to talk openly.

As I pondered this and hesitated on what to say, my phone rang via the speaker in the car. Knowing it was Vanessa, I pressed the dash button to receive the call. "Hey, there."

"Hey," Her voice radiated through the car.

"What's up?" I tried to sound casual.

"Carter's flight got delayed," she stated as I watched Finn slightly shake his head negatively. "Looks like we're going to miss the ceremony but should be there for the reception."

"All right."

"You'll need to get lots of pics of that cute little ring bearer for me."

I looked back at Chance and smiled. "I will."

"How's everything going with—"

"Vanessa! You're on the car speaker," I warned and once again witnessed my husband's head shake.

"Oh, sheesh…" She stumbled verbally. "You oughta tell people that. Hi, Finn."

"Hi, Vanessa," he managed rather civilly, considering I'm sure he knew she was going to ask about our personal business.

I switched the phone to handset and continued talking with my friend…if not privately, at least it was just a two-way conversation. We didn't venture anywhere near the topic of Finn and I. But I was thankful to talk with Vanessa for a few moments. It was a perfect distraction from the awkwardness inside the confines of the car—an awkwardness I feared would only fester if Finn and I didn't get some time alone. And with the eventful day still ahead of us, there wasn't much hope.

***

I was, indeed, capturing pics and video as my precious, and at times precocious, little boy made his wedding ceremony debut. He was walking alongside the flower girl, Gillian, who was almost six years old. I worried that Chance was going to be scared, considering some of his other fears that had arisen that summer. But he must have gotten the performance bug from his daddy since he grinned and strutted the entire way up the aisle. When he got to the altar and handed the best man the pillow, Finn, who was also up there, but a little more to the side, gave him a thumbs up. Chance, self-assured, returned it right back and then ran more than walked to the pew where I sat.

"I did it, Mommy!" Chance semi-yelled, causing a polite, stifled laugh from the audience.

I muffled him into my chest and whispered, "You did"

and then silently praised our decision to have already dropped Arinn off with Summer at our penthouse—there was no way Arinn could have remained settled through a wedding ceremony and reception.

After the introductory spiel from the minister, it was Finn's turn to sing Matthew Baute's "One." I had never heard the song before let alone Finn's version of it. It was so beautiful. His voice was strong and sweet and sensitive. And the lyrics surely resonated not only with the bride and groom but any of the married couples in the church. I noticed how Finn looked at me when the words told how love will get you through. And I prayed his eyes on mine meant something— that he wasn't just "sucking it up" like he obviously thought I had to.

When the song was finished, he cheek-kissed Reese who looked absolutely stunning in a white, strapless gown, flowing with bouncy ruffles from the waist to the floor. Then, after shaking Roger's hand, he made his way to the empty spot waiting for him next to Chance and I. Chance bounded immediately into his father's lap. I smiled a soft, closed mouth smile at my husband and he mirrored my action.

We then watched as the minister united two hearts in marriage. And even though our wedding had been vastly different—everything being much more intimate for Finn and I—I couldn't help but flash back to our personal vows and our magical matrimonial kiss. I purposefully grazed Finn's hand in that pew, and I think he was ready to take mine. But I wouldn't find out because the announcement was made and the bride and groom were heading down the aisle, causing us to rise from our seats.

***

The reception was conveniently only a block away. Everything about that part of the evening was such a contrast to the serene wedding itself, as I knew it should be. We were immediately thrown into the buzz of the celebratory setting—the wedding party being introduced and people mixing and mingling over cocktails. Finn was once again Mr. Popularity, as relatives and friends of the bride and groom found themselves in the midst of celebrity. And that was solely Finn, since the couple of sports figures that Roger represented were unable to attend due to their game schedules.

When I wasn't calling to check in on Arinn or making sure Chance wasn't bothering anyone, I was by my husband's side. But we spoke to the guests and not really to each other. Thankfully, when Carter and Vanessa showed up just prior to dinner being served, I felt a little more at ease.

After dinner, the bride and groom had their first dance, followed by the bride and her father and the groom and his mother. Then the bridal party was called out to the dance floor, which included Chance dancing with the flower girl. Little Gillian did a good job trying to direct Chance into a dance. But our son just had too many fast moves in him, which made for a very amusing display.

While I was recording that, the DJ called for the parents of the flower girl to dance and the parents of the ring bearer to dance. I had no idea we were expected to dance. I stopped the camera phone and looked at Finn horrified—not only because of my detest of dancing, but because I hated being in the spotlight, especially in the arms of a man who was upset with me. He shrugged his shoulders and held out his hand. Not wanting to cause any more turbulence, I reluctantly shoved my phone and clutch purse at Vanessa and made my way onto the dance floor.

Dutifully, I wrapped my arms around Finn's neck and he laid his on my lower back. I allowed my head to rest on his suit-clad chest and looked at our son while softly swaying to the music. I wished I felt as secure and happy as we looked.

"It may be years later, but I'm finally getting that bridal party dance from you." I heard Finn's voice from behind my head.

I tilted to look into my husband's eyes. He was being nostalgic. Long before we were ever a couple, Finn was a groomsman and I a bridesmaid in Olivia and Sam's wedding. We were supposed to dance as part of the bridal party dance, but I had insisted that his girlfriend at the time dance with him instead. And then years and years passed.

After a moment of us simply remembering, Finn spoke again. "It was all worth it."

"Finn…" I said his name softer than I had since he had come back from tour.

"I need to go to batroom." Chance was suddenly between us tapping on our legs and doing a whole different kind of dance.

"Is it an emergency?" Finn tried while looking at Gillian, who was now with her parents.

"Yes." Chance wiggled some more.

"An emergency?" Finn's embrace on my back was getting looser by the second. "You're going to pee your pants?"

Chance's little eyes looked pleading, and I knew that was enough of an answer. "You better take him," I said.

"Yeah." Finn sighed and now had our son's hand in his instead of mine.

Just as they disappeared from my sight and I started to remove myself from the dance floor, Carter came to my side. "The Murphy men bailing on their dates?" he joshed.

"Appears so." I played along and then said, "No. Chance was just doing the pee-pee cha-cha."

Carter laughed and stuck out his hand offering to finish the dance with me. I looked over at Vanessa, who was smiling and had my phone up to take a pic. I obliged, wanting to get in a couple private questions to Finn's best friend and bandmate, anyway.

"Are you hoping that Vanessa catches or misses the bouquet when it's thrown?" I semi-teased, but I *was* curious if their relationship was gaining any serious ground.

"Did she set you up for that?"

"Nope. Totally on my own. Well?" I didn't let him off the hook.

"How about one flower ...not the whole bouquet?" And then added, "yet."

"Way to be decisive." I smirked.

"Ha." He twirled me around in a silly fashion. "Y'know, we really missed you on the road this year, Lara-Li."

"That's good to hear."

"Oh, c'mon. I'm sure Mr. Romantic Big Guy told you that a few thousand times. I'm surprised you two even came up for air—probably humping like rabbits for the past couple of days."

"No," I said plainly, knowing then for sure that Vanessa had kept her word and had not mentioned to Carter about the night I spent at her place.

"C'mon, I know you two," the drummer stated. "And I, for sure, know how your boy was this summer."

"Wh—" I started.

But I was interrupted by Finn, who very firmly, yet discretely said, "Get your hands off my wife."

Carter and I broke from our arm's length dance out of pure shock. "Finn! It's Carter." I was flabbergasted but aware enough to see Chance standing at his daddy's side, looking equally bewildered by Finn's tone. I turned to Carter. "Can you and Vanessa take Chance for a couple minutes?"

Carter locked eyes with Finn—the former puzzled and the latter pissed. I nodded my head slightly up and down to encourage Carter to let it be and then directed our son to tell Ms. Vanessa and Mr. Carter about the church since they missed him doing such a good job. Giving Finn and I a second glance, Carter slowly took Chance's hand and then they both walked over to where Vanessa was sitting.

Finn brought me back into his arms. The music had changed and more couples were now on the dance floor. So at least the attention wasn't completely on us.

"You don't want to dance with me, but you'll dance with him?" Finn questioned.

"That's your best friend," I answered semi-exasperated. "And we were talking more than dancing. And, I *was* dancing with you. And you know what? It had felt really good." God, the tears were threatening. "I know you don't want a scene." I pushed my index fingers into the spaces below each eye. "It's my turn to use the restroom."

"Lara..." His voice trailed off as I gently broke free and weaved through the dancers.

I made my way into the restroom and immediately leaned up against the sink. Looking into the mirror, I realized, thankfully, that I didn't appear as worn or as stressed as I felt. Regardless, I grabbed a tissue from the counter and brought it up to my eyes, dabbing the bottom eyeliner that looked like it was threatening to smudge. I placed my hands around the back of my neck and tried to stand up straight and strong. Whatever was going on with Finn and I, I would not let the crowd in there see. I would not ruin this special day for Reese or give an outsider a reason to spread gossip.

"So things are still a little weird with the two of you?" Vanessa's voice made me turn. She had entered the restroom without me noticing... I had been too absorbed in my thoughts.

Nevertheless, I answered without missing a beat. "I thought we were pulling it off."

"Yeah. You are. Might have even fooled me had you not been at my place in tears two nights ago."

I did a double check glance at the stalls, which I pretty much knew were empty. "Thanks for letting me crash there, by the way."

"You're welcome. It was fun. We should do that more often." Seeing my half-hearted smile, Vanessa continued. "What was that business with Carter just now?"

"I don't know." I sighed.

But I did. I knew. I knew it had nothing to do with Finn's medication. I knew he was taking it. I knew it had little to do with him being exhausted from an extensive road series, but I'm sure it did play into it. It had to do with his love for me. It had to do with Miller. It had to do with his fear of being left. He had only acted similarly one time in our relationship— when we had confronted Macon and Miller about getting tested for the bone marrow transplant. Finn's jealousy and protective stance had always been at full tilt when it came to those Altman brothers. And since that text had, unnecessarily, awakened his fear, he took it out on an extremely innocent Carter.

"Well, whatever it is… whatever's going on, you two will work it out. The love that you have is written all over both of you. Here's your phone back." She handed it to me along with my purse. "Watch the video I shot. You'll see."

"Thanks," I said. "I will. But maybe right now we better get back."

We were no sooner out the restroom door, than Vanessa was off to the open bar. She offered to get me something, but I knew I needed to keep a clear mind. I gave myself a moment to just take everything in. There were couples dancing and others at the bar and still others at tables talking or laughing. I spotted Finn with Chance on his shoulders talking with Carter. From their postures and facial expressions, I was pretty sure there wasn't any more friction between the two musicians, which made me feel relieved.

But that was an easy fix. I knew it wasn't going to be so simple between Finn and I. There had been too much said and too many layers of hurt. I was confident that we could break through it like Vanessa had said, but it couldn't be done in that ballroom, and it simply hurt too much to see him and love him and not truly be with him.

When I spotted Reese in a rare moment by herself, my decision was made. She barely got in a greeting to me when I interrupted. "I'm sorry, but I'm going to head home. I'm a little sick. And I'm tired."

"Oh, Lara, I'm sorry. What's wrong? You're not feeling well? You're not pregnant again, are you?" She nudged me in a friendly way.

"Not sure how that would happen." I thought I had mumbled it to myself but by the look on Reese's face, I knew she heard. "I'm just not feeling well." I tried again with my lie.

"Maybe the flu? You're probably run down. I hope it wasn't us having this wedding. We shouldn't have done it so close to Finn coming back and—"

She was making me feel guilty. "No, it's not you. Believe me. It's not you at all," I added and looked to my left where Finn had suddenly appeared. "I'm going to get a cab."

"We can go," Finn offered. "Let me just grab Chance."

Before I could answer, Vanessa jumped into our conversation with an offer. "Carter and I can take Chance for the night if, you know, you want some time alone."

"No, that's okay. Finn can stay and bring Chance home later. *You* should have some time with your man," I answered.

I appreciated Vanessa's offer, and it really was a good solution, but I wasn't sure. Chance would go to Vanessa and Carter in a room where he knew both of his parents were close by. And he would probably leave with them. After all, Chance was a "tour/on-the-road" baby, and he was used to being around his father's friends. But staying the night? That would probably only cause problems and distress, especially with his newfound summer fears. And none of us needed any more issues to deal with.

"Lara, we'll all go. It's fine," Finn said with definition.

"Yeah, take your wife home," Reese chimed in. "We got what we needed from you— a song and an adorable ring bearer. I see too much of you as it is!" Reese was glowing. It was easy to see it in her light demeanor and the way she looked as her newly-appointed husband joined our mini-gathering.

Finn gave me an inquisitive look, wanting to confirm our joint departure. And when I shrugged my shoulders to affirm, he said, "I'll go get the car."

CHAPTER SIXTEEN

"Did I suck it up enough for you? I'm not used to performing like you are." We were on route to the penthouse, and the tension that had mounted over the past few hours, nonetheless the past few days, had hit a limit for me. I unleashed what I had been wanting to say since leaving our suburban home much earlier in the day. And I was able to because our first-born was asleep as soon as his little head hit his car seat, making it the first time we were alone.

"C'mon…" Finn sighed.

But, he knew me. So I'm pretty sure he knew it was coming—us hashing it out. He had, after all, in a way encouraged it when he insisted that we leave the wedding together.

"Finn, I love you. Don't ever say that I don't. That was the cruelest thing you have ever said to me, and I really hope you don't believe it. Because if I didn't, none of this would matter. Neither of us would be so upset."

"So this is now going to be all about one comment I said at the house?"

"Yes!" I instantly sprayed and then slowed. "I don't know…maybe. That definitely hurt." Especially when I thought the night before we were making progress.

"Fu—!" He cut his cursing short but slammed his hand into the steering wheel.

"Pull over," I said after recovering from my body jumping at the shock of his outburst.

"What?"

"Pull over. I don't want you driving if you're upset."

"Yes, I'm upset. I hav—"

"Pull over…please," I added in a slower tempo.

Because it was later in the evening and a weekend, a holiday one at that, traffic was at least very light. He eased up on the accelerator and looked at me. I thanked him silently by blinking my eyes once.

"The park," I suggested as a discrete place to pause and cool down…for both of us.

When the car came to a definite stop, Finn and I both took the moment and breathed in some long, individual breaths. I finally looked over at my husband. He continued to stare out the front windshield.

After one more breath, it was me who spoke again. "Can we talk outside? There's no one around and Chance…he'll be all right." I needed the air—not confinement.

Finn's answer came via the opening of his driver's door. He looked back at Chance, still asleep, and exited. I followed suit, making sure to stay only feet away from the open car window.

"I shouldn't have said what I did earlier." Standing across from me and near the park bench, Finn was now calmer. "And the shit with Carter…"

"That was wrong," I stated simply.

"I know it was, Lara. I apologized to him. It wasn't about Carter. You're refusing to talk about what it is about, though. You walked out the first night. And then yesterday? Yesterday you went all towering igloo on me. Icing me out is not helping. Quit making the snide comments, and let's get it out."

"Fine."

"Fine?"

"Fine. What do you want me to say?"

"I want you to understand how it makes me feel that you're in contact with him."

"Like Audrey," I offered as it clicked in my head.

"Jesus. I don't talk with her, text her... I don't even have her number." Finn was instantly agitated because he thought I was being accusatory.

I wasn't, though. I tried again. "I'm just trying to understand how you feel. That's what you asked me to do." I realized Finn probably felt about Miller the same way I felt about Audrey. And if that was the case, I could empathize with his emotions, just not his accusations.

He took a purposeful, hopefully clarifying, breath. "Well, imagine if I was in contact with Audrey and you didn't know. And you know that's not the case. Any time I have accidently run into her—and that hasn't happened in years—I've told you." Before I could concede at least that much to him, Finn spoke again. This time it was softer...more reflective, but, nonetheless, filled with hurt. "You know why Audrey and I broke up."

Audrey had been seeing someone else behind Finn's back. He had had no idea and had been blindsided by the broken engagement. I knew that. I hurt for him back when he had told me, and I knew how her leaving had intensified his already deep-seated fears of being left. I also got the connection to today...to us. I understood that seeing Miller's texts—knowing of our correspondence—created flashbacks in his mind. I knew it created unnecessary doubt. But it shouldn't have—not with us ...not with our love.

So even though it wasn't necessarily the correct answer or, most certainly, the one he was expecting, I rolled the proverbial dice and repeated something he had told me a long time ago. "Because it was always going to be me." I managed to look him in the eyes.

Standing there, with his tie hanging loosely around his open collar and the beam of the park light the only illumination on our bodies, Finn softened. His exhale came through his nose before he offered me a slight smile. "Yeah."

"I will never, ever do that." Without directly mentioning cheating or leaving, I got my intention across. And then I added with resolute, "Ever."

"I know."

"Do you?" I asked because that was the crux of everything we had been going through in the past couple of days.

"I do," he confirmed. "It doesn't change the way I feel about you talking with him, though. Maybe I handled it wrong."

Maybe? Maybe! I pushed away the urge to repeat his word back to him. This was one I needed to let go.

"I just…everything is happening at once…"

"I know," I agreed. "You've said things are changing. But this summer? This summer, Finn? It's been hard for me, too. I mean, God, I not only missed you, but dealing with the kids nonstop…and on top of that, I quit my job. Everybody went back to work a couple weeks ago…"

"I—" He started to say something, and I could tell it was going to be empathetic.

But, I was on a roll. I needed to get some stuff out. "When we first started dating," —I saw softness creep into his eyes on our mutual remembrance— "I was so independent and thought I was fine with it. I was," I clarified. "And even though I missed you when you were still living in Tennessee, we didn't know any other way. That was our relationship. And then you moved here and…and I got used to that. I got used to—and loved— that you were around more. I started to need you more because you were here."

"Lara, that's all right. It's okay to need somebody."

"I know." I sighed. "But since you've been on tour and

away, I couldn't go back to not having you around. It's…"
I tried to make a comparison. "It's like the cars. All these
heated seats and steering wheels and windshields and the
navigation systems and cameras and hands-free calling. I
can't just go back to driving—" I cut myself off, knowing I
might have started to ramble. "Finn? I lost myself this
summer. I didn't have us."

"You di—"

"Not the way I was used to. And I didn't have my old
self. Everything seemed to be in a tailspin
especially…especially after the bank. That really…it
messed me up," I finally admitted. "Not just for a couple
days. I was having nightmares all the time. Really, if it
weren't for the kids, I probably wouldn't have even gone
out of the house. Maybe I should have called Dr. Bartola."

Finn slightly bent his knees so that he could urge my
eyes up to meet his. "You seemed okay after…" His voice
trailed, surely recalling that horrific day in July. "Why
didn't you tell me?"

"You were away, and I didn't want to worry you," I
answered.

"Baby…" He sighed, using a concerned version of his
term of endearment for me—a first since he had been
back.

"But I've gotten better," I offered, still trying to protect
him from unneeded worry. "I couldn't wait for you to
come home. Nobody I would ever talk to on the phone or
in person could make me feel loved and secure like you.
Do you get it? Do you understand? I didn't—"

I saw the recognition of my words in his face. "Of
course I understand. You are that to me." As an older
couple walked past us hand in hand, Finn nodded a
general greeting to them and then said to me, "Can we go?
Lara, please. I'd rather do this at the penthouse…in our
home."

"Yeah," I agreed, knowing Finn was now calmer.
"Sure." Being back at the penthouse seemed like the ideal

place to, hopefully, finish what needed to be finished.

I went for my car door. But Finn got to it first. He showed me his kinder, more gentler side by opening the passenger door for me and shutting it after I entered.

We drove in silence for a few minutes. It wasn't the same silence that had filled the car on our initial trip out that morning. There wasn't as much anger, but there was definitely still an awkwardness.

That was relieved momentarily by the sleepy musings of a love-struck three-year-old. "Gilli pwetty," Chance mumbled midst dreamland.

My eyes got big. And when Finn and I looked at each other, we both busted out a quick spurt of airy laughter. I brought my hand up to my mouth, and Finn shook his head back and forth.

"He gets that from you," I tried to keep things light. "This girls are beautiful business."

"Not all girls. Just one," Finn said and purposefully looked at me. When the compliment left me speechless, he resorted back to neutral family business. "Call Summer. Let her know we're almost there. I'll wait for her in the car to take her home if you can get Chance up to the penthouse."

We were both very vulnerable and still a little upset. But our conversation in that park helped us gain some perspective from the other's point of view. And, hopefully, that was going to be the bridge to recovery.

***

After tucking Chance in and checking on Arinn, I changed into my pseudo pajamas— a black pair of sweats and pink tank—and went back downstairs to the living room. My bare feet were curled up on the sofa when Finn returned from dropping Summer off at the apartment she and Ingo were now sharing on the lower east side. I watched as Finn entered and placed his keys on the hook.

He looked more weary and more relaxed at the same time. His face showed me the hours and days of stress, but his attire was now stripped down to just the button-down shirt and slacks. Entering the living room, he tossed the jacket and tie he had been carrying onto the arm of the high back chair and slid his phone onto the coffee table in front of me.

When I stood up to greet him, I hadn't considered what I was going to say. But for the first time in a while, my immediate thoughts weren't harsh and cruel. They were right and honest. "Finn? We're fixing this, right? Please. I don't like fighting with you."

"Lara, I love you."

He could have stopped there. Because even though I knew it, I had needed to hear it. And once I did, I was pretty sure I knew the answer to my question. And it was the one I wanted.

"Seeing that text threw me," he continued with honesty. "I'm scared to death of losing you. There are so many days when I simply can't fathom how I was so lucky that you not only reentered my life but that you weren't with someone else."

"I never told you this, but that spring?" I mimicked his subdued tone. "The year we were dating? That's when I realized…I didn't know it, but I think I was subconsciously waiting for you. I had been waiting for you to come back into my life. Sure, what happened that summer out of high school with the pregnancy and Macon had guarded me to relationships, but I think I also, somehow, knew it was always going to be you. There was no one else for me. There never had been and there never would be."

"Lara," He paused at my sentimentality, taking a physical and emotional mini-step forward. But he stopped and got back to what his current concern was. "I don't think I can handle him being in your life." He spoke of Miller. "I'm sorry. I know that makes me weak or whatever…"

"I should have told you," I admitted and conceded. "I should have told you all along. But I swear to you, Finn, I never thought of Miller as anything besides a friend…maybe not even that—an old acquaintance. I will stop talking with, texting, everything altogether. He means nothing to me." And I meant it. I didn't need to be stubborn. No matter of the innocence of the act, I didn't need to cause my husband pain.

His phone had, ironically, started buzzing at the tail end of my pledge. He had it set on vibrate for the wedding and reception and had yet to switch to the ring mode. He looked at me first and then down to the phone before picking it up and swiping it to see the caller ID.

I watched as his face seemed to twitch before he said, "I…" He hesitated. "Let me see about this, okay? I…okay?"

"Yeah."

I tried real hard not to sigh. It was something I, unfortunately, had been quite used to since we had first started dating—the interruptions, the demands. But the inopportune timing right then really bit. Finn looked at me for a long second more and then walked outside to the wraparound balcony.

I went into the kitchen to find some tea. Even though I would have much rather preferred coffee, I wanted something more calming and easier to make. A couple minutes of boiling water in the microwave and an additional few minutes of dunking the tea bag, and I was set. I sat back down on the sofa and sipped my hot beverage while watching my husband through the glass balcony doors. He had his back toward me for most of the conversation, but he turned at the end. Now looking right at me, I could tell he was still talking to the person on the other end, but I had no idea about what or how he was feeling.

A moment later, he reentered the living room with the

disconnected phone in his hand. "Listen, I've gotta…I've gotta get out of here. I can't breathe right now. I need to breathe. I need to get out."

I immediately stood up. "What? What's going on?"

"Nothing."

"Nothing? You were pissed at me when I left a couple days ago and now we're in the middle of—"

"I can't." He pleaded more with his eyes than his voice.

"What's wrong? Who was on the phone?" Something had changed, and it seemed to have happened with that phone call.

"It's too much."

"Finn…"

My anger at him wanting to bail on our serious conversation was now turning into concern. This was totally not like him…at all. He was not one to go when the going got tough. Especially when it came to me and especially when I was telling him what he wanted to hear.

"You all right?" he asked, subconsciously playing with the phone in his hands.

"Yeah," I answered in an automatic but confused way. I didn't know what else to say. I wasn't all right because our conversation had just taken another abrupt U-turn. But, in a way, I felt slightly better than before due to the mere fact that Finn was asking about my well-being. In that sense, he was being more like the man I knew.

"Yeah, okay." Satisfied, I suppose, with my response, he started walking toward the door and his keys.

"Finn?" I followed him still confused by what just happened. "Can you at least tell me where you're going?"

"I don't know."

"Are you doing this to get back at me?" I nearly whispered as the thought crossed my mind.

"What?" He was distraction and confusion rolled into one.

"For leaving the other night." The tears were pooling behind my eyes when I said the words. I could feel their heaviness like the air in the room.

"No," he answered immediately. "But, Lar, this is one of *those* times." His eyes darted back and forth on mine, wanting me to understand that on rare occasions his PTSD triggers made him feel like it was too much, and he didn't want me around it. "I'm going to bust. I'll be back." He leaned in and kissed me on the forehead. "Okay."

It was the first time his lips had been on my body for weeks, and I tried to hold onto that feeling and hopefully positive meaning. But I was still even more confused by the action of his sudden departure that accompanied it. No cup of tea or even bottle of wine, if I had dared, would be able to calm my nerves.

I stayed awake, trying to replay our conversation every which way—trying to figure out where he went and why. And, yet, I had no resolution. But the fact that I was mad that he had gone without explanation stopped me from immediately investigating further. Eventually, though, worry took over.

I was debating whether to text him when I picked up my phone and remembered the video Vanessa had said she had shot of Finn and I on the dance floor. I pressed play and watched the opening image of Finn drawing me into his embrace. I saw our natural fit despite the tension I knew was lingering inside. And I saw how my face seemed to relax in his arms. Most importantly, I saw what I couldn't have seen in person—I saw his face behind my back. I saw the peacefulness grow as the dance progressed. And even though you couldn't hear the words we spoke to one another, I could see how his comment about dancing with me was spoken in love. I replayed it a couple times, wanting to treasure that moment because so many moments around that one had been quite the opposite.

***

It was a little after one a.m. when I heard him

stumbling around downstairs. I was glad I hadn't turned on the security system as, in the state he was in, I'm pretty sure Finn couldn't have disarmed it. I sat on the top two stairs and just watched as he haphazardly kicked off his shoes, nearly knocking over a ceramic model of the first stadium he had headlined. He swore at it in a chuckling kind of way... in a drunk kind of way. Finn was more drunk than I have seen him in years...possibly ever.

I don't think I made a sound, but I could have. Exasperation mixed with relief probably warranted some kind of exhale from my body. Regardless, it was then that his head did a messy swirl, and he looked up at me.

"Ah, there's my wife. I should see my wife." He pointed his finger at me like he had made a presidential proclamation—one that appeared to have been dictated by someone else. "Hi, wife."

I was processing...processing everything— his actions, his drunk state, his words. My brain wasn't working fast enough to know how to react or what to do. I was happy that he was home and that he was safe. But still, the mystery of what had made him leave in the first place—the reason I was witnessing the scene— troubled me. He had said it wasn't to get back at me. But, was it still about me? Or was it that phone call? And, if so, what was that about?

When he stumbled coming toward me, I cautioned, "Finn, stop! You're going to fall." And I got up from my perch on the stairs.

Thankfully, he did stop. "No, *you* fell." There went the pointy finger again. "You're the one who fell. You...You like almost di – ied."

"I know," I softly agreed, recognizing that he would never get that image—one which *I* still had no memory of—out of his mind. The one of me falling in our suburban home...of me losing our unborn child...of me in a coma.

"Lar..." He started both verbally and again with his clumsy feet.

But I was now down next to him. "C'mon, let's get you on the sofa."

"I don't want to be on the sofa." He whined like he was Chance's age.

"Well, I can't get you upstairs," I argued, trying to encourage him to see my rational option while simultaneously walking us toward the living area.

"You don't want me up there with you."

"What? Finn," I started, but he almost fell over nothing but his own two uncoordinated feet. "Sheez," I lamented, holding him. "Sit down."

He obeyed my directive, flopping in a very uncoordinated way onto the sofa. It took a moment, but he was able to focus his gray eyes on me once I sat down next to him.

"You didn't drive, did you?" I vocalized my fear, thinking of all the ways that abusing alcohol had affected my life.

"No. She wouldn't let me."

She? She? She who?

Finn brought his finger up to the corner of my mouth and tried to force me into a half smile. "Junie," he answered the question I know I didn't ask aloud.

"You were at Eoin's?" I asked.

I should have known that Finn would have gone where he felt family, even though we both knew his uncle was away on a purchasing trip. His uncle's restaurant was a place where people knew him and would look out for him—not try to take advantage of his stardom. And, admittedly, although not usually the jealous type, I was glad the mystery woman was Junie—who besides being Eoin's girlfriend, was also the restaurant manager.

"Yeah. That new bartender really knows how to pour. But he's also a narc." Before I could question, Finn clarified as best he could. "He didn't have to call Junie down."

"I'm glad he did. And I'm glad that's where you went."

I paused for a second and then said more decisively what the previous two statements really meant. "I'm glad you're safe."

"Lara." He said my name with such love and melancholy, I felt the slightest of shivers.

He brought his hand up to my face. Coarser from a summer of strumming a guitar, he glided it along my cheek. And then he kissed me. It was far from being magical, but even in its sloppiness, I could sense the love.

"We would be so good together." Finn was flashbacking to our first unofficial kiss— on the sofa in college. And even though it had taken us years to reconnect after that, that had been our start and those had been his words back then. Why was he being so nostalgic? What was troubling him so? Surely, he knew that we already were —we always had been—good together. "Why didn't you tell me how you were feeling after the bank?"

"I—" I started, trying to keep up with the change of subjects.

"I'm sorry you felt that way. I'm sorry I wasn't there for you. I know all about fear and pain."

"Finn—"

He wasn't letting me get a word in. "You're okay now, though, right? I need to know you're okay. Promise me, Lara. Because I couldn't handle it right now if I thought you weren't."

"You need to sleep." I began spreading the Americana blanket, which had been draped on the back of the sofa, over his body.

"Lar?" He still needed his answer.

"I'm all right." I reassuringly patted his leg and started to get up.

But my husband pulled at my hand with his. "Don't leave," he practically begged. "Everybody leaves. Everybody is—" His voice faded, and I could swear he was almost about to cry.

I sunk back onto the cushion. I couldn't leave. I

wouldn't leave. "Share the blankie."

He looked at me, knowing that I was back on that sofa in college with him, too—reciting another line he had used all those years before. "Okay," he managed and spread out his legs so I could fit between them. I had no sooner rested my head on his chest and readjusted the blanket, than he passed out into a very drunken snore.

CHAPTER SEVENTEEN

I didn't sleep well. It was due to a combination of his shirt buttons agitating my face, my fear of falling off the sofa since his grip on my body had become lax as soon as he passed out, and the fact that my mind was still racing. It didn't matter, though. I was up in a matter of a few hours or so, anyway. The kids made sure of that.

Finn didn't stir as I got up and saw to the kids in their rooms. Chance seemed to immediately leave off where he had the night before. He was bound to retell every moment of the wedding. I was glad that they were all happy moments for him…if not for his parents.

When I couldn't keep them entertained upstairs any longer and knew they needed some sort of breakfast, I brought the kids downstairs. I cautioned Chance, telling him that his father was asleep on the sofa, and we needed to be super quiet for daddy so he could sleep. I told him that we were playing a quiet game, and then a sudden flashback of my early childhood crashed into my brain. I had forgotten all about those similar days when my mother had tried to keep Lane and I hushed around our father's hangovers.

Midway through Chance's bowl of marshmallow-enhanced cereal, Finn started to moan in protest to, I am sure, a raging headache or just the effort of opening his eyes. Chance noticed right away. Our little boy, who had been away from his father for most of the summer, was eager to spend any moment with him. Quiet game was over.

"Daddy!" He popped up from his booster seat in the kitchen in record time.

"Chance!" I loudly whispered, but it was no use.

Running toward the sofa, Chance called out, "You awake now."

Finn mumbled in response, "Give me a minute."

"Daddy, I won quiet game. Arinn—"

"No." Finn was mono-syllabic as he tried to get up.

When Chance bounced on the sofa on top of Finn, that's when it happened. That's when our world was turned completely upside down. That's when I saw what I never, ever imagined I would ever be witness to.

"Damn it, I said, give me a minute." Like thunder and lightning crashing at the same frightening time, Finn's hand suddenly met Chance's face.

Leaving Arinn in her highchair, I hurried into the open living room where Chance, after a hitch in his breath, had started to cry. I buried him into my arms and hauled him away from Finn. The whole world seemed to stand still for a minute. I knew my son was crying, but I couldn't hear him. There was just a low, dull buzzing…and Finn. He was sitting up now, much more alert. His eyes were wide, and they were on us.

And then I snapped out of it. Or, I just snapped. I pulled Chance just slightly away from me, shushing him with as much calmness as I could muster. I looked at his face. It was a little red but not bad. I know he was scared, though. So was I. Scared and beyond mad.

"You're okay, Little Man. You're okay," I cooed, trying to soothe both him and myself.

I glared at Finn, who had yet to say a word. Once

Chance's sobs slowed, I asked him to meet me at the bottom of the stairs. He did as he was told, still looking shell-shocked. I then quickly gathered Arinn in my arms and took Chance's hand to walk up the stairs…to walk away.

Once upstairs, all I wanted to do was cry. But I couldn't. I was the mom. I needed to make sure my kids were not scared. I checked my son's little, innocent face again. The pinkness was already evaporating. But the shock was not.

Before I knew it, I had a plan in action. I didn't even think it through. I just did. It was instinct. It was something my mother never did. I was leaving.

I asked Chance to put the things he had brought in his little overnight bag the day before back in, and I went to the master bedroom to find the special direct number to call Graham at the building's front desk. As the phone rang, I felt like my insides were on fire—spinning, burning fire. I managed to take a deep breath just as Graham answered.

"Hi, Graham. It's Lara." I think my voice sounded normal. How had I managed that? It must have been a learned behavior from living with a performer so long and dealing with being in the public eye. "I need a favor," I continued.

"Sure, Miss Lara. Whatever you need, ma'am."

"Can you call a car service for me? It'll need two car seats." I couldn't drive. I had never driven in that bumper car speedway called Manhattan. But, most of all, I couldn't drive because I was way too emotional.

"Of course. For when?"

"Right now. As soon as possible. We'll be going back home."

"I'll do that right away," he said as I walked back into the next room to see my kids.

The anger began to boil again from its just-above-simmering state. That's when I added a little amendment to the thrown-together plan. "Graham? I'm sorry, but there's something else. Would you mind if Chance came down and you watched him for just a few minutes? I'm so sorry—just Chance for a few minutes, and then I'll be ready for the car."

"No problem, Miss Lara. I would love to have the little guy. I'll be up in a minute to get—"

"No. No. I can bring him down." I hated to bother him even more. "You don't need to—"

"I need to stretch. Besides, Niven is here." He spoke of one of the janitors. "He'll watch the desk for a few. On my way, ma'am."

I hung up, knowing any argument I was going to have was not going to be with the overly-kind front desk man. The arguing was going to be with the man immediately one floor beneath me, and it was going to be huge. It was the reason I needed Chance to be out of the penthouse. Arinn might hear us, but she would not understand. Chance would. He could not be hurt anymore.

I explained to my son how he was going to be Graham's little helper for a few minutes and played it up as quite an honor and special event. Chance liked Graham. So, not only did he not question the proposal, but it got his mind off what had just transpired in the living room. I checked his bag and was throwing some of Arinn's and my things into mine when I heard the door buzz. Sheez, Graham was quick!

I was walking down the steps with Chance, Arinn, and our bags as Finn was answering the door. I was kind of surprised he was up and functioning. He opened our private door knowing it would be Graham, as no one else would have access without our knowledge first.

"Morning," Graham greeted.

"Graham, what's up?" Oblivious to my calling Graham, Finn tried to act normal.

But I think anyone would have noticed he was off. They might not have known whether he was upset or hungover, but there was definitely something. I knew it was both.

"Morning, Miss Lara...Miss Cutie-Pie." He motioned to Arinn in my arms and then said hi to Master Chance, who giggled.

"Good morning, Graham." I responded, setting Arinn and the bags down. "Thanks. I really, really won't be that long." Without looking or, even in the slightest way, acknowledging my husband, I encouraged Chance to go to Graham.

It was then that I think Graham could sense the friction. "That's all right. Whenever. Car is on its way."

I could feel Finn's eyes dart, horrified, in my direction. But I didn't look. Instead, I bent down to our son. "Chance, be good, Little Man. I'll be down in a minute."

"I get to watch the special TVs?" Chance asked excited.

"Yeah, and say 'good morning' to everyone." Graham agreed, taking my little boy's hand. "I might even let you share my donut." As Chance's eyes lit up at that prospect, Graham asked a question. "Would you like me to take those bags, Miss Lara?"

"Um, yes, please." I agreed, handing them over to Graham and thinking it would be much easier to just carry Arinn when I left.

Graham took the bags and started leading Chance through the door. When Finn called out our son's name, I glared at him so strong, he stopped mid-way. Instead, he nodded his head to Graham and closed the door.

"Lara?" Finn asked immediately. When I didn't respond but to walk a few steps away, he tried again. "Lara? What are you doing?"

"Never!" I swiveled around and yelled in such anger, I even scared myself. "Never. Ever. You f-ing want to hit me? You hit me. That..." I stumbled on my words because they were spilling out so fast. "Your son did nothing but want to love you. So help me, Finn..." I didn't know what my threat was, but he didn't give me a chance anyway because somehow, some way, he was going to try to explain.

"I didn't mean to hi—"

But I knew that statement was absurd and didn't deserve to be finished. "You didn't mean to?" I mocked. "Your arm involuntarily wound up in open air and struck him in the face?"

"Jesus! No!" he hollered back. "I was—" He cut off his own words, grabbed at his head, and squinted his eyes in obvious hangover discomfort. "Slow down," he tried while witnessing me shoving things in a plastic bag. "I—"

I didn't. "It's me you're mad at and for no reason. Grow up. Get over it. I talk with a guy every so often. A guy who sav—never mind! You will not see your kids. You're not getting anywhere near them."

"Lara…"

"No! God, I never, ever…no matter what…I never thought you would ev—" Geez, this was the worst pain ever. I couldn't keep this up. I switched gears so I could come to my conclusion. "If you need something from the house, make sure I…that we're not around."

That was it. That was my "so help me." And as much as it hurt and I never imagined in the most crazy, messed up scenarios that I would be saying it, I believed it, and I meant it. What happened had trumped any concerns about his neurosis of being left. My traumatic past surely factoring in my decision, I was determined to do what was right for my children first and foremost.

"Lara, don't. I need you. I need you to understand," he tried.

"No. There's no explanation."

Surprisingly, I had no tears. Not because I wasn't hurt. There was no pain greater. But, because my emotional walls were suddenly so high, I wondered if the clouds were too low to even see me. With that, I scooped up our innocent little girl, who started belting out "da-da" as if she knew the finality of the situation, and I didn't look back.

***

We were a wreck. There really wasn't any other way to describe it. We were like a three-legged dog hobbling along…capable but pitiful. I knew what was missing and so did the kids. They knew, especially Chance, that it was different this time. It wasn't just Finn going away for a few days or even on the road. They could sense it. Arinn was a lot more fussy, and Chance had a billion questions. He wanted to know where Finn was, when he was coming back, and why he hadn't called. No matter what, in the past, Finn would make a point to correspond with us in one form or another on a daily basis. I tried my best to answer my son, but I simply didn't know the answers. When he asked why Finn was suddenly non-existent in our lives, I wanted to scream, "because he's a possessive, messed-up bastard." But, I didn't.

Chance didn't mention the slap or that awful, awful Sunday morning, while I couldn't forget a single second of it. Did Chance forget or was he just so willing to forgive because he wanted his dad around? Did my little man see that I was protecting him? Did he know that even though nothing felt right, it *was* the right thing? Most likely not. He was a little boy wanting his daddy— a daddy who, except for one incident, was the most caring, giving man we all could ask for. But that incident and the days immediately leading up to it had changed so much. They had to. I had lived that life for my first eighteen. I would not let my kids do the same.

I did find it odd that Finn hadn't called or stopped by the house. He was not one to give up, especially when it came to his family. But that was exactly what he seemed to do.

While he may have been fine without talking, I wasn't. I needed to get some of it out, and I certainly couldn't burden my three-and-a-half-year-old and ten-month-old. I knew Lane would understand the most. But I didn't want to tell him. He was my protective older brother. He would want to fly out and beat the crap out of Finn. I didn't need that. And, quite honestly, neither did Finn. Despite everything, I knew no matter where my husband was, he was most likely emotionally beating himself up over what happened with Chance.

I did talk to my mom, but I didn't mention what had happened. She would have been the opposite of Lane. She would have done what she had her entire marriage—rationalized the situation. She would have seen Finn's side—the "just a bad moment, good man" side. And I wasn't ready for that, either.

That Thursday night, with the kids asleep, I tried to occupy my mind with cleaning and following up on correspondence. Sleep had pretty much evaded me the four nights since leaving the penthouse. So I knew not to try for it too early.

With the chores complete, I turned on the TV around ten p.m. That, regrettably, was a mistake. I had forgotten what night it was.

On the screen, two teams were colliding on a lengthy green field. It was the first Thursday night game of the NFL football season. And, of course, Cincinnati was playing. And, of all ironies, they were playing the Jets. It was those same two teams that Finn and I had made our original bet on years before... just after we got engaged. And that wager became an ongoing one. If Cincy lost, fan Finn gave me a massage. And if Cincy won, Finn got to lick chocolate off my body.

It was because of that—because of that silly broadcast on national television— that I cried my first post-penthouse tear. Then I looked at the score. Despite the game being half over, it was still 0-0. Both teams were losing—how ironic. I turned off the television and cried some more.

***

Less than a week later, it was Finn's birthday, and Chance was well aware of it. He was good with his calendar skills because of our multitude of countdowns that summer. And Daddy's September eleventh birthday was displayed prominently on it. Despite my denials and kindly-worded protests, Chance had convinced himself that Finn was coming home for a birthday party that day. My heart, which I had been so carefully guarding, broke into pieces knowing that my son's was going to do the same when his wish didn't come true. I tried to distract him by letting him watch his favorite movie and by taking the kids to the library's story hour.

When we reentered the house afterwards, though, Chance zoomed around in search of, without saying it, his father. I gave in then. I decided to call Finn and let Chance talk with him. Besides, if I admitted it, I wanted to make sure he was okay, too. While at first I had been relieved that he hadn't contacted us, my emotions now teetered between mad that he didn't care to and concerned why he hadn't.

But Finn's phone went straight to voice mail. Stunned that he didn't pick it up, I tried again, getting the same result. With my preschooler's big eyes anxiously looking up at me, I explained that I would try again, but that he would have to leave a message. Chance seemed disappointed, yet accepting of the compromise.

As the phone was dialing that third time, I asked Chance if he remembered what to do. He nodded his head up and down as I handed him my phone. "Wait for Daddy's voice to stop and then you can talk."

"Hi, Daddy." Chance spoke into the phone and looked up at me proud for following the directions.

"Why are you calling him?" I asked, nodding to the phone still up to his cheek.

"Happy birthday, Daddy. I sing to you." Chance

looked up at me again, and I started him off on the traditional Happy Birthday song.

While our mini-lyricist sang, I picked up Arinn, who had begun fussing. But now I knew why —she was getting two more upper teeth just to add to the misery. "Anything else?" I prompted Chance when he had finished his serenade.

"I miss you." Chance spoke honestly into the phone. "Arinn is cwying and sometimes Mommy, too."

God, I thought I had been good about keeping that undercovers. "Chance, you need to finish," I said once I regained my bearings.

"I love you. Bye, Daddy." He obliged and handed me the phone, which I promptly hung up.

***

My emotions were rolling like the pirate ship ride at the amusement park that always left me sick. First of all, I couldn't believe he wouldn't pick up the first time. But then to see that I had called three times in a row? And then to hear Chance's sweet little voice singing to him and telling him how much he missed him? Why didn't he call back? So, okay, maybe he was in the shower or recording, and he didn't hear the phone. But, it was now the next day and there was still no return call from my husband. I was furious…until my brain flew to the other end of the spectrum. What if something had happened to him? What if he was hurt or…God, who knew? Well, the world knew. He was Finn Murphy, after all. He couldn't hide. Everyone would know if he had been hurt. And just as I was thinking that, the phone call came in.

I answered immediately. I wasn't playing games. I was pissed that it had been twenty-four hours since Chance had left that message, never mind a week and a half since speaking with him at all.

"You're calling back now?" I didn't give a glimmer of a

traditional greeting.

"I misplaced my cell yesterday," Finn stated plainly.

"Really? How could that happen? It's always glued to your hand." My response was coated in pure, sugary sarcasm.

"Lara…God, give me a break."

"Give *you* a break?" I bellowed. "Why haven't you called?" I was doing figure eight after figure eight around the entire first floor.

"I told you."

"Before the phone missing," I clarified.

"You told me you didn't want—I was trying to respect that. I can't win. Nothing I… Nothing is—"

"Are you drunk?" I asked, hearing his rambling starting.

"What if I am?" That was enough of a confirmation.

For one thing, it was what time of day? For another… I cut my own mental frustration short. I didn't need to answer his question. It didn't deserve an answer.

"Good-bye, Finn."

He jumped in with his interjection. "I want to talk with Chance."

"Are you kidding me? No. No way. He's sleeping," I semi-lied.

There was a fifty-fifty shot that our son was awake vs. sleeping. His afternoon naps were really going to the wayside. But at least he was up in his room keeping quiet, which had been our Mommy-needs-naptime-too deal.

"Is he—" Finn started.

"You're not talking with him. It's bad enough that the last time he saw you…" I let my voice fade, not wanting to even vocalize the words myself. "Now to be drunk? I'm not doing this."

"Baby…"

"Don't. I'm not your ba—I'm not—"

"Lara, please, I'm glad you called."

"Well, I hope you enjoyed it. Sober up, Finn."

I didn't give him a chance to respond. I promptly hung up and sunk to the floor in that random spot where our telephone conversation had suddenly come to an end. God! How had our beautiful life become this?

CHAPTER EIGHTEEN

"What's going on? He's cancelled everything. Everything! And, he won't return our calls— no one's. I even had Carter try. Are you okay? Are the kids okay?"

As I listened to Reese's concerned, harried voice, I was almost sorry that I had picked up the phone in the first place. But I figured if she was calling my private cell phone, there might be something that affected Finn's personal life. I didn't want to have to explain anything about what was going on between the two of us to Finn's crew…even someone as close to us as Reese. That was for him to deal with. Yet, listening to her, haunted me. It seemed that Finn had not only shut down from me and our kids but, apparently, the rest of the world, too.

"Lara?" she called out my name, interrupting my internal thoughts.

"Yeah," I answered. "Yeah, we're all fine." Well, that was a lie… at least emotionally.

"Then what's going on? I've never, ever seen him like this, and I've been through a lot with him over the years."

"I know."

"Even with Wyatt." Reese brought up that horrific time when his nephew was killed, which also, unfortunately, coincided with the only other time in our history that Finn and I had argued so badly that we separated.

"Yeah," I said with grieving recollection. "Reese? You'll have to ask him."

"I'm trying. I've been trying for days. Can you just put him on the phone?"

"I can't."

"Well, if he's standing there, can you at least tell him to call me? He needs to make a statement about the noms."

"What nom—" I started, only realizing I should have known about the CMA nominations, which would have been announced that week.

"What do you mean what noms? Song of the Year and Male Vocalist, of course."

"Not Entertainer of—?" I asked of Finn's customary nomination. I'm sure that was a mini-blow for my husband's already fragile state.

"Lara," Reese cut me off, identifying my neglect of the situation. "What's going on? Are you—"

It was my turn to interject. I didn't want to answer a direct question, especially to someone— even a genuinely nice someone— in the publicity world. "I know you're worried, but I can't help. You'll need to find a way to talk with him."

"You can't?" she asked much slower, for sure putting some pieces together.

"I'm sorry. I gotta go." I wasn't going to answer any more— that was up to Finn. "The baby is—"

But, I hated using my own child as a lie. It seemed like bad karma. And I certainly didn't need any of that.

"What?" she questioned.

"I'm gonna go. Bye, Reese."

***

And it wasn't just Reese calling. Carter, Carter via Vanessa, others…were concerned about Finn. But I didn't return their calls. I couldn't keep up the façade of everything being all right. But I also couldn't reveal the truth. In that sense, I was becoming as much of a recluse as Finn was.

But why? What was going on with him? I mean, I knew he was upset about the whole Miller thing. But I thought we were getting past that. I thought we *were* past that. And then he left that night...out of the blue. And he was drunk...so drunk. And the hit. I shivered thinking of it.

I had thought about that morning so many times. But, as time passed, I believed the encounter with Chance had been a weird, isolated incident— a terrible thing where worlds collided at the wrong moment. I knew it wasn't on purpose or with deliberation. And knowing him like I did, I was sure he was extremely remorseful.

And I loved him. I did. I wouldn't even try to deny that. For as angry as I had been, I still couldn't fathom a life without him. But I wouldn't—couldn't—do it if he was more interested in drinking and not making an effort with us. Where was the Finn I knew? What happened to him?

And then... I got the call from Nola. As par for my recent telephone behavior, I didn't pick it up. I let it go to voice mail. But when I did listen to her message, out of all the phone calls, hers concerned me the most.

"Lara? Lara?" Her voice started on the recorded message. "Hey, listen. I know you're probably ignoring my call and, first of all, I hope you know, you're more than a sister-in-law to me. I don't know what went down with you two. Finn won't tell me. But I'm sure it had to be something big for you to leave. I'm not... It's not my place, I get it. But you need to put all of that aside. Please. I didn't know that Finn didn't tell you."

It was like all those years ago—when we had broken up and Nola was being cryptic telling me I didn't know everything. Back then, it was that I didn't know Finn suffered from depression and PTSD. I didn't know he took medication and had therapy for it. But I did now. So what did she mean that he didn't tell me? It couldn't be that. And Finn and I told each other everything... no omissions. I pressed replay because I realized I had blocked out her voice as it had continued.

"Lara? Lara? Hey, listen. I know you're probably ignoring my call and, first of all, I hope you know, you're more than a sister-in-law to me. I don't know what went down with you two. Finn won't tell me. But I'm sure it had to be something big for you to leave. I'm not... It's not my place, I get it. But you need to put all of that aside. Please. I didn't know that Finn didn't tell you. You need to talk with him. Everything's a mess. It's—" It was then that I could hear her stifling tears. She continued, "But Finn's not. He's all right now. He's been here since Friday... showed up really early. Lara? He's been with us. And you need to talk with him. If not for him, for the kids and for Mom and Pop."

Damn it if I didn't play that again two more times. And each time I got more confused and even more concerned. It was Thursday. She had said he had been with them since Friday. That was almost a week. Friday was a day after I had spoken with him. What was a mess? If it wasn't Finn—which would have been my number one guess— what was it?

Her call had come in just as the kids and I had finished lunch. I had been set to drive them to preschool so they could have a couple hours of socialization and I could get some errands done. Needing some time before reacting to my sister-in-law's message/plea, I decided to proceed with my plan.

But after I dropped the kids off, I sat in the preschool parking lot and added one more to-do to my list. I needed to know. I wanted to know. And although I wished he— especially if he was in town—was the one to do it, I decided to call Finn right then and there.

But I got his voice mail. Exhaling out of frustration,

relief, and nerves over what the conversation was going to hold, I left a message. "Is there something going on that I don't know about? Reese has been calling, and now Nola left a message that I need to talk to you. I want to talk, Finn. I don't understand what happened...any of it. We need to talk. But you need to be sober and you need to be...Are you okay?" That was enough. I couldn't handle any more, especially when I had no idea how receptive he was to any of it.

As I sat in the still, quiet car wondering what to do next, his text came in. *I'm @ Dr. Bartola's right now. I've been here every day this week. He can call U if U need 2 confirm it.*

I believe U. I texted back, feeling calmer that he was in the right place.

Can we do this in person?

And that calmness skyrocketed to nerves. I knew his suggestion was best, but it still scared the hell out of me. We hadn't seen each other in just shy of three weeks. And I knew this wasn't going to be a reunion like when he was away for a similar amount of time on the road. This was going to be gut-wrenchingly serious. But I prayed it would conclude with a positive resolution.

Can you come to the house now? Just dropping the kids @ preschool. Don't want them 2 B a part of this. I texted, admitting to myself there really wasn't a better time. We needed that time alone.

It seemed like it took him a long time to respond, but maybe it was because I was just anxious about confirming that we were actually going to meet. *It'll B at least an hour. I'm in the city.*

OK

This time his answer was immediate. *I'll B there.*

***

I don't think it even registered where I was awaiting his arrival until I actually heard his car pull into our drive. I was curled up on the built-in bench in the foyer. It was the same spot I usually claimed when he would text me that he was on his way home from a trip. Even if it was in the middle of the night, I would pull myself, blanket in tow, and wait for him there because I couldn't wait the other seconds it would take for him to find me in the house. Weird how I found myself right there at that moment. The cause of Finn's absence had been for a completely different reason than ever before, and, consequently, the anxiety I was feeling was also a different strain. But that bench, I suppose, had brought me some sort of continuity…some sense that some things don't change.

I think I had been sitting there almost the entire time since driving home directly from the preschool. I don't remember doing anything else. My mind had been so muddled since our texting and the prospect of seeing him again. The sound of his car engine coming to a halt and then, a couple moments later, a car door being shut, made me look at the decorative hall clock. He had gotten to our house in decent time—not too fast to make me worry that he was driving unsafely and not too late to make me fear he wasn't coming at all. I shook my head, trying not to care that much. I needed to remain semi-stoic. There was a lot of hurt and pain to get through, after all.

Right before he opened the front door, I realized he had parked in the driveway. He hadn't used his remote to go straight into his spot in the garage. Why was that? Was he making for a quick getaway? Or, did he feel like a guest in his own home?

I know he was shocked when he saw me sitting there on that bench. He stopped immediately in his stride. Was he thinking of all the times I had warmly greeted him in that same spot? Or was he thinking he still had a moment or two to collect himself before facing the proverbial music? There were so many questions. We had always known what the other was thinking and feeling more than ourselves. And now it didn't feel that way at all.

Finn looked put together on the surface. He was wearing new black boot-style tennis shoes, gray slacks, and a tight black T-shirt. But when he took his sunglasses off, I could see the other half. His eyes, looking more muted than bright gray, were worn, and he was paler and scruffier than usual.

I'm sure I didn't fare much better. Even though the preschool knew me as Chance and Arinn's mom, I also knew that every time I stepped out of our home, I was Mrs. Finn Murphy. I might not have the intensity of flashbulbs, etc. that Finn had to deal with, but I was always aware of being a representative. So, I had on the comfort clothes of dark gray leggings and a long, bright pink, V-neck hoodie that I felt like hiding under. But I also splashed it up with a snazzy black and gold belt.

Somehow, I found my feet and stood up. Finn took a step toward me. But it felt too close. God, my husband felt too close and he was feet away.

My reaction wasn't unnoticed by that man in front of me. "Oh, damn. This is so hard," he admitted and then, in the silence that followed, asked, "How are the kids?" There would be no traditional "hi, baby" and loving hug as a greeting.

"They're all right." I couldn't stand there— it felt too closed in. "Kitchen?" I suggested, which I am sure seemed completely out of the blue to him. "Or do you want to talk in the great room?" God, he pulled his car in like a guest, and now I was acting like the hostess.

"Yeah," was all he replied but followed me.

After he sat down on one end of the sofa, I rested up against the opposite end's armrest. But I couldn't sit still for even less than a minute. Standing once again, I instinctively crossed my arms over my chest and said, "First of all, you're okay, right? Your meds...drinking..." I sensed that he was, but confirming it would make a much more solid launching point.

"Yeah. Better." His demeanor was so internal.

I plowed on. "Then I deserve some answers."

His exhale was noticeable but not exuberant. "I know."

"Finn, why won't you look at me?" I thought about the fact that even in his lowest moments, even after what happened with Chance, Finn had always been able to meet my gaze. "What? Why won't you look me in the eyes?"

"I have to tell you something." He had hardly spoken since entering the house. And, before that, he had texted me in lieu of an actual verbal conversation. And now…now his eyes were on anything but me. What was he trying to avoid?

Oh, God…a sickening thought screeched through my brain. "Finn?" I asked, knowing that in just that one slow syllable of his name I was asking so much more.

And then came the answer to the unsaid question— the answer I hadn't wanted to hear. "I'm …God, I'm so sorry." Finally on mine, his watery eyes spoke of pain, guilt, and pure emotion. "She didn't mean anyth—"

"Oh…oh, God." I cut him off with my nearly unintelligible words. I suddenly felt like I couldn't breathe. Putting my hands to my knees, I was trying hard to just stand nonetheless inhale, live, and comprehend. I knew I had asked it, but I, honestly, hadn't expected the answer. "Please tell me you didn't."

"Lara…" I have never heard my name pronounced— not only from him but anyone—in such a gut-wrenching manner. And it was all he managed to get out.

"Really?" I was starting to move past my denial, even though my question didn't appear so. "Really?" I cried out. "When? Who?"

"Lara…"

"When?"

How could I have not known? How, all of a sudden, was it so apparent on his face? How was this happening?

"On the tour?" I sputtered in a voice I hardly recognized as my own. "When I…because I wasn't there?"

"No!" he exclaimed vehemently and then, "Last…last

week."

My hands still braced on my knees, I tried, with limited success, to erect my body to a semi-standing position. "We...we're apart...We're not together because of something you did—not me—you. And you think...you just went and made love to someone else?" I was going to say more but dry heaves were violating my body.

He was more adamant now as he stood. "I didn't make love to—"

"What?" I managed to regulate my body enough to challenge him. "You—"

"Oh, God. God. Lara, I only want to make love to one woman, and that is you."

"Don't lie to me, Finn!" I screamed, shaking my head and glaring hard and strong. I knew what he had just admitted. And I could see the guilt branded all over his face.

"I'm not. I'm not," he countered. "That's why I'm telling you. I ...God, yeah. God help me, I let some newbie singer...she gave me a blowjob and then I stop— It made me sick." He was talking now, and it was kind of a good thing because I couldn't. "I know that doesn't help you. But I was messed up. I know it's not an excuse, but I was drunk, off the meds, and...I was angry. I was so angry. I wanted to hurt. And, yes, she wanted me to fuck her and I...I couldn't. I wouldn't. I couldn't hurt you. I knew I needed help. So I went straight...I went straight to Nola's. Besides church and Dr. Bartola's, I've been there this whole week. I've hardly slept because I knew I had to tell you. I can't lie to you even though I know it is hurting you beyond all boundaries. I promised you I would never lie to you. I...I know I threw away the best thing I have in this world. I knew it then. And I knew it when I...when...with Chance...God. I'm telling you, Lar, I didn't mean to do that to him. It was an accident. I sat up as he..." Finn stopped and then, sounding even more defeated, continued with, "But I knew it didn't matter. I knew when we talked last week, you would never forgive me for what happened with him. I had nothing…nothing in this world. And I wanted to hurt."

"You deserve to hurt." The venom was in my words and in my piercing eyes. I certainly wasn't afraid to look at him.

We both took a moment to breathe before Finn said, "I know this probably doesn't matter, but it was once…the…the woman. And it will never come out. I made sure. She's not going to be anywhere near me—"

"I don't give a damn about her!" I belted out. "You're the one I gave a damn about, and you are the one who broke vows, promises…trust. You are the one who hurt me. I can't believe you…you…Oh, my God!"

Finn momentarily closed his eyes and then slowly opened them again. "I know," he spoke in the softest of voices.

"Finn, why? Why did you do that? Go to someone else?" I was trying not to cry. I had been hoping the afternoon was going to be so much more but, yet, the punches kept coming. "God, didn't you know that I was just protecting us—our kids, me, us— by leaving? I was mad…for good reason. I don't know if it was an accident or a hangover ramification, but I do know that what happened with Chance wasn't you. And once I cooled down and things settled, I knew we would be able to turn it around."

"You have more faith in me than I do."

"I guess so," I answered plainly.

And then I watched as Finn pretty much just went to pieces. He sank back down onto the sofa and started rubbing his eyes. I knew there were tears coming then, and I couldn't help but pause at the rarity. Alongside the loss of his nephew, this was the lowest I had ever seen my husband. And I knew there was due cause—the destruction of our vows— but the tiniest part of me ached for him.

"I can see you are trying again. I know you," I offered because both of those facts were undeniable. "What derailed you? What led to this—the drinking...the...What happened? It couldn't have just been me talking with Miller. I at least deserve to know what led to this...what destroyed us."

Finn's low, aching, grunted sound told me that my words had cut him to the core. But, all of them were the truth. Even in the midst of my own agony, I knew from years of loving him that something had shaken him so bad that he hadn't been able to keep things under control. And, I needed to know what and why.

"Finn?" I asked with just a tad more kindness. "What?"

"I need you, Lara. And I know I don't deserve you." When I didn't acknowledge his statement, he confirmed that there was, indeed, a missing piece of the puzzle—a very big and devastating piece. "Pop's sick. The cancer...it's returned."

"Whaaat?" The word seemed to take forever to come out of my mouth.

I understood, but I didn't. I knew, but I couldn't accept. I couldn't deal with any more. Yet, this eclipsed everything. Zak Murphy had been sick the year before Finn and I had become a couple. I hadn't known my father-in-law as anything but healthy.

I sank onto the coffee table, not wanting to join him on the sofa, yet not being able to stand any longer. Between Finn trying to gather himself back together and me just wanting to absorb the news, we both seemed to need to take a moment before I asked, "What are they doing?"

"It's metastasized."

"Oh, God. Oh, my G—" I was trying to resist my own tears. "That's what Nola meant about me needing to know."

"Yeah," he said quietly.

"I...Oh, God, Finn, whatever happens with you and me, that man is my father. He—"

"Please don't say that."

"What?" I asked, slightly taken aback that Finn wouldn't recognize how much I loved his family. "He is more of a dad to me than mine ever was. I love him. I—"

"Don't say whatever happens with us." He clarified his previous statement and then emphasized with, "Please…Please."

"I…God…Oh." I wasn't able to put anything together. Every emotion had been thrown at me in the matter of a couple minutes—hate, sadness, fear, love. "When did you find out?" I finally managed.

"They called a couple days before I came back. He had been sick and wasn't getting better. They kind of blew it off, but I could tell they were worried because they were going to the doctor." While Finn went back to his sad, less hurried voice, I thought about the timeline of what he was saying. On top of missing the pills right before coming home, he had found that news out. It was the reason he was so anxious right after the tour…the reason for how he reacted to Miller. "Then the night of the wedding…" He stumbled verbally while recalling. "The phone call I got…they confirmed it."

"Oh. Oh, baby…" The loving moniker fell out of my mouth naturally as I not only hurt for him but realized exactly what phone call he was referring to.

Maybe I had been right and we had been making our way back to one another that night. Finn hadn't gotten drunk because of his anger toward me and my correspondence with Miller. It had been because of his dad and that call…the devastating news of cancer.

"Why? Why didn't you tell me?" My voice was softer, too. "Finn, is your dad…is he getting treatment?" When Finn silently shook his head in a negative way, I felt the tears well up in my eyes. "Is he…?" I started but couldn't finish.

"There's nothing I can do. There's nothing anyone can do. I love him, Lara. I won't know what to do without him

240

in this world. I won't know what to do when he is gone. He can't...he can't." He had no problem looking at me now—most likely because he was stripped emotionally bare and needed support.

It dawned on me then what Finn had been drunkenly slurring after coming home from Eoin's bar. He asked me not to leave because everyone was leaving. I didn't know who he was referring to then. But I sadly did now.

I tried to gain the strength to put aside my own grief, on top of the resentment and anger, to say something encouraging to him. "All you can do is be there for him...and your mom. Just be their son." I thought about the next sentence before I said it but did anyway. It is what needed to be said and done. "And I will be there for him...and for you."

"I lo—"

But there was no way I was going to be able to hear that. "Don't." I verbally stopped him. "Let's just get through this. Let's help your dad."

"But I do. I do love you, Lara. I—"

"Stop, Finn," I said a little more adamantly while standing and physically backing away. "That hurts too much right now." I couldn't handle his declaration of love. It muddled my already murky, messed-up mind.

"Lara?" When I didn't do anything but take another retreating step, he stood to meet me. "Lara?" He conceded with my next step. "Okay."

Despite knowing about my father-in-law or maybe because of it, my anger started to boil up again. Finn's father was going to die—probably soon from what I could gather—and it made me angry to lose such a vital, loving, giving, strong human being. But there wasn't anything I could do about it.

I *could* do something, however, about my anger that raged because of his son's stupid, drunken, hurtful choice one night a week before. Letting loose of all my emotions, I started smacking, smacking, smacking Finn's chest at the same time as my tears started. "How could you? How could you jeopardize us? I hate you so much for that."

Finn took the blows straight on while trying not to flinch. I think it was the part of him that he had said wanted to hurt... wanted the pain. When I eventually slowed my assault, Finn tried to pull me into his chest. I struggled in his arms, wanting to deny him, yet craving the act of being comforted. Breaking free, I turned from his grasp, not wanting him to see any more of how much I hurt.

After a moment of regulating our collective breathing, Finn said to my still-turned back. "I'm sorry. I understand. I'll go."

My hands, which had been hugging my body, rose up to my face to create a covering escape. I waited another moment, slowly turned, and then let my hands fall to my sides. Finn had started to walk away.

"Don't." My voice was just above a whisper. When he turned to face me once again, I said, "Stay." I took a deep, deep breath, mentally accepting what I was saying. "I have to pick up the kids. They need to see you, and I think you need to see them. You are...you are okay now, right?"

Finn's surprised but grateful eyes met mine. "With meds ...anger? Yeah. Yeah. I promise. How's Chance? Is he mad or scared or—"

"He's fine. He misses you. Kids..." I emphasized the word so he was sure to get the point that my offer was about the kids ...for the kids. And then I repeated it for the same purpose. "Kids have a remarkable fortitude to forgive."

By the look on his face, I knew he understood. "I would really like to see them."

"Okay." I pushed my fingers underneath my eyes, willing the last remnants of the water show to stop. "I'll go get them."

"Lar," He paused with tentativeness. "Let me. Let me get them. I want to."

I agreed for the simple reason that I needed time. I needed legitimate, uncontested time to myself. I needed time to think about everything that in the matter of virtually minutes had gone down in that great room. And having to obey the rules of the road or listen to a three-year-old reenact his afternoon or a ten-month-old babble endlessly didn't match the requirements.

CHAPTER NINETEEN

But it didn't matter. Finn's commute back and forth to the preschool wasn't enough time. I hadn't gained any perspective. In fact, I think I was even more frozen than when I had initially been waiting for him in the foyer. I wondered if there would ever be enough time to understand how I was supposed to feel when my whole world was completely falling apart around me.

I don't know if Chance reacted to seeing his dad for the first time in weeks by growling at him like a dog or running to him like he was the best gift ever. I knew he missed Finn, but I wasn't sure how he would behave, especially when it was a complete surprise. Regardless, by the time I ventured in from the cloud-covered patio and joined them in the great room, they all appeared to be in good humor. Both kids seemed to delight in the fact that their dad was around again. Arinn's giggles were showing off her new teeth, and there were no visible ramifications of the incident at the penthouse between Finn and Chance. I wondered if Chance even remembered it. I wished I could forget. I wished I could forget so much.

When Finn glanced at me upon my arrival, Chance must have sensed something. Not only by his choice of words but by the way he said them. "Daddy, you going again?"

I could see the guilt screech across my husband's face. I wasn't sure if it was guilt for what he did or guilt that he was going to leave. So, before he could answer, I said, "Of course not."

My words not only surprised me but they also shocked Finn. He looked at me again to mentally confirm. I blinked once. I could not let Chance or Arinn go through seeing him leave again so soon or be away for an extended period of time. If I knew nothing else, I knew I had to protect their little psyches. How was it going to work? I had no idea. But it needed to.

"Yay!" Chance bounced into his father's arms...and I walked away.

Finn found me just a few moments later with my arms wrapped around my legs sitting on the bed and staring out the window stricken with fresh raindrops. "I can leave," he offered. "I can explain to him that—"

"Do you want to?" I slid my hands down from my knees onto my shins.

"God, Lara, no, of course not."

"Okay, then. I'm just going to bring a few of my things upstairs." I stood up and went toward the armoire.

"I'll go up." He was sad but resigned.

"I said I'll do it." I spoke more definitively. I didn't want one more thing to argue about. And no matter how many years we had been married, somewhere deep down, I still considered the houses, the wealth—all of it—Finn's. So, I would be the one to relocate but not leave...neither of us could leave.

***

That night, I retreated to the guest room and its bed early. I mumbled something about forgetting to call someone and just walked out of the room, not returning that night. Finn would have to figure out how to put Chance and Arinn to bed. After all, it had to be his turn. I had been a single parent far too long.

I slumped on the bed and turned off the side light. It didn't take much for one tear to turn into a deluge. It was going to take a whole desert for the monsoon to stop.

***

Finn wanted to go into the city that next morning for his Friday session with Dr. Bartola. I had never known him to go on a daily basis. He rarely, in fact, went at all. The meds, meditation, his life—it had all been working. Until…until it didn't. I'm sure they had a lot to talk about and sort through. And, since seeing me, Finn most likely had a whole new list of discussion topics. I was glad that he was going for a couple reasons—the obvious one being I knew Dr. Bartola would help him and keep him on track. But also because we couldn't be in the same house together for any lengthy period of time. The stress and the strain was enormous. I needed to be there for him, for my in-laws. and for my kids, but I couldn't be present in the way I used to be. There was too much clutter. There was too much pain. There was simply too much.

So once Finn returned from his appointment, admittedly a little more zen-like, he agreed to watch the kids while I went to my old workplace. I had been wanting to visit with my ex-colleagues and answer any questions my replacement might have. But every time one of them asked about Finn, my stomach knotted and I limited my talk to quick semi-truths. Then, afterwards, I ran some errands that I had been meaning to do while the kids had been at preschool the day before. Ironically, picking up my automatic birth control reorder was on the list. That made me laugh and cry.

Once I got home, we tried to spend some time together by eating dinner with the kids. Thank goodness

Chance was in a chatty mood. I wasn't sure exactly what he was talking about, though, because my mind was so clouded. I was back in that tunnel from after the bank. I wondered if Finn was, too. He had the same glaze in his eyes that I knew must be in my mirror. Afterward, we went our separate ways. I took an extra-long shower and played games with Chance and Arinn, while Finn went off to call his folks and Nola.

Before the incident at the penthouse, when we were angry and hurt with one another, we knew it and we talked about it. And even though at times it felt like we wouldn't get through it, I knew deep down we would. But this…this felt so foreign…so odd…so different. I was so hurt by Finn's actions that I was emotionally numb. I was simply concentrating on just putting one foot forward at a time. I knew there had to be pain and anger, but I couldn't even feel it. And if I allowed myself a moment to think about what Finn was going through, I knew it was probably double mine.

***

After waking up in the middle of the night and not being able to get back to sleep, I decided to go down to the kitchen and make some tea. My laptop was down there, too. Maybe I could play some games until I felt drowsy again. Throwing on my fluffy gray slippers, I ventured down the stairs only to find Finn, in white boxers and a T-shirt, stretched out on the sofa. His hands were behind his head and he was simply staring at the ceiling.

"Couldn't sleep either?" I said, surprised that I even was asking.

He shifted his body to a more upright sitting position. "The bed doesn't seem natural without you. I'm… I'm not used to that…there."

"I am," I said with a mix of honesty and cruelty—it was a fact that Finn was gone a lot.

I made the decision to sit down on the sofa with him. I believed the offer was implied by his new body arrangement. And things seemed calmer...softer. Perhaps it was because it was the middle of the night. Perhaps it was because there weren't two little darlings running around. Perhaps because we had given each other a little space.

"Why didn't you tell me about your dad?" I asked still not understanding and a little hurt.

He sighed. "Think about it. I got home and, God, seeing that text was the last thing I needed."

Crap, we weren't going to rehash Miller again, were we? That should be the last of our concerns. "But—" I started.

"Nothing was confirmed, anyway," he interjected, obviously not wanting to take that bend in the road, either. "He had a cold— ears, throat, runny nose, headache, backache..."

"But when it was confirmed, Finn. Why didn't you—"

"That night? The night of Reese's wedding?"

"You could have told me. I thought we were...I don't know. I thought things were getting better. Even if they weren't—"

"They were. We were. Oh, Beauty..." My heart skipped a beat hearing him call me that— a name I hadn't heard in so long. "But my folks calling like that? It just slammed me. I couldn't handle it. I still can't. But then? Right then? After days of us—you and I— being angry with one another? And after grueling months on the road. I needed an out. I needed to process. I needed to deny it for at least that night. I was wrong. I know that. It was a bad decision that led to even worse ones. Of course I was going to tell you but..."

"...everything snowballed." And then some.

"I'm so, so sorry, Lara."

I wasn't sure how to reply. So I asked another question. "What are you going to do about your dad?"

"I wanted to go see them. Nola went for a couple days.

But I couldn't—not with how things were."

"No. You couldn't let your dad see you off. He doesn't need that worry," I agreed. "I know Nola knows, but do your folks know that we..." My voice trailed because what...what were we?

"No," was his simple but succinct answer.

"Good." That was another worry I knew they didn't need. "I want to go to Louisville with you. I want to see your folks. And if you think it's all right, I want to take Chance and Arinn." It was something I had been tossing around in my head just moments before when I was unable to sleep.

"Really?" Finn seemed surprised.

My answer may have come across a little blunt, but it was the cold, hard truth. "The kids are going to lose a grandparent. Chance is at that age where he's only going to partially understand. He'll think he does and then—"

"*I* don't understand." His honesty was heartbreaking. "Arinn for sure won't, but Chance probably won't even remember Pop, huh?"

I knew it wasn't the answer my husband wanted but, again, I spoke with candor. "That's a good possibility. But what he does remember will be good. It will all be good memories," I added in case Finn was thinking about his own grandmother dying when he was a similar age and how she had left him.

"Thanks for doing this. I'll let them know, and I'll make the flight arrangements first thing in the morning."

"I love your parents," I said right away so he knew what my concentration was on. "Your dad, he—" But I couldn't get any more out.

"He's one-of-a-kind. And he loves you very much, too," Finn's acknowledgement made the tears that had been threatening actually materialize. "Lara? I know this is a lot. And knowing you're still struggling with what happened at the bank...Why? Why didn't you tell me that?"

I closed my eyes and slightly shook my head. "I guess we both chose the road of denial...and crashed and burned."

"Baby?" His voice seemed pained at seeing me in distress. "Please let me hold you."

Even though his offer was probably the one and only thing I craved at that moment, I hesitated and resisted. My defensive walls were too sturdy. "No. No. I can't." I denied him and started to get off of the sofa.

Finn managed to brush my hand with his before I made my way back toward the steps. "I love you, Lara."

***

Finn noticed the little wrinkle my nose made when I looked at the caller ID of my ringing cell phone. "Why didn't you pick it up?" he asked after I placed it back on the arm rest of the patio chair I was sitting in.

It was the next day, and he had just emerged from our pool with Chance. We were trying a united bond for the kids' sake. Lucky to have gotten a swim in that late into September, Chance looked secure and happy, already running around trying to catch butterflies. Finn did not. Because I didn't immediately answer his query, he peered up from playing with Arinn on the blanket beside me. Although he was trying to disguise it, I could tell he was starting to seethe.

"You have no right. You understand me? None—not after what you did." My voice purposefully dipped in volume but not in attitude.

I knew he thought it was Miller. And it was no longer the wee hours of the night where all was soft and serene. It was the middle of the day, and all the other things that were complicating our relationship were as blazing as the sunshine above.

I waited a moment, letting what I said to him sink in, and then I replied. "It wasn't." I paused again, knowing I had never called Miller back. "It was Reese, and I'm not the one who should be picking up. You are."

I think I actually saw him physically swallow his guilt— guilt for thinking the worst of me *and* for not talking with Reese. Sitting in the chair next to mine, he asked, "Did she leave a message?"

I looked to the phone. "No. What else can she say to me? She just wants you to call her so she can do her job."

"I know."

"Congrats on the noms," I conceded as the harshness in my voice faded a little.

"Thanks," he replied quietly. "I was hoping for more, but it's all relative."

We looked at each other for an extended moment... our kids adding a playful, happy, natural soundtrack in the background. It *was* all relative. But it was also all real... too real.

***

Later that night, he did call Reese back. And I was privy to the entire conversation by happenstance. The kids were both asleep, although Chance was fighting it, and I heard Reese's unmistakable voice coming from Finn's cellphone speaker in our master bedroom.

"Thank goodness for caller ID. I probably wouldn't have recognized your voice it's been so long. And that's not a good thing for a singer," she said with an extra dose of sarcasm.

Finn obviously didn't appreciate it. "I don't need that shit right now."

But how was Reese to know? She was completely in the dark when it came to all recent things Finn. "Well, excuse me. I don't need to be fending off angry people you are blowing off, especially right after my honeymoon."

"Sorry, but you're just going to have to do it for a while longer," Finn answered as I quietly leaned up against the doorframe undetected.

"What does that mean?" she queried.

"It means, I'm out. I'm out for the foreseeable future." He was walking around the room packing some items into his carryon for our trip to Louisville early the next morning.

"I need to know more than that." I spotted Finn's phone, with Reese's voice coming from it, on his nightstand. "I need to be able to say something or to give some sort of timeline or—"

"It's personal." He stopped her.

"I get that!" she exclaimed and then took another approach. "Tell me what's going on and you know that it will be just between us. I just need to know so I can deny or spin away..." There was dead space on her end and then she asked, "Is it Lara? Are the two of you—"

"Listen to me," He stopped mid-jeans folding and turned in the direction of the phone. "You need to lay off her. Our relationship is our business. My career is yours."

"I told you, I get that," she bounced right back. "I'm asking as a friend. I thought all three of us were that."

"There's a lot, Reese," he admitted and started rolling his belt and socks. "It's not just one thing. Look, we're going to Louisville tomorrow morning."

"Who 'we'?"

"Lara and the kids and I."

"Oh." Reese's one word sounded like relief since the "we" included his wife— too bad I wasn't as sure as she was.

"I'll call you when we get back. We'll only be there for a few days. I'll have a better grip on everything then." My husband landed a final shirt in the carryon.

"Finn?" she called out.

"Yeah?" He was in the master bath now gathering his toiletries.

"I hope everything's going to be all right," she said.

"It's not," he answered plainly. "I'm sorry for not

calling."

"I'll take care of what needs to be done. And if anybody asks, 'no comment.'"

"Thanks." When he turned around to enter the master bedroom and formally hang up the phone, even though Reese already had on her end, he saw me climbing into our bed. I know he was shocked to see me, but he tried not to show it. He confirmed that the call was dead and looked at me silently for an explanation.

"Don't make this out to be anything more than what it is."

"Okay?" His voice was leading, obviously wanting more information.

"Chance noticed where I was sleeping, and I don't want him any more confused. And I'm assuming we're going to be in the same bed at your folks." We wouldn't have to be. There was another bedroom, but that would raise questions we didn't want asked.

"Yeah."

"Then I'm going to sleep. Neither of us slept well last night, and it's an early start tomorrow."

"Yeah." He wasn't saying much. It was like he didn't want to jinx the fact that I was in his bed.

"Do you have your alarm set?" I asked.

"Yeah," he said the same word once again and then shut off the overhead light. "Six o'clock all right?"

I almost laughed…almost. I always needed more time than him, especially since we had kids. "Give me another twenty or twenty-five minutes. Between the kids and traffic…"

"Okay." He slid into bed and fiddled with his phone's alarm.

I couldn't deny the pull of our bodies even though we were carefully minding our own sides of the ginormous king-sized bed. It was awkward. But, at the same time, it felt like home.

"Good night, Lara," he said behind my now turned

body.

I waited a beat and then recited, "G'night back."

"I love you." He didn't get anything in reply that time.

***

To further intensify the stress I was under, I had to board a plane— one of my absolute least favorite things in the world. And then I had to put up with the overly-zealous, friendly—dare I say, slutty—flight attendant. She personally took us to our seats while catering/swooning to everything F-i-n-n. I'm sure she would have done him Mile High style if Finn would have let her. But he wasn't the least bit interested. I could tell. It wasn't because I was standing there scowling or because he had other things on his mind. It was because he truly never showed any interest in anyone but me. That's why I believed it when he had said that night over a week before had meant absolutely nothing to him…except pain.

Finn asked the flight attendant to help me get Arinn secured at the seat by the window after I shut down the blind. It was a small plane with only two seats on either side of a single middle aisle. I would sit next to Arinn and Finn would be with Chance. How he managed to get four seats in a row on such short notice amazed me. But I guess it shouldn't have. He was country music's charming crooner, after all.

"Can I sit at da window, Daddy?" Chance asked with eager anticipation.

Chance loved flying, much to my chagrin. And he had been a pro at it since birth. This, however, would be Arinn's first, and I hoped she would be just as successful.

"All yours, bud." Finn accommodated our little guy, buckling him in and then sitting in the seat next to him, which was just the small aisle away from me.

In typical Finn Murphy fashion, we had barely made the flight. Although they probably would have held it for us, knowing my husband. The good part of that was, I didn't have to sit long at the terminal or on the tarmac and have my stomach churn and churn. The anticipation of flight was maybe worse than the actual experience for me.

As the engine began to roar and we eventually started coasting down the runway, I could see Chance getting excited and stretching his little head to look out the window. In contrast, I instinctively clung to the arm rests and subconsciously looked over at Finn. I had to, on occasion, fly by myself, but, most of the time, I had him as my security blanket. Not saying a word, he reached across the aisle and flattened his hand on top of mine. He then curved it so that our fingers interlaced. And he squeezed...securely and reassuringly. I was glad he didn't speak. I think he knew better. It would have ruined it. I might have been forced to tell him to let go. And although we still had so many things between us, I was so very thankful for that hand.

Once we were smoothly in the air, I squeezed back, released my hand, and whispered, "Thanks."

"I'm available for landings, too." Finn tried to keep it light.

I caught his eyes and then looked away. I had planned on pretending to sleep for the approximately two hour flight. But, while watching Arinn peacefully, thankfully, slumber, I somehow managed to legitimately do the same.

That was, until I felt the jolt of us descending. We were ready to land. My eyes popped open. I hated landings the most. They always seemed the bumpiest... just like my life. But there was my husband's hand again and the silent squeeze just when I needed it.

CHAPTER TWENTY

Surviving inside a tension-filled enclosed tin can miles and miles in the air was probably the easier part, though. What came next...that was the hard part. The hard part was all the pretending that took place over the next couple of days.

We were pretending that everything was the same. When it most certainly was not. It was a balancing, taxing performance on both of our parts. But we didn't want to let either Finn's folks or our kids sense that anything was awry. Finn, being an entertainer, was perhaps a little more used to a façade. But this was his family. They knew him best. Luckily, but sadly, the focus was not on us, though. It was on my father-in-law, who already had that sickly look in his once vibrant, lively eyes.

"Never as in 'never, never'?" Mr. Murphy exclaimed.

"No, Pop." Finn shook his head, clearly amused by his father's insistence.

"And you neither, Darlin'?" My father-in-law asked me for the second time.

"No. Sorry," I admitted.

"Thalia, we have failed as parents." Mr. Murphy mocked to his wife.

"Pop, it was way before our time."

"It's a classic," was the elder's response.

"I'd love to watch it," I chimed in from the parlor floor where I was playing with Chance.

"Well, good. Because that's what we're doing." From the comfort of his recliner, Mr. Murphy pointed the remote in the direction of the TV. *Splendor in the Grass* was just starting. "That Natalie Wood...she was quite a beauty."

"Mommy is Beauty," Chance mumbled next to me.

I chuckled, knowing our son was referencing the name Finn often called me. Sitting behind us on the sofa, Finn fluffed Chance's hair while cuddling Arinn in his lap. I turned my attention back to a subdued Chance.

"Now that is good parenting," Mrs. Murphy complimented from a recliner that matched her husband's.

"Thanks," I replied and looked up awkwardly at my husband. We were good parents even if we weren't much more at the moment.

"How good of parents are we being if we let a three-year-old and a nearly one-year-old watch something called *Splendor in the Grass*?" Finn questioned.

"It was filmed in 1961! You have things that are ten times worse on those videos of yours." Mr. Murphy certainly had enough energy yet to razz his son. "Bikini clad women and hands everywhere."

"Pop!" Finn groaned, and I felt his foot scoot over to rest on the side of my seated bottom.

I knew he was doing it to make sure I was secure and not upset about the mental image of some of his music videos. Normally, I was okay with it. But considering the recent revelation, it admittedly bothered me.

"It's their bedtime, anyway," I offered as an excuse to extract myself from the conversation. I felt Finn's foot try desperately to inch closer, but I lifted my body up and said, "C'mon, Little Man, it's nighty-night time."

Finn stood up. With an extra-long pleading stare, he

transferred Arinn into my arms. "You want me to—"

"No." I cut him off. "I got them. They're both tired. I shouldn't be long." And after a couple toddler goodnight kisses, I grabbed Chance's hand and we started our way up the old Victorian steps.

As we did, I heard Finn say to his father, "Pop, I just sing in those videos. I'm in the background...the side. There are actors who are doing that other stuff."

"I know that. Geez, you can't take a joke anymore?"

"No, I...no." I heard him sigh as I closed the door to the room where our two babies would slumber for the night.

***

When I made my way back down, I no longer had the sanctuary of sitting on the floor to play with Chance. With both the recliners occupied, the only place left to sit was on the sofa...with Finn. However, as I prepared to sit down by pushing off my shoes, Finn got up and walked into the kitchen. Not questioning, I propped my back up against the arm of one end of the sofa and bent my legs, placing my feet on the middle cushion of three. This purposefully, only left one place for Finn to sit—on the opposite end of the sofa—a fortress wall away from me.

When he reentered the living room, he handed me a chilled glass of white wine. I hadn't asked for one, but it was, indeed, exactly what I needed at that moment. I took it and immediately swallowed a hearty gulp. On that motion, Finn somehow manipulated another spot for him to sit. Carefully lifting my tented legs, he sat upright on the middle cushion before replacing my feet on his lap. I took another gulp as he rested his hands on my bare feet. I knew he was doing it on purpose, knowing that I wouldn't alter the situation in front of his parents.

"How's the wine?" For the first time since he sat down, he turned his gaze at me.

"Good," I admitted. "Thanks."

"Where's yours?" Mr. Murphy proposed.

"Not drinking." Finn affirmatively nodded his head up and down at me with what I determined was a mixture of guilt and desired redemption.

Not wanting his parents to question any further, I gave my husband the assist by teasing, "Shhh boys, unless you are telling me what I missed."

***

"That's it? That's the end?" I lamented.

"Yep," My father-in-law confirmed.

"But they didn't get together. I thought it was a love story."

"You wanted the happily ever after?" Finn's father questioned me.

"Well, yeah. I…"

"It doesn't always work out that way, Darlin'. Maybe they weren't ever supposed to be together. I mean, she might actually have been better off after—"

"Fuck!" Finn burst off the sofa and proceeded straight out the front door.

Both of his parents turned their gaze from their son to me, shocked by his sudden departure.

"He's…you know, it's a lot." I offered up a lame excuse, hoping they thought it was solely about Mr. Murphy's illness and not a hero in a movie screwing up his relationship with his one and only. Putting my shoes back on, I said, "I'll go check on him." I didn't necessarily want to. I didn't want to talk about what caused his outburst. I didn't want to see the pain he was in—self-induced and otherwise. I wasn't ready, and it certainly wasn't the place. But it was my role, and I needed to.

Leaning on the rail of the iconic white front porch, Finn immediately acknowledged me joining him outdoors. "I'm sorry, Lara."

"I know." If I knew anything right then, I did know that he was sorry. But, the fact was, it didn't solve or fix anything.

"You would have been better off without me." He looked and sounded as defeated as Warren Beatty's character after realizing the damage he did to Natalie Wood's heroine.

"That's not true," I immediately rebuffed, standing more in his line of vision and leaning now against the railing myself. "I know you're hurting right now, but don't defile everything we had."

"Had?" He jumped on my use of tenses.

"Finn…" Tired, stressed, and certainly emotional, I sighed, not wanting to have to clarify… if I even could. "Concentrate on being here. It means so much to them. They need you. They need your strength as a son and as a father."

"But I'm a husband, too." He didn't plead, but it was close, and it did affect me.

Managing to hold the tears at bay, I said, "I know we have a lot to talk about but once we get home, okay? My emotions are too high right now." I was proud that we were able to at least look at one another throughout the tense conversation.

"I love you."

And, just like that, my eyes failed me. I couldn't look back into his. While those words had usually lit me up warm and happy and blessed inside, I couldn't bear to hear them since his confessional. They hurt. They confused. But he repeated them… day after day.

"Why do you keep saying that?" My voice rose in a semi-whine. "Why do you keep telling me you love me when I say nothing back?"

He partially sighed. "I'm sorry that you don't want to hear it. But I have to tell you. I have to tell you that I love you. It's how I feel. And even if I don't deserve it, I hold onto the hope that there's a part inside you that feels the same way— a part that doesn't think all that is us is now in the past...a part that believes in the glory of the flower." When he recited that part of *Splendor in the Grass*, I managed to look up. The vulnerability was not only in his eyes but in his deflated posture.

"I'm upset. I..." I started without any idea how I wanted to finish.

Perhaps not wanting to hear one more rejection, Finn offered, "It's all right. You don't have to explain. In fact, I'd rather you not. I'd rather you just think...please." He stepped forward and opened the front door for us to go back inside.

"Don't stop saying it," I practically whispered.

He looked at me as if his ears had deceived him. But I wasn't about to repeat it or even acknowledge that it had been said in the first place. Instead, I walked back into the house just as confused and hurt but in love as ever before.

***

Both kids fell asleep on the car ride home from the airport. So it was an easy transition for their bedtime. But it wasn't just their soft breathing that made our home so quiet. There was an additional stillness in the air —the sense that we were back to another reality...a reality that Finn and I had to confront. It was the reality of us.

After each of us taking a child to tuck into their respective rooms and beds, Finn and I met in the upstairs hallway. He caught my eyes with his and blinked slowly once. It seemed so ironic—how well we knew one another...how without saying a word, we knew exactly what the other was thinking...how our connection was that strong. Yet the pain and hurt was a current, unfortunate rival.

Finn stuck out his arm motioning for me to go down the steps first. When we reached the great room, I decided to continue into the kitchen. It seemed further away from where our children might hear and yet close enough that we could hear them. And it was not a conversation I wanted to have in what had normally been our sanctuary—the master bedroom.

After both Finn and I sat on the tall kitchen counter stools, I stated the truths that weren't a surprise to either of us. "I am so hurt. I am so mad. I am so confused." I waited until he closed his eyes for an extended moment and then opened them once more. "I know that what happened with Chance was a reaction—"

"It was my fault." He beat his chest hard with his palm. "Even though it was an accident—I didn't know he was so close—I still wasn't in control, and that is so on me. That is me. That is my fault and something I will never, ever be able to forget or forgive myself for."

"I know. I realize that—all of it." I did, and I was at peace with it. "I know I came down hard about that because…" I hesitated on my own past which he very well knew.

"…because you had to and you should have."

"My point is, you need to forgive yourself for that. Chance has. I have."

I dipped my eyes momentarily. This was hard…all of it. I had to voice *everything* out loud, though, if we had even a semblance of a chance to survive.

"But, God, Finn, what you did with her? Even though I know the circumstances and I get your pain… that…that still hurts." I had to take a deep breath just to continue. I had never been one to openly share my innermost thoughts and feelings. Between growing up with an anger-driven father and keeping the secret of a teenage pregnancy, I had learned to be reserved. That was until the man sitting next to me …until I trusted someone so implicitly that all of those walls were imploded and freed of debris. And now, once again, I was struggling. I knew he could tell, and I even knew he wanted to help, but it was still my words that needed to get out. "It hurts so bad.

I want to hate you."

"Do you?" he tentatively queried.

"I can't," I admitted. "I'm trying to reconcile the contempt that is festering inside my soul with all the love I have for you." That broke me—the 'L' word and the truth of what I was saying…of what I was admitting to him, as well as, really, myself. A tear found its way almost simultaneously down my previously dry cheek. Wiping it quickly, I continued. "I don't know how to do it. And I'm trying to remember everything that is going on with your dad and—"

"Don't," he interrupted me firmly but not with anger. "Whatever you do, Lara, don't pity me."

I knew that was something he detested from anyone. I started to try to rephrase. "I—"

But he continued to talk. "Or do something because Pop is sick."

"But he *is* sick, and I do worry about you," I spoke honestly.

"Don't," he answered again with the same intensity. "I love you, and God knows I am lost without you. But don't do something because… only if you forgive me. Only through trust and love."

"I do love you." It was easier to say that time, but there was still so much else in the way. Watching his gray eyes slightly light at my words, I paused, trying to really comprehend what I was feeling and how it had or had not changed over the past couple of days. "And I do, oddly enough, trust you. I just…I'm hurt, and I'm angry. You know what that's like." I tagged on at the end.

"I do," he agreed easily, and his eyes seemed to once again turn a little more dull gray.

It wasn't quite a sigh that left my mouth. It was more of a whimper because I was realizing things that I hadn't before. "I'm angry at you, and I'm angry at myself for not being what you needed or wanted when you were hur—"

"God!" He raked his hands through his already unruly

hair and stood up. After a half turn, he looked back at me. "Don't say that. Don't." With an almost plea, he started to bring his hands toward mine which were clasped tightly and anxiously together on the counter. When he saw me flinch ever so slightly, he retracted them and continued. "What I did was not a reflection on you. It wasn't. I was mad at cancer… at the world. I was mad at myself for what happened with Chance and for how I had treated you after the tour. And I couldn't face you because I didn't deserve anything good. I didn't deserve you."

I knew that feeling. I *lived* that feeling… for years. I didn't think I deserved happiness after the destructive decisions I had made that resulted in giving up a child as a teen.

"But, Lara…" He bent slightly and leaned forward to gain even more of my attention, like he didn't already have it fully. "Lara, you are always *all* that I need."

He was adamant on his stance, and I even saw his point of view. But, I still felt that twinge of guilt. I still felt like because I loved him so much, I should have been able to have seen that there was more to his sudden change of persona, attitude, and demeanor a few weeks prior. I hadn't, though. I hadn't.

"I drove you to it," I voiced. "I didn't listen to you at the penthouse or on the phone."

"Baby, you had every right to hang up on me. I was drunk. I wasn't on my meds. Don't do that to yourself. It was on me. I …I…" He stood a little straighter again. "Fuck… I shouldn't have gone out. I shouldn't have…" Finn couldn't say the words.

My self-pity was starting to mix with anger toward the poor decision he made —one that recalled his wicked, messed up past …before he was diagnosed and before me. "Gone back to back seats and blow jobs."

"Don't, Lar."

"Why? It's the truth."

He breathed out an enormous breath. "I know you

must have questions."

I did. The knots in my stomach since finding out were tearing me apart. But I wasn't sure if I wanted the answers. I didn't know if I could handle the answers. Yet, how could I ever move on? I stood up to meet him. "How did it play out?" The first question had started out semi-calmly, but anger and hurt were definitely taking a stronger hold on the follow up. "Where were you, Finn? *Was* it the back seat of a car?"

"Lara…"

"I need to know." When he didn't readily respond, I prompted again. "A car? Your car?"

"No." He spoke a bit more subdued as he gave me the facts. "I was at a club in mid-town. I didn't know her. She introduced herself after her set. I was wasted."

"Where, though?" I pressured for a more exact location of the scene of the crime.

He took a deep breath and spoke with obvious shame. "In the back alley behind the club."

"Did you kiss her?" Did I want to know? God, the images…

Momentarily squeezing his eyes shut like a vice was flanking his head tightly, he said, "It was more the other way around. But not a lot."

"Is she young?" Painting my mental picture was a form of self-torture.

"Younger," he said plainly.

I was imagining this "younger" woman with my husband doing something so personal…so intimate. It made me want to throw up. I brought my head sharply back and forth a few times trying to physically shake away the mentally embedded image. And then, suddenly, I became almost possessed with what I knew and didn't want to know. "Did she fall down to her knees like this?" I dropped down on the kitchen floor in front of Finn. "Did she work your buckle?" My hands on his belt were suddenly and rapidly doing the things that I had been imagining since he first told me. "Did you get excited and help her?"

I was just about done with his buckle and ready to string the belt through when Finn must have broken from his stunned state. "Stop it!" he bellowed, grabbing my wrists and pulling me up to equal him. "Stop!" he repeated, a little yes yelly.

With his hands wrapped around mine, we were very close in proximity, but I couldn't look at him. I was embarrassed and vulnerable and needing a break. Or, to just actually break. I started to cry. But it wasn't a straggling tear this time. It was more of a deluge.

"Stop," he said much, much more kindly as he pulled me into his cotton shirt covered chest. "God, baby, I love you so much. I'm so sorry I hurt you. I can't stand that I did this to you… to us."

I made a big, spontaneous decision then. I thought if I kissed him—if I put my lips on his— maybe a part of me could feel better. Maybe it could ease my racing mind. I tilted my head up to let our mouths merge. Finn instantly, softly reciprocated my movements. But I was so hurt. I was so mad with the images of the two of them doing just that. I wanted her erased. I wanted her gone. It should have been me…only me. But, when my tongue started to invade a little more hungrily, he halted our action.

"Lara, I'm not sure this is a good idea." He gently pulled me away.

"What?" The instant sting of rejection felt like a follow-up slap across the face.

"I don't think—"

"You don't want me, but you let some two-bit wannabe take you—"

"Stop!" His voice rose once more and his arms outstretched onto my shoulders. "That's exactly why not. I want you. I always want you. But I'm afraid you think you need to prove something."

"Maybe I do," I said quietly. I did. I wasn't quite sure

what, but it definitely centered on my insecurities of being worthy of love.

"No." He punctuated each word. "You. Don't."

"I'm…" I released myself from his arms and took a step away. After a moment of settling my thoughts and wound body, I tried to focus on why I had acted like that…what I needed. "Finn…" My words came out in a plead. "Promise me," I said and then reiterated, "Promise me that was it. That was all you let her do—" I choked on the words. "She put her mouth on you, gave you a—"

He couldn't stand for me to say it out loud either— it was noticeable every time. "I promise. I promise on my life…on whatever you want me to swear on. Lara?" He bent slightly again to make sure he was directly looking in my eyes. "This…damn… telling you about it was the hardest thing I have ever had to do. But I'm telling you the truth. I'm not trying to talk around it. I was so out of my mind drunk and emotional that it didn't even seem like me when it was happening. But when I realized…I stopped it. I was so sick."

I believed him. I could even, during that retell, kind of relate. It paralleled in a lot of ways what had happened to me that summer post high school—too much alcoholic punch, an aggressive kiss, not knowing up from down. I knew what one reckless night could do. And Finn had a series of them leading up to his night. I could empathize. I could kind of understand. But, yet, the air in the kitchen, the house…my life was still so heavy.

"I need a break." God, did I ever. I started to move away from him.

"Don't go. Let's talk through this."

"What's there to talk about? You say it made you sick and how sorry you are, and I believe you. I get it. I do. But it doesn't undo what happened. I'm still upset, and I still see it in my mind. And I don't want to. I want to see us. But when I go to touch you, you push me away like I make you sick, too." Everything was coming out jumbled because my words were mimicking my state of my mind.

"Lara!" He swiftly narrowed the gap between us. He took his hand and lifted my chin up so that I had to look in his eyes. He kissed me softly, slowly, lovingly. But, once again, he stopped. "I told you, I love you." Although obviously full of his own emotions, he spoke calmly. "But only when you have forgiven me. Not like this."

I was beyond torn on how to feel and what to do. Completely spent, I reclaimed my face by putting both hands up to it. Flanking my cheeks, I slowly shook my head back and forth.

"Lara?" Cautiously, he prompted me to tell him how to proceed.

"I can't...I can't forgive you...yet." I added. "It's tough."

"I know," he acknowledged. "I will do everything I can to earn your forgiveness."

I knew he meant it, and I wanted it to come to fruition. But, at that moment, everything seemed so far out of reach. Everything seemed sad.

"Concentrate on your dad," was my answer, as it honestly should have been.

"I will," he agreed, and we stood looking at one another for an extended moment. The days, months, years of knowing one another said so much without a sound being made.

Finally, I was the one to break the silent bond. There really wasn't anything else to say. "I think I'm gonna go to sleep."

"You'll stay in our room, right?" And then he tacked on, "Please."

"Yeah." If we had managed, however awkwardly, to sleep in the smaller bed at his folks, we could do it in our own home.

"Good. I'll be in in a bit."

"Okay."

"I love you, Lara."

Oh, God. There were those words again. Somehow, when I had just previously strung them in a sentence intermixed with some explanation and anger, it seemed all right. But to just lay those three words out there by themselves as an echo? To admit it so openly? I was too vulnerable yet.

"You know I feel the same way," I voiced instead.

His subtle, closed mouth smile was worth me saying at least that much. It was the most relaxed I had seen him since maybe the Hamptons. It helped me, too. While I still had a blizzard of emotions ravaging my mind, I was confident that our foundation of love was still intact even if above it a fortress still remained.

***

A few nights later, I awoke to find myself cradling Finn's T-shirt covered back. We were both laying on our sides, and I had one arm draped over to his stomach while my other arm was beneath my head and pillow. I hadn't consciously done it. But, somehow, between the time I went to sleep and 3:21 in the morning, my body had managed to eliminate the gap that had become accustomed between Finn and I in bed. Internally admitting to myself that I liked and missed the feeling of our bodies bonded that way, I breathed him in, letting my soul rest for a moment. Then, knowing the truth of the situation, I sighed and started to pull away.

Finn's sound was also a sigh. But it was also partially a moan. I knew he wasn't awake. Just like he could tell with me, I knew the difference between his sleep breathing and his resting or awake breathing. But his body, consciously or not, was aware that mine was leaving his. And it was that act that he feared the most.

I froze for a second and then melded right back into position. I needed his touch, his warmth, his presence just as much. I let my breathing sync with his, feeling it through the cottony fabric of his covered back. I think he may have murmured my name, but the relaxing rhythm of our chests rising and falling had me drifting off to sleep at just about the same time.

CHAPTER TWENTY-ONE

If he had been aware of it, Finn didn't mention the nighttime embrace and neither did I. He had been the first one up that next morning, which was a rarity, so I wasn't even sure if we had remained in that position for the rest of the night. He did seem slightly happier, though, as we made our way through the trials of those days following our trip to Louisville.

Finn got back to work contacting Reese and finally filling her in on his father's status but not on ours. He worked on new material and did interviews that he could do over the phone. And he started making arrangements regarding the CMA Awards, which were to be held in early November— just about a month away. Finn had agreed to perform a short acoustic piece because it wouldn't involve extra practice and commitment with his band. He hadn't said much to me about it, and I pretty much knew why. The CMA Awards were our thing. It was our tradition …our faux anniversary. That night had always been special to us. And he feared, I am sure, what this year would bring.

Things were still tenuous between the two of us. But we were making progress. After our honest kitchen conversation and the unexpected cuddling, we were becoming closer through kinder words and touches. At first, it felt a little forced. We did things in front of the kids to show that we were still united as a family. But I knew deep down those two precious little ones were just an excuse for me to chip away at my Lara wall and put myself even more out there. I would purposefully touch his hand when passing food or a remote or a piece of paper. And when I saw that he was feeling low or when things got to him—a call from his parents, a work situation, or just watching me with the kids—I would go over and give him a hug. He was silent during most of those interactions, letting me take the lead. But, he was always consistent with those three words that I knew but still needed to hear. And, he would kiss me. At first, it was tentative like our first real kiss outside of the bookstore years before. And then he gained confidence when he saw I not only didn't reject the motion but even slightly reciprocated it.

***

Finn was in Manhattan for most of the day on the fifth of October. He had an appointment with Dr. Bartola, then a photo shoot for his upcoming album, and finally dinner with Reese and Roger. He had asked if I wanted to come. But I declined. There wouldn't be anything for me and the kids to do for the majority of the day. Plus, I wasn't ready for the penthouse. Even though we shared so many magical memories there, including it being the place where we had gotten engaged, I still had the image of that last time I was there— Chance and a hungover Finn. I knew I would be able to embrace our second home again but not until we were on more stable footing. I didn't tell him all of that. But I think he knew and understood. That was the good part. We were getting more in sync with each other...and not just in our breathing patterns. It was the first time he left—albeit only for the day—since moving back, and we were both okay with it. There weren't any worries of mind-changing, jealousies, or other insecurities.

I knew he was back home later that evening because of the garage door opening and closing and then the security system announcing the entry into the house. But I didn't see him when I came down the stairs after putting the kids' laundry away and double-checking that they had both fallen asleep. I thought of looking in our bedroom for him. But then I realized the place he most definitely would have gone to...especially on that day and after being in the city.

"How old would he have been today?"

On my voice, Finn looked up from his desk in his downstairs studio. He wasn't necessarily startled to see me, but I know he hadn't heard me enter, either. "You remem—" He started and then almost immediately changed his dialogue. "Of course you did." He stood up and put Wyatt's photo back in its place on the shelf behind him. "Fourteen, right?" He turned back around to face me.

"Yeah," I agreed in reference to what would have been his nephew's birthday. "That awkward teen stage." I tried to bring a little levity to the topic.

My husband's head bounced in light laughter. "Yeah. He would have been giving Will and Nol all kinds of hell."

"And running to his cool uncle Finn to understand."

"I still feel him, you know?"

"Yeah. He was special."

Wyatt had been an awesome kid—the whole seven years he had been on this Earth. He was well-behaved, funny, smart, kind, curious. But he was also special in another way...because he had been the one that had brought Finn and I together.

"He was," Finn agreed quietly.

"Did you call your sister?"

"I did." He smiled at my directive tone, knowing that every year I told him to call Nola. "On the drive back," he confirmed.

"Good." I returned his smile. "How are they doing?"

"She's more concerned about Pop." He paused and then added, "And us."

With the room going instantly quiet, I forged forward with the sudden change of topic. It was something I wanted to talk about, anyway. "Can we sit?" I asked.

"Yeah. Sure," his voice said, but he didn't look so sure. Regardless, he followed my lead by sitting down on the studio sofa.

I crossed my legs and sock covered feet beneath me and adjusted my body so that I was facing him. "I need to ask you something. I need to put it to rest."

"Okay. Go ahead." He was calm, but I know he was also curious. The putting to rest comment surely had to intrigue him, particularly since we hadn't spoken since that night in the kitchen about what had brought us to the semi-separation. We had just been taking it one day at a time.

"She's gone?" I asked, trying to maintain eye contact but still hating the emotional pain of the topic. "Really? And she'll never—"

Not having to question who the "she" was, Finn interrupted me while reaching out for one of my hands. "Lara, I promise. Right after it happened. I…look, you want to know?" He let go of that hand simply because he was becoming a little more animated. "I called in a favor. I had another label sign her, but she had to promise to never leak any of it, or I told her I would make sure she was dropped."

"Could you do that?" I don't know why I was shocked. I should have been used to Finn's outreach of fame and connections. And, more than that, I should have known how fiercely he would want to protect his privacy and his family.

"Yeah," he admitted nonchalantly.

"Are you paying the label?" I didn't like the thought of that.

"No. No money. Nothing like that," he said

reassuringly. "I have nothing to do with her. There won't be a situation where I will see or correspond with her in any way. We're in two different genres, labels, statuses."

"But you did… at that club." I wasn't saying it to be accusatory. I was just stating the fact.

"Yeah. But that wasn't my scene. It was the upcoming indie slash pop crowd. You know I was messed up. Do you think I'll ever go near there again?" When I dipped my eyes down, he gently tipped my head back up to meet him. "Honestly, she'll probably fizzle out of the business. I don't think she's that good of a musician. It really was a favor."

"Okay. That's all I guess I need."

"You've never asked her name," he said more as a question than a statement.

"I don't want to know, Finn. I don't want to search for her name online and see and…and know." Don't get me wrong, I had thought about it many, many times but knew not knowing was for the best.

"Believe me, I would like to forget myself. But she's gone. I promise. I know I've said it before, but, I'm so, so sorry, baby."

"I know." I exhaled a lengthy breath and then took my phone out of my wristlet and handed it to him. On his inquisitive look, I explained. "Search the contacts, last numbers dialed, whatever, he's not in there."

Once again, no further explanations, clarifications, or definitions were needed for Finn to understand who "he" was. But the difference was, Finn knew Miller's name, and I wanted to make sure he saw that it had been erased from my phone. "You didn't need to do that." Without even glancing at the device, Finn handed it back to me.

"I didn't need to, but I don't want it between us. It hurt you, and I need to recognize that." God, had we been able to settle the Miller issue sooner, would any of this have happened?

Sure, Finn's father would still have cancer. It wasn't a

karma thing. But Finn probably would have been able to tell me about it and not bottle things up and…and the drinking…and the meds …and that nameless tramp. I knew it wasn't all my fault. And I still believed I was doing nothing wrong by speaking with Miller. But not listening, not wanting to talk when he wanted to, didn't help. And now, holding onto Miller's number or contacting him in any way held no purpose but to have something between me and my husband. It wasn't worth it.

"What about the kid?" Finn interrupted my internal thoughts while speaking about the child that I gave up for adoption all those years ago—Miller's nephew. "I don't want to ask you to—"

"You didn't," I objected. "I did it because they are my past. I have never had a right to that boy and if, God forbid, he should need anything—bone marrow again or whatever—it's Miller, not me, who is a match…who can help. Miller hasn't heard about him for a while now, anyway. If he does, and he leaves me a message, I want to know, sure, but I'm not going to call just to catch up. I—"

"Thank you." He kindly forced a conclusion to that subject.

And I was glad. I wanted to talk about Miller as much as Finn did…which was not at all. Just like I didn't want to talk about the girl from the alley. I wanted to find a way to move on. And, ironically, the past was going to assist me. I pulled a folded envelope out of my wristlet.

"What's this?" Finn asked, taking it from my extended hand.

"It's okay. Open it up," I prompted.

Unlike his usual rapidly-rip-open-presents self, Finn was meticulous when unsealing the envelope and then carefully pulling out the concert flyer. "Huh…that's from one of my gigs in college." He acutely assessed, examining the date on the tiny piece of paper.

"Yeah," I agreed. "My mom just sent me a box of my old memorabilia. She's been going through things…cleaning house. I think what's going on with your dad has even affected her."

I had spoken at length with my mother after I found out about Finn's dad's diagnosis. As a nurse, she knew all too well the grave situation that Mr. Murphy was in. As a parent, she empathized even more.

When Finn's mouth curled in sadness, I tried to redirect the conversation back to what it was meant to be. "Anyway, she sent that. I know that's the first show I went to of yours…the first time we met."

"Why did you keep that?" he asked, surprised, and I noticed just a bit more glimmer in his eyes.

"I don't know," I admitted. "I didn't even know I had. That's the weird part. It wasn't like you and I were together."

"Nor did you show any interest."

Finn liked to tease me about that. Back then, I hadn't realized that our mutual friends, Sam and Olivia, had been trying to hook Finn and I up. Finn had figured it out, of course, but I had been oblivious. So much so, that Finn hadn't even showed any pursuit. But we had ended up as friends because we both hung out with Olivia and Sam so much.

"No." I smiled. "I did have a good time, though. I think it was one of the first times I had tried to let go since giving the baby up for adoption."

None of them had known that secret then, and only Finn knew now. They hadn't known that was why I came across as so standoffish. Finn had even admitted that he thought I was stuck-up when we first met. But it was just that I had been so afraid of trusting anyone again after becoming pregnant that summer after high school.

And, now, it was up to me to start trusting once more. "It's kinda foretelling, though, huh?" I continued. "I had no idea how much that flyer would change my life."

He pierced his eyes at me trying to decipher my comment before giving me his wishful interpretation.

"Hopefully as well as it did mine."

"Like the lottery and chocolate factory all rolled into one."

He didn't even try to disguise his exhale of relief. He brought his lips back in together and got up. "I have something to give you, too."

"Yeah?" I asked, starting for the first time in what seemed like forever to actually relax.

"Hold on." He opened his top desk drawer. Pulling out a legal sized manila envelope, he started back over to the sofa. "I was going to give you this when I got home from tour and, well..." His voice drifted off, recalling the terrible turn that his first day back took.

Taking the envelope from him as he reclaimed his seat next to me, I opened it up and pulled out a notebook. "What's this?"

"I wrote to you," he explained. "There's a letter or song from every city. Not a selfie. I wrote something each stop."

I think my jaw actually dropped. "I didn't think you..."

I had asked him to write to me that night before he initially left on tour. We had actually been in the studio we were in now. But he had acted like he didn't understand or had too much on his mind.

"Of course I did. Even if you hadn't asked, I would have. Being away like that, I had to write. I told you, you are always on my mind."

"Thanks," I said, feeling a loving warmth spread throughout my inner core. I put the notebook back into the manila envelope and held it up to my chest.

"You're not going to read them?" he asked clearly astonished. When Finn had written things like that for me in the past—our first year of marriage, etc.—I had always dove right into their words.

"I will," I answered and tried to explain. "Just knowing that they exist means more than anything right now."

It meant that at times when we were both stressed and

lonely, he always saw me as his home base. We were always connected. I may not have felt it all the time, but our bond was always there.

"You're my forever, Lara… no matter what you de—"

I wouldn't let him continue, though, because that was all that needed to be said. "Forever …your girl." I said, feeling that final piece of the forgiveness puzzle clicking in.

"God, baby. I—" He stopped himself this time and scooched in closer to me.

Cupping my face in his hands, he kissed me then. It was different than the soft, quick ones we had been experimenting with over the past few days or so. With that one kiss, it was like he was making up for all the real kisses we had missed during the miserable month plus that we had not. It was strong, passionate, and begging for revival. He stopped almost as suddenly, though. Not dropping his hands but intensely looking in my eyes, he was silently asking if everything was, indeed, back to where it belonged. I confirmed by kissing him with the same intensity.

He took my hand in his and helped me off the sofa. Leaving the notebook and his concert flyer behind, Finn silently led me up the stairs and straight into our master bedroom. He kissed me again and then started unbuttoning the front of the white sleeveless shirt I was wearing. Letting that fall to the ground, he pulled one of my bra straps off my shoulder and nuzzled his lips on the now bare skin. My head fell back, relishing his soft lips that I had missed so much. He broke that insatiable touch just so he could make haste with his own shirt—a green button down he still had on from his trip into the city. It was a green that matched—

"Finn?"

"Yeah?"

"Baby, do you mind? Your…your eyes."

"Oh." He only realized then that he still had in his fake green contacts. They were a must for the country superstar's photo shoot and probably for being seen out with his publicist but not for his wife who preferred the real person behind the performer's mask.

"I want *you*. I want 'my Finn.'"

"Damn. Yeah. Hold on." He scurried into the adjoining bathroom where I heard the sink water run momentarily. And, within minutes, he was back in front of me.

"Thanks." I stood up on my tippiest of toes to pull his head toward me and kiss his two closed eyes.

I went then for his gray slacks still strung together by a leather belt. Unfastening it, I started to pull his pants down his long, firm legs. I froze, though, just before I was going to have him step out of the pants that were now puddling at his feet. I was on my knees and I couldn't help but imagine "her." Damn it.

"Lar?" Finn asked perplexed at the halt in my action.

I put my hands up to cover my face for a second or two. When I removed them, I was about to go for his hips when he knelt down to meet me. He now understood. He knew what I was thinking. He kissed me softly and then pulled back just enough so that I could see his glorious, sincere, loving, natural gray eyes. He shook his head slowly back and forth. I wasn't exactly sure what it signified, though. Was it that he wanted me to put it out of my mind…erase it? Was it that he was sorry that the club incident happened in the first place? Or did he not want me to do what had crossed my mind—let me be the memory that he has of someone on their knees … it would be my mouth, not someone else's.

He pulled me to him again kissing the thought out of my head. Then, after caressing my face with the soft side of his hand, he finished taking off his pants. With a gentle grip, he scooped me up and carried me straddled against him like he would our son when he was too tired to walk. We sat down in that same exact position—Finn seated upright on the mattress and I wrapped around him on his lap. I leaned my head onto his chest taking in the moment—feeling the love and strength of that man in my arms, knowing that there was no other place I wanted to be.

"I'm sor—" His voice vibrated from behind my back and through his chest.

I pushed my palm against his bare torso so that he would not only stop talking but so I could back up. I wanted him to see me but not break our embrace. "All I need to hear is that you love me."

"Oh, Beauty, I love you so much. It was always you…and it will be forever."

"I love you, too." Repeating those three words brought me such relief and peace.

I stood and quickly discarded my jeans. His body elongated as he stood up between me and the mattress. While he kissed me, I felt his hands go to the back clasp of my bra. I helped him finish the task and then guided his hands down to my panties. Just the touch of his fingers there threw my emotions and body into overload. I loved, wanted, and needed him so much, and I knew by his soft touch and words, the feeling was mutual.

"You are so beautiful," he whispered, bringing a teardrop to my eye, but this time it was one of happiness.

We cascaded together onto the mattress. Our hands intertwined and he kissed me softly, tentatively a few times. Even though we were both eager to be connected again in that special way, we took our time rediscovering each other, almost as if it were our first time. But then again, in a way, I suppose it was. In a way, we were being reborn.

SNEAK PEEK AT
THE PLACE I BELONG
BOOK 5

CHAPTER ONE

A phone call in the wee hours of the morning—
before the sun would dare begin to rise or the birds begin
to chirp— is never a good thing. Through the darkness of
the master bedroom, illuminated only by the bubbling ebb
and flow of our red lava lamp, I tried to adjust my eyes,
and then my ears, to pinpoint whose phone it was. Of
course, it was my husband's. Finn's cell seemed to beep
more than the rush hour taxis in nearby Manhattan. But
the ringtone was the one he had assigned to his parents,
and the unusual time, combined with my father-in-law's
declining health, was troublesome.

"Finn," I spoke softly in the otherwise stillness of the
room. "Finn, baby, wake up...your phone."

On my voice, he opened his natural gray eyes to meet
mine. A quick but undeniable glimmer of recognition
flitted in them. It was a mixture of a tiny bit of shock and a
whole ton of happiness. I knew he was thinking of the
night before and the fact that I was not only in bed with
him but that we had made love. Despite tumultuous weeks
of pain and mistrust, we had landed back where we
belonged. It was because of our core... because of the
solid, forever love between us.

Finn leaned over and kissed me quickly, but with
adoration, before reaching to his nightstand and his phone.

"Hello?" he answered. "Mom, it's all right. What? What's going on?" The silk bedsheet fell a little further down to his waist as he sat up straighter. "Yeah, of course. She's right here with me."

Finn turned his arm slightly and reached for my hand. I took it, thinking how glad I was that his parents had not been wise to our arguing and mini-separation. It was a moot point now, and definitely a stressor that my in-laws didn't need, especially since learning of Finn's father's terminal cancer diagnosis. Keeping my one hand entwined with my husband's, I wrapped the other around his body and onto his well-defined abs. As he continued to talk with his mother, I leaned my chest and head onto Finn's bare back. I wanted to cocoon him with me because, undoubtedly, he was going to need my comfort and support.

Now Available

Want to read about how Lara and Finn? Check out the first book in the Country Roads series.

A young woman content with her solitary life.

A rising country music star.

They were friends once …until their lives took them down separate roads.

Now, years later, when a child volunteers his uncle to sing for a fundraiser, LARA FAULKNER realizes it is none other than her college pal, FINN MURPHY. As the two get a chance to reconnect, Lara reveals to a compassionate Finn details of her shocking past and the traumatic decision she had to make.

Through trust and love, the bond between Finn and Lara deepens as the country singer manages to get an emotionally scarred Lara to let down her self-proclaimed walls. But will secrets, lies, and tragedy cause a bumpy detour on their road to complete happiness?

ABOUT THE AUTHOR

There really wasn't any other path. Grea Warner knew from a young age that she wanted to write. She was born to write. First it was in diaries with little metal keys and in written tales that she slipped to friends in study hall. School newspapers, a college television drama, and internships in the soap opera world were next. After producing and writing a local show, she decided to delve into the world of the novelist. When her fingers aren't tapping out her latest book filled with angst and romance, Grea can be found hiking the trails or jamming to her favorite country artists on the radio.

Website: http://www.greawarner.com
Facebook: https://www.facebook.com/grea.warner.7
Twitter: @grea_warner
GoodReads:
https://www.goodreads.com/author/show/17230140.Grea_Warner